QUEUING
FOR THE
QUEEN

QUEUING
FOR THE
QUEEN

SWÉTA RANA

An Aria Book

First published in the UK in 2023 by Head of Zeus,
part of Bloomsbury Publishing Plc

9 7 5 3 1 2 4 6 8

A catalogue record for this book is available from the British Library.

ISBN (PB): 9781035900183
ISBN (E): 9781035900152

Typeset by Siliconchips Services Ltd UK

Printed and bound in Great Britain by
CPI Group (UK) Ltd, Croydon CR0 4YY

Head of Zeus
First Floor East
5–8 Hardwick Street
London EC1R 4RG

WWW.HEADOFZEUS.COM

For every mother and daughter who make each other laugh, hurt each other deeply, and love each other no matter what.

Hour 1: Southwark Park

Where were you, when you learned the news?

Perhaps you were out and about. Perhaps you were late for an appointment, and you were hurrying along the street a little faster than usual. Perhaps you didn't notice when your mobile phone buzzed in your pocket with a notification. When you finished your appointment, you retrieved it from your pocket, intending to check your fastest route home. Then there it was, flashing on the screen, in unambiguous finality.

Or maybe you were working late. Maybe you saw the story unfurl across social media websites in the afternoon. Maybe you got a sense of foreboding when you saw the vague announcements, the tension of the coverage. Maybe you knew that her family flocking to Balmoral could only mean one thing. Yet, in the early evening, as the text sprawling across the TV in the office changed from speculation to certainty, it still caught you by surprise.

Possibly, like me, you were at home. I was curled up on the sofa, chatting nonsense with my fiancé as he prepared dinner in the kitchen. Over the day I'd seen what the headlines were saying, and I flicked to the news every so often, in between watching some familiar sitcom or other. And so there I was, curled up on the sofa, when the newscaster's grave face filled the screen and he spoke the words. Her Majesty Queen Elizabeth II has died, aged ninety-six.

And how did you feel, when you learned the news?

I saw a vast range of reactions online, from despair to indifference – and sometimes, harrowingly, celebration. Some people wrote of their intense, leaden, consuming grief over losing a figure they'd come to love and admire. Others wrote scathingly of the monarchy's utter irrelevance in these modern times. Some posted jokes; others prayers. Many simply didn't acknowledge it at all, and just went about posting their regular memes and film reviews and emphatic opinions on football.

Me? I didn't know what to feel. I've never been particularly invested in the monarchy, and I'm not entirely convinced that having a king or queen makes much sense any more. Nevertheless, this wasn't some abstract concept of a ruler. This wasn't some theoretical notion from a textbook. This was *the* Queen. The one and only – the woman on our coins and banknotes, the woman we celebrate in our national anthem, the one families gather around the television to watch each year as she gives her Christmas address to the nation. The woman whose sheer length of reign afforded us jubilee street parties and extra bank holidays.

A woman who was loved, across the country as well as within her own family. A woman who lived and breathed, who fought and laughed and collected outlandishly colourful hats – until she didn't any longer.

I never met her, and I never particularly followed royal news. When her death was confirmed, I didn't know what to feel. My emotions seemed to pause, frozen and unsure. Was I sad? I didn't believe so. But I felt something within me shift. Something ineffable, a gradual turning of the tide, perhaps, which told me things would never be quite the same again.

'Love?' I called through to Jonny in the kitchen. 'The Queen's died.'

'Ah, that's a shame,' he called back. There was a pause for a few moments, during which I could only hear the sounds of sizzling on a frying pan. 'Are you all right?'

'Yeah, I'm all right. You?'

'Yeah.'

Another pause. Then Jonny called again:

'Dinner's ready in five minutes, love.'

And so we followed our unchanged routine. Perhaps we chatted a little less than usual while we ate, but fundamentally our evening continued as before.

Later, when the Queen was brought to London, I heard about people queuing across the city to view her lying-in-state. I was quite indifferent to the whole affair. Personally, I couldn't imagine ever going to all that effort simply for thirty seconds in the presence of a coffin. But who was I to judge? Each to their own. No one was dragging *me* out to shuffle from Southwark Park to Westminster through an interminable sequence of barriers, navigating awkward conversations with strangers, like an outdoor airport queue run amok. So why should I complain?

Perhaps, years from now, I'll look back on today and realise there was only ever one person who could have convinced me to be here.

'Tania, did you remember to bring a scarf?'

And perhaps, years from now, I'll look back on today and wonder why I ever let that person drag me here.

I sigh. 'No, Mum. It's only September. I don't need a scarf.'

She's now unfurling a woollen jade-green scarf from around her neck: 'Here, take my scarf.'

'I don't *need* it, Mum,' I hiss, trying to push her hands away.

It's 11 a.m. on a Friday. Here I am, clad in my burnt-orange autumn coat and some old faded black jeans. My new shoes aren't sexy boots or kitty heels, but trainers, light grey with shocking pink laces. They're cute, if I do say so myself, but they're much more practical than they are stylish. Not my usual choice at all. Today, I had to select footwear which would see me through several hours of walking, standing, and perhaps even occasionally stomping a foot in impatience.

It's 11 a.m. on a Friday, and I've been dragged out to shuffle from Southwark Park to Westminster in slow motion, part of an epically long human chain snaking along London's spine, the River Thames.

It's the last place I would've expected to be. I should be working from home right now. Jonny set up a 'home office' for me (in other words, a big wide shelf screwed into the corner of the living room with a swivel chair next to it), where I'd normally be spending my Friday morning looking at stats and preparing a weekly report. My marketing job pays the bills, but it's not exactly glamorous.

It's a nice change of pace to be spending the day outside instead. Here in Southwark Park, the fresh early-autumn air is crisp and cool on my face. The park itself is full of towering trees, and the dazzling sunlight is giving everything a lively glow.

It's just about warm enough not to need a scarf. Just about.

Mum is now reluctantly wrapping her scarf back around her neck and letting it fall against her thick black coat, though she seems poised to thrust it back towards me at any moment.

Neither of us is alone in our choices. In the mass of fellow members of the public surrounding us, I see some wearing hats and gloves along with their thick winter scarves. Conversely, several people have donned lighter layers. One, presumably crazy, man up ahead seems to be wearing a vest and shorts.

The last time I read about it, the queue to view the Queen's lying-in-state was taking about six hours. I suppose vest-and-shorts man will be home before it gets dark, at least.

'Well,' I say. 'We've got a long day ahead of us, haven't we?'

'Yes,' responds the diminutive woman by my side. I'm not particularly tall myself, at five foot four, but I'm not sure my mother even graces five feet. Unlike me, she's skinny; she always has been, but now she's in her sixties it seems there's barely a gram of fat left on her. The crevices around her mouth and eyes seem more obvious than before. She carries herself like someone much bigger and tougher and younger, though: her back is always ramrod-straight and her chin held high. Her long, dyed-black hair is pulled into a ponytail, which reveals the beginnings of silver-grey roots at her temples.

'I'm glad to be here,' I continue. 'This is such a historic moment.'

'Yes.'

'Elizabeth was Queen for my entire life. For your entire life, as well. It's weird to think we have a king now, isn't it?'

She doesn't even bother saying anything this time – she just nods.

'Thank God for that,' pipes up an elderly male voice from

in front of us. 'About time we had a man running things around here.'

'Excuse me?!' I exclaim.

As he turns to face us, his weather-beaten face indicating he's in his late seventies at the very least, I see there's a twinkle in his eye. He's wearing a shabby, shapeless, ancient-looking khaki-green raincoat, buttoned up to his chin. Wispy white hair sits atop a face bearing deep creases, suggesting he wears a smile more often than not.

'What's the problem?' he says, grinning widely. 'Can't handle the truth?' He's got the faintest hint of a Yorkshire accent.

His grin is infectious, and despite myself I reflect it back at him. 'Oh, I can handle the truth,' I say. 'And the truth is that women are much better at running things.'

I raise my arms, indicating the flock of activity around us. Southwark Park is probably as full as it ever has been, or ever will be again. Aside from the queuers, zigzagging their way across the span of the park, there are also officials in high-vis jackets dotted around, doling out wristbands and shepherding newcomers to the right places. Some vendors have set up stalls along the sides, flogging hot drinks and pastries. There is constant noise: talking, laughing, shouting. Occasionally, I catch a sob, too. People of all ages, of all races, from all corners of the country, have congregated here in Southwark Park. Inhabitants of our very own pop-up kingdom, in which there's a whole lot of standing around.

Still gesturing at our surroundings, I ask: 'Could a man have inspired all this?'

The old man chuckles warmly. 'When you put it that way, you certainly have a point.'

I nod. 'My name's Tania. It's nice to meet you.'

'Hello, Tania,' he says. He pronounces it 'Tanya' – most people do. 'My name is—'

'*Tania*,' Mum interrupts suddenly.

He turns to look at her, still grinning. 'Oh, and here I thought my name was Harold.'

'My daughter's name is pronounced *Tania*,' Mum says, pronouncing it the correct way: a long 'taa' with a very light flick of the tongue for the T, followed by a short 'nee-yuh'.

'Tania,' he says slowly, but he still says it more like 'Tanya'.

'Yes, that's fine,' I say hastily, just as Mum repeats: '*Tania*.'

'It's really fine,' I insist. 'Please don't worry about it – call me whatever you want.'

'No, no, I want to get this right,' Harold says, leaning towards my mother and watching her lips move. '*Tania*. Is that right?'

I give a half-hearted shrug, as Mum beams and nods. 'Very good,' she tells him.

'Excellent,' he says with obvious delight. 'It's nice to meet you, Tania. And what's your name?'

'Rani,' Mum answers him. 'Rani Kapadia-Nichols.'

'Rani,' he says, getting the pronunciation correct instantly this time. 'That's a beautiful name.'

My mum gives a short nod and blushes, before fixing her gaze on the path below.

'It's very nice to meet you both,' Harold says. 'Here, at the end of the Elizabethan Age.'

'Welcome to the Carolean Age!' bellows a passer-by in response.

'The what?' I ask, but the person's already drifted into the throngs.

'The Carolean Age,' Harold affirms. 'That's what it's called, when someone named Charles is monarch.' He gives a mischievous smile. '*Carol*-ean. Sounds like women are still calling the shots after all, doesn't it?'

'Thank God for that. So, are you here all by yourself?'

He gives a curt nod.

'Not any more,' I say. 'You're with us now.'

'Well, that's good to know. After all, I'm just a useless man.' There's no malice in his voice, and he gives me an exaggerated, theatrical wink, his eyes slightly crossed. I burst out laughing at the goofy expression on his face.

'Excuse me!' A middle-aged woman with short blonde hair standing in front of Harold has turned around sharply. She's wearing a dramatic black velvet dress, which has already gathered bits of soil and crumpled leaves around its hem. 'You *do* know we are here to mourn? You shouldn't be laughing.'

The whole park is fizzing with laughter. It's like getting shushed during the trailers for talking, even though everyone else in the cinema is talking too. 'Yes, of course,' I mumble nevertheless. 'Sorry.'

'Yes, sorry,' Harold adds in a good-natured tone. 'After all, the Queen absolutely hated laughter and joy, didn't she? Such a tyrant.'

The woman shakes her head in mute disapproval, before turning her back on us again.

Harold and I catch each other's eye, and we both laugh this time, while Mum gives a shy smile.

Hour 2: Bermondsey

Once upon a time, the idea of slowly queuing across London with my mother might not have seemed like much of a novelty at all. When I was small, I was always at her side. I would've followed her anywhere, she was so pretty and caring and wise. My tiny hand would slip eagerly into her big warm one, hers just a bit darker than my own.

Then my other hand would be taken by my father, his pale knuckles covered in brown-red fuzz. There I was, in the middle, my brown-pink complexion the perfectly balanced blend.

I would never question where they led me. Because where they led me was always full of joy, and excitement, and love. We moved forward in synchronicity, the three of us a single unit, never to be torn apart.

That was once upon a time. But things are very different now.

Back then, the three of us would take holidays to various UK seaside towns. Once, we went to Llandudno, in north Wales. With its pebbly beaches, its flashing and hooting arcade games along the pier, and brightly coloured cable cars gliding through the mountains, it became a firm family favourite. And so after that, we returned every year.

Dad would drive the four or five hours from Watford;

although Mum has a driving licence, she always felt nervous behind the wheel. I was safely belted into the back seat, and then we'd set off.

For long stretches, Dad would play I-spy with me, or join me in pointing out passing fields of cows. Or we'd both tunelessly sing along to the tape player: he got to enjoy a hit from the seventies for every Spice Girls song I insisted we put on. If he bellowed his song at the top of his lungs, I'd make sure my next performance was even louder.

As we were screeching and shrieking away, Mum's quiet voice would suddenly cut through: 'Jim, should we stop for lunch?'

We'd park at the motorway services, and I'd scoff down chips practically swimming in salt and vinegar. Mum would hand me some crayons so I could fill in the little puzzles at the back of the menu. Then we'd be back on the road, for more games and singalongs. The holiday hadn't even officially begun yet, but already my cheeks and ribs ached from laughing.

Whether it was me or Dad being the boisterous entertainer, our audience was a constant. Mum would listen intently, and smile and laugh along in all the right places, always swept up in our stories and our roleplays, but never participating herself. She sat back and marvelled in silence; she never attempted to contribute her own piece.

Until: 'Jim, do we need more petrol?'

Dad would dutifully take the next exit to fill up the tank. Then, in the car on the way to our holiday rental once more, he'd start regaling me with some silly story about the dragon on the Welsh flag and all his adventures. Mum wouldn't say another word, until we'd reached our hotel and she had to remind him which bag he'd packed his wallet in.

So it should be no surprise to me that, after an hour of waiting, slowly filing out of Southwark Park and reaching Bermondsey, Mum has barely said a word to me besides, 'Is your mobile phone fully charged?' and, 'Are you sure you don't want my scarf?'

In some ways, things are very different now, compared to 'once upon a time'. In other ways, nothing has changed at all.

It's past midday, and the sun has risen high above us, beaming down from an almost cloudless sky. I've taken off my coat and slung it over my arm, carrying it along with my handbag. Yes, I tell my mother yet again. I'm sure I don't want a scarf.

Now that we're out of the park, the queue's path takes us along the Thames, from east to west then bending south. We'll be following the river all the way until we reach Lambeth Bridge, a few miles along the way.

From this vantage point, we can't see too much of the city across the river. The bobbing heads of other queue-dwellers often obscures our view, because Mum and I are too short to see over most of them. It's incredible: when I try to look out at the river on my right I can see a seemingly never-ending mass of people, far beyond my vision towards Westminster. When I look to the left, I see almost an identical scene: people, people, people, an eternal stream from Southwark Park. I can scarcely comprehend that we're only at the back of the queue; it feels more as if we've been plonked in the square centre of a single-axis, but infinite, crowd.

All the much taller people inhibiting her view don't seem to stop Mum gazing towards the river, though. Meanwhile Harold, the top of his spine slightly hunched over as it is, also struggles to observe much beyond other people's backs.

When I catch a glimpse, though, I remember why this area of London is so loved and sought after. Our road is taking us past quaint, squat little houses, built in a mellow sandstone. Bright purple fuchsias spill out from the hanging baskets decorating the local pub on the corner. There's a patch of grass on the other side of the road, and though it's clearly battled the summer's unprecedented heatwave, flashes of its greenness still stubbornly linger. This part of London, with the lazy Thames drifting nearby, feels plucked straight out of some tiny rural village.

'It's nice here, isn't it, Mum?'

'Yes.'

What else did I expect? I should start talking to one of the hanging baskets instead – it'll probably have more to say than Mum.

'I love this architecture,' says a dark-skinned man in front of me.

His companion begins replying, but I get in there first: 'Me too,' I say pointedly, stepping somewhat rudely in between them, inserting myself into their unit. If I'm going to take this slow, winding road along the Thames today, then I demand games and singalongs.

They're both well-groomed and annoyingly handsome. The white one looks quite perturbed at my sudden presence, but the other smiles.

'I'm Denzel,' says the darker-skinned one, 'and this is my husband, Colin.' Denzel sports some artfully-shaped stubble, while Colin has the clean-shaven, fresh-faced look of a teenage boy. They both appear to be in their early forties or so, and each is impeccably dressed in a tailored designer coat. Both also have backpacks at their feet, with Colin's twice the size of his husband's.

'Planning to set up camp?' asks Harold cheerily.

'How can you like this architecture?' Colin chides his husband, blithely ignoring Harold and the rest of us.

'It's pretty,' I say, before Denzel can answer. 'It's so quiet and peaceful here.'

Colin rolls his eyes so hard I worry they may pop straight out of his skull. 'Please. You're young, you should be craving lights and noise.'

'I like lights and noise, too,' I instantly qualify, but Colin doesn't seem to have heard me. He's shaking his head in dismay.

'This place is very old-fashioned. This isn't what London's all about. I much prefer the hustle and bustle of the real city.'

'Like it's possible to have more hustle and bustle than what we have right now?' Denzel retorts, looking around at the rest of the queue, our concentrated line of people heading towards Westminster. The buzzing atmosphere of Southwark Park hasn't remotely abated; the noise of our hubbub must carry across the Thames. Anyone hoping for a quiet pint in the pub today will be disappointed. I hope the kill-joy in the black velvet dress brought earplugs.

'You know what I mean,' Colin sniffs. 'The big glass buildings. The cocktail bars and restaurants and clubs. That's what this city is about: modernity.'

'Yes,' Harold laughs lightly. 'I thought the very same thing, when I moved here to be with my wife. Nothing historical about this place. St Paul's, the Tower of London, the Houses of Parliament – not important at all really, are they?'

'Exactly.' Colin seems to miss the very obvious sarcasm,

and is instead surveying our picturesque surroundings and looking as though he's bitten into a lemon. 'If I lived here,' he announces loudly, 'I'd be miserable.'

An old lady with a walking stick is shuffling along the opposite end of the street. She's heading towards Southwark Park and is clearly not a part of the queue. At Colin's declaration, she starts, before raising a fragile, papery fist in the air and shaking it in his direction. 'Don't live here, then!' she screeches.

'I won't!' Colin hollers back fiercely, ignoring his husband's fervent attempts to shush him.

'*Fine!*' shrieks the old woman, still shaking her fist.

'*FINE!*' roars Colin, his voice so loud that my ears begin ringing.

'Bloody hooligan,' she spits as she hobbles away.

'For God's sake,' mutters Denzel, slapping a hand to his forehead. 'I can't take you anywhere.'

'Just take me to the Golden Jubilee Bridges, honey,' Colin says, his voice shifting to a rather theatrical and commanding tone. 'Then you don't have to take me anywhere ever again.'

'Why?' I ask. 'What's at the Golden Jubilee Bridges?'

'You'll see,' he says, with a strange nod and a wink. Colour me intrigued, Colin.

'Which ones are the Golden Jubilee Bridges?' asks Harold, frowning. 'I don't think I've heard of them.'

'The Golden Jubilee Bridges were built in 2002.'

We all turn around. A few places behind us stand a harried-looking woman and, presumably, her son. He looks about nine years old and he's wearing a cardboard crown, crudely cut out from a cereal box. He's standing straight, arms stiffly at his sides.

'The bridges were named in honour of Her Majesty's fiftieth jubilee,' the boy continues, his voice squeaky and earnest.

'Sorry about him,' calls the woman, her Welsh accent even stronger than her son's. 'He's a bit obsessed with the monarchy.'

'I'm not *obsessed*,' the boy barks back, his cheeks reddening.

A few queue-dwellers step aside so the mother and son can walk over to chat to us more easily. The mother gives us all a tired half-smile. 'I'm Elsie. And this little eejit is Owen. We came down from Anglesey this morning.'

Owen looks up at us, wide-eyed. As he takes in the mass of new people in front of him, all looking at him, he visibly loses his nerve. 'Nice to meet you, goodbye,' he yelps, and moves to hide behind his mother.

'It's nice to meet you too, Elsie and Owen,' Harold says. 'Owen, I'm ashamed to admit it, but for the life of me I can't remember the Queen's birthday.'

Owen's wide, bright blue eyes peer round from behind his mother.

'Do you think you could remind me?'

Owen gazes up at his mother. Elsie is a pretty woman, but the faint bags under her eyes and her slightly limp, dull brown hair betray her exhaustion. When she smiles, though, her entire face seems to light up like a firework. She nods at her son.

'W-well,' Owen stutters, taking a half-step out from behind his mother. 'Do you want to know her real birthday, or her official birthday?'

'Her real one,' Harold says, as Mum simultaneously speaks: 'Her official one.'

Owen looks utterly alarmed.

Mum and Harold exchange glances, then speak in unison: 'Both.'

Owen gives a timid smile. 'OK. Her real birthday is April the twenty-first.'

'You mean it *was* April the twenty-first,' Colin says gloomily. '*What?*' he adds sharply, after Denzel's elbowed him in the ribs.

The fragile beginnings of a smile have evaporated from Owen's face, replaced with a look of confusion and deep sadness. 'Oh, right. Um, her real birthday *was* April the twenty-first.' He clears his throat and blinks hard. 'I guess Her Majesty doesn't get to have birthdays any more.'

'It'll always be her birthday,' Elsie reassures her son gently. 'Even though she's gone, the day she was born won't ever change.'

I turn to catch Mum's eye. She raises her eyebrows enquiringly.

'Remember that time Dad forgot Grandma's birthday?' I ask her in an undertone.

It was a late afternoon, back when I was a teenager. Dad was lounging about merrily on the couch, singing along to his favourite hits on Magic Radio. He was in the middle of bellowing to Fernando that there was something in the air that night and the stars were bright, when Mum offhandedly asked him what he'd bought his mother for her birthday.

I've never in my life seen a man move as fast as my father did in that moment. He bolted from the sofa as if it had electrocuted him, his budding romance with Fernando abandoned forever. Once he'd thrown a coat over his shoulders, he dragged us all out to the local petrol station, to pick up a bottle of Champagne and a cheap keyring, which read 'MUM' in glittery pink lettering. Mum suggested the keyring might be a slightly insulting present for an elderly matriarch, but was proved wrong as we witnessed Grandma enthusing over it an hour later. Grandma never did have particularly good taste.

By contrast, Mum has always had beautiful taste. She sticks to classic looks and effective splashes of colour. Today, for example, the jade scarf she keeps insisting I need adds a pop to her black coat, black jeans and grey jumper. She's also wearing neat black flats, which I don't think I've seen before.

That's unusual. Mum knows I have a vested interest in shoes, and she always, without fail, asks for my opinion before purchasing any of her own.

'Did someone give you those shoes?' I ask.

'I bought them a couple of months ago.'

Of course. With all this reminiscing and revelling, for a fleeting moment I'd forgotten just how long it's been since Mum and I last saw each other, let alone had a normal conversation. There was a time when she'd have sent me pictures, with accompanying shoe emojis and question marks. But that was then – once upon a time – and this is now.

Perhaps I'll never get a message like that from her again. It feels a bit as if a hard stone has lodged in my heart.

'The Queen had a pair of custom shoes made for her coronation by Roger Vivier,' Owen informs us all.

'*Really?* I love Roger Vivier,' Colin says in delight, just as his husband shakes his head and mutters under his breath, 'Who the hell is Roger Vivier?'

My phone buzzes in my pocket. 'One second,' I say,

retrieving it and excusing myself as I see I've got a text from Jonny:

> Can't talk, busy lunch shift, but how's it going? x

Jonny's a chef, working at a local gastropub. Having a fiancé who's a professional chef is an incredible thing. I should probably be stricter about portions, as I've gone up two dress sizes in the four years we've been together, but it's worth it to eat his incredible food. He made me a croque monsieur before I left the house and I can still taste all its delicious cheesy hammy goodness lingering on my tongue.

I quickly type back:

> It's going good. We're moving a bit slow but there's some funny people here x

My phone buzzes again:

> Funny as in fun, or funny as in they're complete weirdos?

> Funny as in fun. For now at least…

> That's great to hear. Bet no one's as fun as you though x

> Obviously I am the one and only queen of fun, long may I reign x

I pocket my phone again.

I wish I hadn't thought about that croque monsieur. I want another one now.

'Guys,' I say, approaching the makeshift circle that consists of Mum, Harold, Denzel, Colin, Owen and Elsie. 'What shall I get my fiancé to make me for dinner?'

'Your fiancé makes you dinner on demand? Lucky,' Colin says, with a pointed, stern glance at Denzel.

'He's a chef, so he loves it. The world's my oyster. Except,' I add, after a thought, 'I don't like oysters. So I guess my world is anything *but* oysters.'

'Hmm,' says Harold meticulously. 'How about steak and kidney pie?'

'You are hilarious,' Colin deadpans. 'Forget that nonsense, Tania. You should ask for something refreshing, like a big salad.'

Denzel lets out a bark of mirthless laughter. 'A salad? Honey, you're insane. Tania, ask your fiancé to make you something rich and indulgent. Like a big, creamy pasta dish.'

'I hate pasta,' Owen pipes up, making a face. 'It's all slimy.'

'My pasta is not slimy,' Elsie says with a wry raise of an eyebrow. 'But personally, if I could pick any dish, I'd ask for a perfect roast lamb. As long as the chef's good enough to pull it off.'

'What do you think, Rani?' Harold asks. 'Is Tania's fiancé a good enough cook?'

Mum has been gazing towards the river again, seemingly lost in thought. Since the river's been in sight she seems to be constantly distracted by it, even more reserved than normal.

At Harold's question, she turns around, opens her mouth to answer, then glances at me and closes it again.

'He's a brilliant cook,' I insist, mortified by Mum's silence.

'Yes,' Mum adds quickly. 'He is very good.'

'What should he make for Tania, then?' Denzel asks.

Mum shrugs awkwardly. 'I don't know much about food.'

That's not true at all. Mum is a good cook, and she knows it, too. It's not food she's avoiding talking about – it's Jonny.

'Pick one of your favourite traditional dishes,' I suggest. 'Daal? Dhokla? I'll get Jonny to make it, and then you can try it out.'

'That's not necessary.'

'He's a brilliant cook,' I repeat, frustration creeping into my voice. 'You're not giving him a chance. You've never given him a chance.'

For a fraction of a second, I think I see something resembling shock flash across my mother's face. Her eyes widen and her jaw drops, as though she's offended, or surprised, or perhaps even hurt. But I think I imagined it, because now all I see is an unyielding expression as she gazes blankly at me.

There's yet another awkward silence. So much sitting between us, unspoken – and as ever, my mother simply looks at me and refuses to engage.

Harold clears his throat. 'Owen, you never did say what food you like.'

Owen bites his lip. 'Um, we live by the sea, so we eat lots of fish and chips. I think that's my favourite.'

Mum's eyes linger on Owen momentarily, and her face softens. Then she turns her back on all of us and looks out towards the river again.

Sixty years ago

R ani Kapadia was, normally, a sensible little girl.
     On this particular morning, just like every morning, she got up early to make a vat of tea for the household. She made it the way her mother taught her, carefully boiling a pan of water on the stove.

While she stirred the tea, the lingering dregs of sleep made her clumsy. As a result, she wasn't careful enough.

'*Ow!*'

Still shrouded in a haze of dreams, Rani had gone and splashed a small wave of boiling water over her hand.

Already, the skin on the back was turning an ugly raw red. Though it was confined to a small patch, the pain was unlike anything Rani had ever felt before. It felt as if the heat had seeped right into her bones.

Rani took a deep breath, ready to scream, stinging hot tears threatening to spill over. But then she bit back her sobs. This was her own fault. If she'd been paying attention, like a good and smart girl should, then nothing would have happened.

She was wary of exaggeration, but she knew herself to be smart. She was much smarter than her friends. There was Geeta, sporting a new sari practically every day.

There was Aniya, whose singing voice was so mesmerising that all the neighbours said she should sing for the films one day. And there was Neha, whose wiry legs meant she always won the race to the bazaar and got to pick the juiciest oranges.

She loved her friends dearly, but Rani knew none of them was as smart as she was. Yet she was the one who'd stopped paying attention, who'd stopped being responsible. So what did that make her? What would her parents say if they learned she was incapable of simply making some tea, without causing herself harm?

Rani filled up a bowl with cold water and plunged her hand in. She blinked hard, refusing to let a single tear escape her eyes. After all, crying never solved anything.

When the angry glow on her hand had subsided a little, she finished making the tea, placed two steaming glasses of it on a tray, and carried them up to the bedroom. Afterwards, she settled under the shade of the big fig tree in front of the house to read a book.

The latest one she was reading, in English, was about a group of adventurous children who went exploring and foiled criminals. As she read, she was transported to a smugglers' cove, sea salt borne by biting winds stinging her eyes. In the throes of peril and adventure, she almost forgot about the painful throbbing in her hand.

She was learning to read three different languages: Gujarati, Hindi and English. It required a lot of concentration, but Rani liked it. She didn't like to be bored. Having nothing to do – simply standing still and waiting – would be her worst nightmare.

She sat under the baking morning sun, whose rays

glimmered and danced on her dark brown skin. The air was fragrant, the scent of figs and mangoes pervading the atmosphere. Soon, her mother's cooking would fill the house with sumptuous spices.

Rani was deep into her story when her mother came out to find her by the tree. 'Rani,' she said, crouching down and smiling at her daughter. Her mother spoke Gujarati, the primary language of the household. 'Can you help me in the kitchen?'

'Yes, Ma,' she said, only slightly reluctantly, slamming her book closed.

Rani's mother was an extraordinarily pretty woman. Where Rani's hair hung straight and limp, Ma's bounced in big cascading waves down her back. Her eyes were naturally large and expressive, with no need for kohl. As she looked down at her daughter's book now, they grew even larger.

'My daughter!' she exclaimed in dismay. 'What's happened to your hand?'

Rani felt her cheeks turn as red as the burn in question. She tried to hide her hand behind her back. 'Nothing.'

'Did you burn yourself?' Her mother tenderly pulled out her hand and peered at it intently.

'Sorry, Ma,' mumbled Rani.

'Don't say sorry, my poor daughter. Accidents happen. We must put some cream on this, so you'll feel better.'

Before Rani could reply, a cry came from the neighbouring house: 'Oh, hello there!'

Mrs Shukla had emerged onto the street, with a basket of wet washing under her arm, ready to hang it up on the wire in front of her house. 'How are you today, Mrs Kapadia?' she called.

'Fine, thank you, Mrs Shukla.' Rani's mother grinned through gritted teeth.

'Oh dear,' Mrs Shukla tutted, plonking her basket to the ground and striding over. A few sheets spilled out of the basket as it dropped, each one gaudier and uglier than the last. 'Rani, your hand is burned!' she cried out, loudly enough for the entire street to hear.

'I know,' Rani said quietly.

Mrs Shukla shook her head. 'Did you hurt yourself in the kitchen?' she asked, still not lowering her voice. 'Mrs Kapadia, I keep telling you – if Rani buries her nose in books all the time, she'll never learn the important things. How will she ever look after a husband or a child if she can't even look after herself? My own dear daughter is four, but she knows how to make tea without any silly accidents.'

'She can't string a sentence together, though,' Rani muttered under her breath.

'What?' snapped Mrs Shukla.

'Thank you for the advice, Mrs Shukla,' Rani's mother smoothly cut in. 'We're going to put some cream on this burn now.'

A little while later, Rani made to follow her mother into the kitchen to help her prepare the day's meals. But her mother stopped her.

'Don't worry, my daughter,' she said, smiling. 'Why don't you read your book some more instead?'

'I won't make another mistake in the kitchen,' Rani said.

'I know that,' her mother replied. 'I trust you. But you need your hand to stay clean and dry while the cream does its work. Go and read for a little while.'

Rani couldn't say no.

She spent the entire day finishing her adventure book, and then beginning a mythology collection for children, written in Hindi. The first story was the *Ramayana* story about Rama and Sita, and how their enduring love had the power to conquer evil.

Sometimes, Rani wondered who she would fall in love with one day. She hoped her future husband would be handsome and suave, like Dilip Kumar, who always looked so appealing in his films. She hoped he'd be tall, and brave, and strong, just like Rama. She hoped he'd like to read books, too.

The day went by in a flash of stories and enchantment. By dinner time, Rani realised her hand barely hurt at all. As she gathered at the table with her mother and her father, she ate her food contentedly, shovelling potatoes greedily into her mouth.

'Rani,' her father said, between bites. He was a tall and well-groomed man, his moustache as neat and precise as the angular lines of his jaw. 'I must tell you something.' His style of Gujarati was like his appearance: no frills or fuss.

'Yes, Daddy?' Rani was intrigued – her father didn't usually want to chat much during mealtimes, or indeed, ever at all.

'We are going to move to England,' he said. 'You, me, and your mother. I have a new job there. It will be a very good life. We move next month.'

Conversation finished, Rani's father got up and headed off to the bedroom, leaving Rani and her mother sitting at the kitchen table, surveying the dirty dishes, in silence.

England? A very good life?

She'd heard some things about England. Often it was

cold, bitingly so, but it wasn't pretty and mountainous like the Himalayas. The days were short, and shrouded in blackness in the winter. Everyone had pale skin and hair.

Rani gazed down at her raw hand, which had been soothed over the hours by her mother's balm. *Crying never solved anything*, she repeated to herself over and over again. *Crying never solved anything*.

Then, quite suddenly, she burst into tears.

'Oh, my poor daughter, don't cry,' her mother said, holding her hand gently, although clearly close to tears herself. 'Your father says we will have a wonderful life in England. He'll earn more money, and we'll live in a bigger house. He says you'll even be able to go to a proper school. England is a place of opportunity.'

'So is India.'

'Yes, it is. But England is even better. It's where all the good jobs are. It's where you've got the best chance of a proper education.'

'I don't want to leave all my friends.'

'You can write to your friends. They'll all be so jealous of your amazing new home. And we'll come back and visit everyone, too. Think about it. England has lots of lovely things. We can go to the seaside and eat,' she switched to English briefly, '*fishanchips*.'

'What's *fishanchips*?'

Her mother paused. 'I don't know. But your father says it's delicious. English people eat it at the seaside. And they live in lovely big houses. You'll have your very own bedroom – you won't need to share with us any more.'

Rani had to admit that this was an interesting prospect.

'Will I make friends in England?'

'Of course you will. You'll make lots of friends in school. You'll meet so many nice people. Your father says we'll meet people who are more educated and well-off than the people here. We'll have lots of lovely neighbours and friends.'

Just then, Rani's father called out from upstairs, asking for a cup of tea. Before Rani could say another word, her mother rose, gathered the dirty plates and headed into the kitchen.

Rani had vivid, disturbing dreams that night. Shadowy, gangly monsters pointed at her, drew away from her towards the comforting dark, feared her sun-kissed skin. It took an entire night of tossing and turning, until the dawn bled in through the gap in the curtains, for Rani to realise: in this murky new world of nightmares and gloom, the shadowy figures weren't the monsters at all. *She* was the monster.

For the next few nights, she cried herself to sleep. The very same dreams continued to assail her. Because, after all, crying never solved anything.

Rani shared the small, upstairs bedroom with her parents. They slept in the big bed, while Rani slept in a smaller bed against the window, above which a small brass idol of Ganesh the elephant god gazed down at her. Every night, as she drifted in and out of sleep, she could hear her father snoring rhythmically, contentedly. She couldn't hear anything from her mother.

One early evening, a few days after her father's announcement, her mother came to find her under the fig tree.

'Hello, Ma,' Rani said, shutting her book. 'What are we making for dinner today?'

'We'll start on dinner soon, my daughter. First, I wanted to give you this.'

'A new book!' Rani said in amazed delight. New books were usually a treat reserved for special occasions, like her birthday or Diwali.

Rani examined it closely. It was quite large, and made of the same thick cardboard as her very best picture books. One glance at the cover told Rani it was in English.

'*Welcome to London*,' she read slowly. The big block lettering was accompanied by some drawings: one of a big red bus zooming along a slate-coloured street, and another of a smiling, waving man in a funny, tall, fuzzy black hat, and a uniform as crimson as the bus.

'Your father found it especially for you.' Her mother beamed. 'It shows you what a wonderful place London is.'

Rani opened the book to the first page. First of all, she saw a cartoon map of a city. It was covered in all sorts of buildings and towers, but through its centre, a thick blue-green line curved and wove like a snake.

'That's the river *Tems*,' her mother told her, as Rani traced the line with her finger.

'*Tems*,' Rani repeated. She squinted at the lettering beside it, which seemed to read "Thamis". But she trusted her mother's pronunciation – she'd already discovered that English could be a very confusing language. Sometimes letters were written down which didn't need to be there at all.

She turned another page. On the next spread, there was a bustling street. A red bus dominated the road, and through its windows were silhouettes of different heads: long straight hair, short curly hair, a small child sitting next to their mother. The bus was flanked by black taxi-cabs and pedestrians. The people walking by were clad in all sorts of different bright colours, and each wore the same wide grin.

'London is a very busy place,' her mother told her. 'But everyone's very happy there.'

Rani flipped over to the next page. Here, a verdant field peppered with trees and bushes and a rainbow of flowers greeted her. Every colour Rani could imagine was on this page, from the orange-yellow of the sun's rays in the top-left corner, to the crystal blue of the lake drawn in the middle.

'There are lots of parks,' her mother continued. 'We can go to them and eat picnics.'

On the next page, Rani saw a golden tower, soaring to kiss the clouds, with a clock set at the very top. The following pages contained more pictures of grand stone bridges, ornate spires and castles gleaming in the sun, teeming streets and laughing people.

'Oh, look,' her mother said as she turned another page. 'It's the Queen.'

Here was an immense white palace, with countless windows and mighty pillars. In front was a vast garden, filled with red, yellow and purple flowers. Outside gilded double doors stood a woman, smiling and waving. Upon her head sat a gold crown, flecked with jewels.

'Will we live near the Queen?' Rani asked. England might not be so bad, if this nice smiling woman could be her neighbour.

Her mother smiled. 'I don't know. Perhaps we will.'

'But we will meet her, won't we?'

'I'm not sure. I don't think the Queen meets many normal people. But maybe we'll meet her, one day.'

That night, Rani didn't cry herself to sleep. She drifted off into a pleasant slumber almost the second her head hit the pillow. The faceless shadows no longer haunted her. Instead, she dreamed she was drifting past beautiful gardens, palaces, big red buses, and grand bridges across the *Tems*.

Hour 3: Tower Bridge

More than two hours in, we've made it to Tower Bridge. Its twin stone towers rise high above the Thames. The road connecting them, and the cars crawling along it, are cloaked in their shadow. The bridge's metal railings are painted white and cyan, affording the grand architecture a pop of modernity. On the north bank of the river, there's a whole host of office buildings in shiny chrome and glass, but it's Tower Bridge which naturally draws the eye.

'What kind of work do you do, Tania?' Denzel asks as he sees me looking towards the city.

'I work in marketing,' I say with a shrug. 'It's not very exciting.'

'It has very good benefits,' Mum chips in emphatically.

'Yeah, I guess so. But the work itself is pretty boring. It's all data and charts and statistics. I don't get to talk to people very much.'

'Yes, but you have very good job security,' Mum says, for some inexplicable reason.

'That's helpful,' Elsie says. 'I work in a hairdresser's and there aren't many benefits at all.'

'The job sounds like so much fun, though,' I sigh wistfully. 'You must get all sorts of different customers coming in.'

'Mum cuts my hair.' Owen beams with pride. His short mouse-brown hair is neatly cut and swept into a side brush, only mildly ruffled by his cardboard crown. 'I don't even have to pay.'

'How *could* he pay?' I hear Colin murmur to Denzel in an undertone. 'He's a child, he has no money.'

'If marketing's not your passion, then what is?' Harold asks me. 'What do you do outside of work?'

'Um…'

When I was a little girl, I tried violin lessons. But I gave up after a few months – the strings hurt my fingers and none of my scales or arpeggios ever sounded quite right. When my half-hour weekly lesson loomed, it filled me with dread. It simply wasn't the right fit for me.

I played football in the school team for a while, too. I stopped as puberty began to set in, though. Where I used to run here and there on speedy wiry legs, I now huffed and puffed and loathed every second on the pitch, mortified by my own bulging and sweating body. It wasn't the right fit for me, either.

As a teenager, we were dragged on school trips to museums and galleries. I found the imposed silence almost physically oppressive, while I couldn't understand what there was to marvel at in a painting of a big green square. It just wasn't the right fit.

I auditioned for school plays, but never got a part more important than Gossiping Villager Number Five. I tried poetry classes, but I couldn't think of anything to say. I'm no good at cooking; thankfully I have Jonny for that now. I go to the cinema sometimes, but I'd hardly call myself a cinephile. I read fashion magazines every so often, but I can barely keep up with what's in vogue. I love shoe shopping of course, but I don't think that qualifies as a 'passion'.

Nothing ever seems to quite stick. At thirty years old, I know I should have some kind of hobby, but I don't have any skills to pursue one. It's as though God chose a day to hand out exceptional talents, but I accidentally hit snooze on my alarm and never picked mine up.

The only thing about any of those activities I enjoyed is when I was doing them with other people. But I think Harold's expecting a more profound answer than, 'I like to socialise.'

'Mum, I need to go to the toilet,' squeaks a high-pitched voice suddenly, as I have my mouth open to answer. Saved by the bell.

'Me too,' Elsie answers her son. 'Let's go now, then.'

We all wave as Elsie and Owen detach themselves from the queue and walk off in the direction of Tower Bridge. As they disappear into the throng, Owen's voice carries back to us: 'Did you know, Mum, Buckingham Palace has seventy-eight bathrooms…'

'Did he just say *seventy-eight* bathrooms?' Colin gapes at us all. 'That's incredible.'

Mum looks contemplative. 'I don't think I'd want seventy-eight bathrooms. It'd be far too much to clean.'

'I think, if you have seventy-eight bathrooms, you probably also have staff to do the cleaning for you,' I point out.

'I suppose that's true.'

'I wonder,' chips in Harold, 'whether you'd pick a favourite bathroom, and use that one the most?'

'Definitely,' says Denzel, nodding, right as Colin cries, 'No way!'

Denzel turns to his husband. 'What, you'd use all seventy-eight bathrooms?'

'Absolutely,' Colin says with glee, rubbing his hands together. 'I'd use a different one every single time I needed to go. By the time I've done all seventy-eight, and I'm starting at number one again—'

'A number one in number one?' grins Denzel.

'—it'll feel like a brand new bathroom all over again. That's the kind of luxury I want in my life. I want to never, ever, ever walk into a bathroom and feel like I've used it before.'

'That's a lot to aspire to,' says Harold.

Tower Bridge is still in my peripheral vision. So instantly recognisable, so iconic – not to mention, so often mistaken for London Bridge. No wonder people think it bears the name of the city itself. It's a symbol of London, and all its people. Old meeting new, the grand and imposing design intertwined with modern technology so the bridge can rise and let river traffic through. Cars, bikes, pedestrians, boats – Tower Bridge accommodates everyone, no matter how they choose to get there.

'You know what?' I say eventually. 'I'm getting married next year, and I want everyone I love to be there. If I can have that, then you can keep your seventy-eight bathrooms.'

Harold chuckles approvingly. 'Isn't that nice, Rani? You must be looking forward to the wedding very much.'

I'm keen to hear Mum's answer. But before she can say a word, Colin launches into describing his and Denzel's wedding, which sounds as if it was a pretty lavish affair, and also as if it was entirely planned by Colin.

'We were saying goodbye to our single lives forever,' he gushes. 'It was the end of clubbing and having fun.'

'Gee, thanks,' Denzel says mildly.

'Well, it was,' his husband retorts. 'Don't get me wrong, honey. I'm much happier now.' He gives Denzel's arm a squeeze. 'But I still wanted to say goodbye to the way things used to be. So we made our wedding a huge party. One last hoorah, before our new life.' Colin shakes his head dreamily. 'I still don't quite remember how I wound up shirtless and covered in wedding cake at three in the morning. But it was the best night of my life.'

Denzel smiles warmly at his husband. 'Mine too.' He turns to me. 'Tania, you have so much to look forward to. Everyone you love in one place, celebrating you and having fun. What more could you want?'

I grin rapidly, but turn away before Denzel can see the uncertainty flooding my expression. With things the way they are with Mum – with Mum and Jonny – I have no idea what my wedding's going to be like. Will everyone I love be there? Will everyone be celebrating and having fun? While those questions remain impossible to answer, I can't even begin to imagine myself topless and covered in cake at 3 a.m.

I look at Mum, hoping to catch her eye. Perhaps all this talk of impending nuptials is exactly what we needed, to address the elephant in the room. But she's gazing out at Tower Bridge, an inscrutable expression on her face, resolutely determined to avoid looking at me.

Hour 4: The HMS *Belfast*

Elsie and Owen didn't find us again. In almost four hours we've only moved as far as the HMS *Belfast*. The shadow of Tower Bridge still looms to the east, but our focal point now is this grey military cruise ship, which has been converted to a nautical museum. At the bow of the ship – or possibly the stern, I'm not really sure – is a Union flag on a pole. It flutters at half-mast.

All the flags are at half-mast. They have been for days. Looking across the Thames at this city – this cutting-edge, ancient, ageless city – we can see several masts outside various buildings, flying their Union flags at half-mast. Usually, when they're flying high, they seem so proud and strong, defiant almost. Now they're deflated and drooping, flapping dully, hopelessly, in the light breeze.

'Shall we go on the boat?' I hear. I turn to see Colin tugging at Denzel's arm.

'If you want,' Denzel says mildly. 'But you're paying for the tickets.'

'*Tickets?*' Colin spits in distaste. 'Forget that.'

I look back at the flag on the HMS *Belfast*. It dawns on me: the Queen will never catch a boat again. She'll never visit a museum again. She'll never see a Union flag again.

She'll never again have an excited loved one tugging on her arm, asking her if they can go somewhere or do something. Who will those loved ones turn to now? Will they find solace in each other?

When someone so famous, so beloved, dies, the grief is shared among thousands. One glance at this queue makes that plain to see. The pictures of mourning royals, those who truly knew her as a mother and grandmother and friend, make it even clearer. For the world, for the country, this is a collective loss of a loved one. I can't imagine how it must feel for her actual family.

I look at Mum, shuffling along the river beside me. One day in the future, when she goes, no one will lower a flag at half-mast. There won't be congregations across the South Bank, queuing for hours and hours to mourn her. But those who knew and loved her will find the very fabric of their world torn apart. We will grieve as one, united in our loss.

Spontaneously, I find myself looping my arm through Mum's. She looks at me, wearing a faint expression of surprise. I don't blame her. For too long, Mum and I have been distant. But we have to cherish each moment, and we have to start now. I'm heartened when I see her swallow, preparing to speak, preparing to say all the words I've been waiting to hear for so long. She opens her mouth, and here it comes:

'Are you cold? Do you want my scarf?'

'Um, no,' I mutter. It's true – I couldn't possibly feel cold with this sudden heat flooding my cheeks. I unloop my arm again.

Can pain ever truly be shared? Isn't every crippling wrench of the heart, every cherished memory, a uniquely personal pain? Personally I've been finding it difficult lately, missing my mother, feeling as though something huge and vital has been cut from my life. But that doesn't mean my mother feels a thing. People mourn loss differently, and some people never truly mourn at all.

We are right next to the river now. Our path is taking us directly along its bank, punctuated by classic black domed streetlights. Behind the ship, the skyline of the city of London is coming into clearer definition. The curved Walkie-Talkie building is the tallest in the cluster of shining metal and glass. Meanwhile, to our left on the South Bank stand more office buildings: some are rounded sheets of windows reflecting the sun's light, while others are dull brown and beige cubes.

None of our little group has said a word for some time. Both Mum and Harold are gazing off into the middle distance. Colin and Denzel are linked arm in arm, both of them silently scrolling through their phones with their free hand.

I've resorted to the same, because there's only so much polite, friendly chat you can make with strangers. And I haven't eaten since my croque monsieur. For some reason, I thought it'd be a good idea to Google 'best croque monsieur recipes'. I thought it'd provide me comfort, to imagine I'm eating a delicious meal. So now I'm looking at hundreds of pictures of these heavenly creations. God, look at this one. It's dripping in grease and there's a fried egg on top. It's practically pornographic.

I'm. So. *Hungry*. This was a terrible idea. Not comforting at all.

As if on cue, my mother opens her handbag and,

wordlessly, retrieves a small bag of ready salted crisps. She shoves them into my hand, as she continues staring out at nothing.

How the hell did she do that? I didn't say a word about feeling hungry. Yes, technically my stomach rumbled a bit, but there's no way she heard that. No *way*.

I begin to shovel crisps in my mouth, and feel slightly aggrieved when my phone starts buzzing. I step away from the queue to answer.

'Hello,' I manage through a mouthful of ready salted, stuffing the remainder of the packet in my bag.

'Oh, good, you're eating,' Jonny says. 'I was worried you might not have had a chance yet.'

'Mum gave me crisps,' I say, and instantly feel like a five-year-old whose mum made a packed lunch for their big school trip.

'That's good. I'm glad one of you thought to bring snacks.'

Jonny is very casually, very subtly pointing out that he badgered me to bring snacks myself, and I refused.

'It's not a big deal. Anyway, soon I can come home and have a proper dinner,' I say.

There's a bit of a pause before Jonny next speaks. 'Love, where are you?'

Did he hit his head, or something? 'Um, I'm in the queue, to walk past the Queen's coffin. Where did you *think* I am?'

'Yeah, I know,' Jonny says, with an uncharacteristic hesitation in his voice. 'I meant, where are you geographically?'

'Oh. We're by the HMS *Belfast*.'

'That boat? Between Tower Bridge and London Bridge?'

'Yeah, that's the one.'

'Love,' says Jonny, and I can tell he's being as gentle as he can, 'you've been there almost four hours, and you're not even at London Bridge yet. You don't honestly still think the whole thing is going to take six hours, do you?'

To be honest, for the past hour or two, I don't really know *what* I've thought. Of course what Jonny's saying is obvious, and I'm not a complete idiot. It did occur to me that we'd have to be way further along by now if I was really going to be out of here by five o'clock.

But I shushed that annoying voice in my head. When I've been here for six hours, I'll tell myself that it'll be just one more hour. And when I've been here for seven hours, I'll tell myself it's just one more hour after that. That's far easier to deal with than being told, point-blank, that I'm going to be here for a total of twelve hours, or something ludicrous like that.

I explain as much to Jonny.

'And so, when I've been here for *eight* hours, I'll say, it's just one more hour,' I'm telling him now. 'And when I've been here for *nine* hours—'

'I get it, I get it,' Jonny says. 'But, love, you're way off here. I know you don't want to hear this, but the news is saying the queue—'

'Wait – don't—'

'—is currently taking—'

'Hold on a second—'

'—upwards of—'

'*Don't*—'

'—twenty hours from start to finish.'

What?

What the hell did my fiancé just say to me?

I can't quite articulate it, but my brain does a strange thing here. At the thought of twenty hours of queuing with my mother, it seems as though I suddenly don't have an intact brain at all any more – it's collapsed, it's melted into a puddle of goo.

This can't be happening. It just can't. Reality is flickering in and out. My vision is distorting at the edges.

I know we're British and everything – I know we have the innate ability to turn queuing into an Olympic sport, only with more tea and cake and apologising for something you haven't done – but this is absurd. No one could reasonably be expected to queue for *twenty hours*. Not even British people can queue for that long. It's just not *done*.

Neither of us says anything for a moment, and I can tell Jonny is giving me time to speak first. But right now I can't formulate words. I think my brain has changed state yet again, moving this time from liquid to vapour. I can't quite comprehend the impossible, ludicrous, downright *obscene* nature of what I've just been told.

I look around, to check Mum and my queue buddies aren't within earshot, before I finally hiss: '*Twenty hours?*'

'At the very least,' Jonny says, as though it needed rubbing in somehow.

'Jonny. That has to be a mistake. I can't do *twenty hours* in a queue with my mother.'

'How has it been so far?'

'*Awful*,' I immediately burst out.

This is the moment. Any other man besides Jonny – any other man in the world – would do a particular thing, right at this moment. They'd all do it in a different way, of course, but right here is when they'd do it. They might say, 'I'm sorry to hear that', or they might say, 'I'm sure it's not that bad'. Or they might say, 'Your complaining no longer amuses me and I wish to break up this instant,' like that one very weird guy I dated for about a week.

But they'd all do it. They'd all say something.

In contrast, when I'm like this – speaking before I've really had a chance to think – Jonny doesn't say anything. He doesn't have a go at me, or try to get me to change my mind, or apply unhelpful and irrelevant reasoning. He doesn't make me feel stupid and small. He just waits for my brain to catch up with my mouth.

This is part of why I love Jonny so, so much.

A few beats pass in silence, and eventually, feeling Jonny's silence practically emanating through my phone screen, I sigh. 'Actually, it's not been that bad at all. She's been all right. We haven't spoken about anything serious, but we've been getting on OK. And we've met some nice people. It's actually been quite fun.'

'That's great,' Jonny says with his genuine warmth. 'I hope it stays that way. But make sure to eat properly. And if you feel too exhausted, it's OK to come home.'

'I can't leave Mum here alone.'

'Yeah, I know. At the very least, phone me if you're feeling fed up. Maybe I can come and join you.'

'No.'

'Think about it, love,' he says gently. 'I know you're worried about me seeing your mum, but it could be a good idea.'

'No,' I say again, simply.

'Call me if you change your mind, OK?' I nod, and although he can't actually see me, he knows I'm nodding.

After we've said our goodbyes and hung up, I wander back to the queue. 'That was Jonny,' I tell Mum, and she inclines her head slightly in acknowledgement. We've moved a bit closer to the HMS *Belfast*, and she has a curious look on her face. Not quite sad, but somewhere in that postcode.

'What is it?' I ask.

She nods and clears her throat. 'I was just remembering when we were on that boat together. In Wales.'

It was, to my ten-year-old mind, the greatest and most exotic holiday destination there could ever be. When Dad first told us we'd be spending a few days in Llandudno, in north Wales, I tried my best to pronounce it correctly, before Dad confided in me that he had no idea how to say it correctly either. 'But we do our best, and we keep trying, and we'll get it right one day,' he said to me.

Before Llandudno, my holidays had all been strictly England-based: Brighton, Blackpool, Weston-super-Mare. I couldn't believe I was about to finally enter a whole new country – which Wales kind of is – and expand my horizons so widely. I felt sophisticated, grown-up, positively cosmopolitan. First Llandudno, then New York City!

We stayed in a hotel by Llandudno Pier. I had an initial tantrum at having to share the room with my parents – I got the sad single bed shoved up against the window – but I got over it pretty quickly. We didn't spend much time in the hotel, after all. Instead we walked along the beach, and Dad taught me how to throw stones into the sea so they'd skip along the waves. He showed me that the trick was finding a stone the right shape, and then flicking it so it landed flat, spinning like a frisbee, upon the water.

We bought sticks of sugary rock, which turned my tongue orange. We took cable cars up to the summit of a nearby mountain, and after Mum had fussed over me, making sure my jacket was zipped up right against the wind, we looked at the views all around. The sea to the west seemed to stretch out beyond the horizon, beyond imagination. I was dazzled by the sheer scale of the glimmering vista before me – I had no idea the world could be so big, so wild, so brimming with potential adventures.

Back towards the land, I could see a cluster of boats, all parked together, as though it was where they lived.

'You're right. It *is* where the boats live,' Dad confirmed happily. 'That's a marina. People store their boats there when they're not using them.'

'Can we go to the marina, Dad?' I asked. So that's exactly where we went the next day. There were boats of all shapes and sizes. Some were big and tall, bright white like a fresh sheet in a sketch pad. Others were tiny, dingy, weather-beaten, yet still clearly sturdy and beloved. I skipped along the perimeter, reading out all the names on the hulls: *The Navigator*, *Serendipity*, *Lizzie*.

Dad started chatting to someone about the possibility of hiring a boat, despite his utter lack of nautical skills. 'OK,' he said to us eventually, excitedly. 'There's a boat ride for tourists, which takes us up and down the river. It leaves from town in half an hour. Let's go.'

Huffing and puffing, we followed Dad into town. Then we boarded the boat, and soon, accompanied by fellow travellers clutching cameras and pointing at the sights, we set sail.

I knew almost instantly that it was my favourite ever way to travel. The gentle lulling up and down, the calming sound of the waves, the cool breeze pinkening my cheeks. The tour operator pointed out all sorts of things, like the names of the various towns and valleys, and how this river was home to a rare species of seabird. But I barely listened – I was too entranced by the light dancing on the water, the rhythmic rocking motion of the ship. Why listen to tales of oceanic voyage when you can simply live them?

What did stick with me was the bliss we all felt on that boat. Mum's delighted cry when a particularly big wave splashed up and rinsed her. Dad's enthusiasm in taking a photo of every single landmark we could see. It was one of those picture-perfect days, when there was nothing more splendid in all the world than being with the two people who love you best of all. When we finally disembarked, breathless with joy, we wanted to do nothing but sit on the pier and eat fish and chips. We were suffused with a warm glow.

I remember Mum's face, unabashed happiness as she whispered something in Dad's ear in between munches of battered fish. I wonder what it was about the fish and chips which amused her so much.

'It's a shame Elsie and Owen are gone,' I say now, also looking at the HMS *Belfast*. 'We could've told them all about our lovely time in north Wales. I think Anglesey is quite close to where we went.'

Mum nods, but doesn't say a word.

'Perhaps we should go back there sometime. Back to Llandudno.'

She nods silently again.

I clear my throat and shuffle my weight awkwardly from foot to foot before preparing myself for what I'm about to say. 'But it wouldn't be the same without Dad, would it?'

I used to bring up Dad a lot. I'd talk about him almost incessantly. But Mum never reacted well – if she even reacted at all. Over time, although it broke my heart, I learned to stop mentioning him, because it just seemed so much easier that way.

But right now, as I watch the silently fluttering flags and the queue of mourners saying goodbye to a bygone age, I think life is too short. Mentioning Dad may be a risk, but some risks are necessary.

Mum doesn't shout, or frown, or walk away. She doesn't give a customary nod, or make a sound at all. She's still staring at the HMS *Belfast*, but as I watch her, she wrenches her gaze away and turns her back to it. She exchanges a half-smile with Harold when she catches his eye, but she doesn't acknowledge my words at all.

No one in our group says anything. Colin's not taken his eyes off his phone, and Denzel has only done so to check his watch. As though the time on his wrist will somehow be different to the time on his phone.

Our little group isn't the only one in relative silence – many of our queue neighbours seem to have lost their energy, too. The clamour of Southwark Park is a distant memory.

Then...

'Oh my God! Oh my God! Oh my *God!*'

It's like the parting of the Red Sea. All of us, as if we've been ordered to by a power greater than ourselves, step to our right or left, clearing a line of vision to the woman several places behind us who's emitted this screech.

She's about my age, her blonde hair straightened to within an inch of its life, and she's pointing up ahead, her jaw slack in disbelief. 'Oh my God! *It's David Beckham!!!*'

There's a collective murmur of delighted surprise as we all eagerly turn to see where she's pointing. And, I can't believe it, there he is: tall, wearing an England kit shirt, stubble adorning his jaw, as skinny as a beanpole, blond shoulder-length hair pulled back into a ponytail.

The entire crowd groans in unison. 'That is not David Beckham,' someone mutters quietly.

We all shuffle back into position, a bit red-faced, exchanging sheepish smiles. Fortunately, it seems to have reignited some energy among us. Harold begins to tell us about his beloved Leeds United, while Colin starts prodding Denzel and asking him to explain the offside rule to him, again.

The only one who hasn't reacted, who seemingly didn't notice anything happen at all, is my mother. She's still standing with her back resolutely to the HMS *Belfast*, apparently gleaning great interest from the pebbles on the ground at her feet.

'You loved that boat in Llandudno,' I say. 'You had a great time.'

Perhaps inevitably, silence greets me in response.

'I was a bit surprised by how much fun you had. You must have been used to boats by then, right?'

I almost think she's not going to respond, when: 'What do you mean?'

'Well, you know. You're an immigrant. You came here from India so long ago.' I can picture it now: clutching their battered old suitcases, nothing to their names except the clothes on their backs, their treasured family heirlooms, and a yearning. A yearning for more. 'Your family came to these shores with a dream,' I continue with a deep sigh, 'and they had to travel across the world to chase it. Surely that must've been a much longer, more exciting boat ride than half an hour around the Welsh coast. Why don't you tell me about it?'

I'm still looking at the HMS *Belfast*, and Mum still has her back to it, so I don't see her face. But she seems to take a while to process what I'm saying.

I give up. She's not going to engage. It's as though she doesn't even hear me.

'My daughter,' she says suddenly, and I swivel around to face her. She turns to look at me too. 'It may surprise you to learn this, but aeroplanes did in fact exist in the nineteen sixties.'

I hear Harold and Denzel snorting with laughter, and my cheeks flare up with heat.

Well, whatever. Personally, I think a boat ride to your new life, being ferried along by the very life force of the planet, is much more romantic and epic than hopping on some plane. Can you blame me?

Fifty-six years ago

R ani Kapadia wasn't sure what to do.

The boys were lurking outside the newsagent's again. There were four of them, all about sixteen or seventeen years old. They were tall, much taller than Rani. Two of them wore denim jackets while the other two wore leather; all four had a lit cigarette clasped between their fingers. They talked over each other, boisterously, and each sentence was punctuated with a scornful sneer.

Her old beloved picture book had promised her streets full of smiling people in brightly coloured garb, waving and welcoming her. But in the years she'd been in England, she discovered most strangers didn't smile or wave. They frowned and barged past her, sometimes sucking on cigarettes, often wearing drab, ugly clothes in black and brown and khaki. Her picture book never mentioned anyone like these boys, who shouted things, frightening things, in her direction.

When she'd boarded the plane to come here, she had been beyond excited at the thought of soaring through the air, touching the clouds. But the flight was underwhelming. The bright blue of the sky above the clouds seemed promising at first, but then it became repetitive, never-ending. Her picture book had promised joyous sunshine in England, and its one drawing of rain showed an anthropomorphised cloud sporting a jaunty grin. Rain was supposed to be charming and fun. As Rani descended the metal steps off the plane, she discovered that rain in England wasn't anything of the kind – it was just wet.

Her picture book hadn't lied about the lush parks or the majestic towers, but Rani barely ever got to see them. Once or twice her parents took her into the city, and she could wander along the weaving *Tems* taking in all the splendid sights, smug and satisfied in the knowledge that this was her home. But then her father would shepherd them back into a train station. Rani would carefully hold the handrail as she descended, only to find her palm coated in dirty soot. They coughed and cleared their throats as the soulless metal tube dragged them back to north-west London, to the house they shared. It was a pleasant home, but it looked like everyone else's. It had none of the grandeur or grace of the London her book had promised her.

The one thing her picture book seemed to have got right was its portrayal of the Queen. Rani had glimpsed Buckingham Palace through the imposing black gates, but it looked every bit as majestic and graceful as her book suggested. Her mother said they'd go and visit properly one day, when her father had the time, and Rani looked forward to that day very much. In the meantime, from newspapers and television screens, the Queen truly did smile and wave at her subjects – at Rani. Just like her book said.

Rani often thought about that little drawing of a refined, content and jolly Queen, waving out at her. She seemed to have so much poise, so much courage.

What would the Queen do now? Faced with these

intimidating, aggressive boys in her path, what would she do?

Rani knew she couldn't cry. Crying never solved anything. She had to remain strong.

She gripped the straps of her school backpack, under the two bunches of hair her mother had plaited for her in the morning. She'd selected an unassuming, plain grey backpack, to match her drab school uniform. She didn't want anything that stood out too much.

She took a deep breath, looked downwards, and began to walk.

At first, it seemed the boys didn't notice her. They continued their own conversation, each one speaking more forcefully than the last. Rani had nearly passed them, when:

'Oi.'

She kept her gaze fixed on the pavement, and quickened her pace.

'Oi!'

Rani was past the newsagent's now, but she didn't slow down or turn around.

Then one of the boys yelled a word at her. She'd heard it before; they'd called her it a few times. It was harsh and plosive, and they spat it from their mouths with visceral contempt. It was a coarse, ugly word, and it showed just how much these young men wanted Rani to leave their streets, leave their shores.

Still with her head bent down, Rani finally turned onto the road she lived on. It was a small, quiet street. The semi-detached houses were a decent size, although her father sometimes complained that they had to park their small car on the street because there was no driveway or garage space. The houses were all dirty white, with rust-coloured sloping roofs.

The boys hadn't followed her; they never did. But that word still echoed in her ears.

She wanted, desperately, to be strong. But how could she, with such vitriol being flung at her? How would the Queen possibly deal with something like this?

'Is everything OK, Rani dear?'

Rani halted abruptly and looked up. She'd almost walked straight into her neighbour, a middle-aged widow who lived alone next-door.

'Oh, hello, Mrs Woodward,' Rani said.

Mrs Woodward had a small, pointy face, which always reminded Rani of the drawing of a mongoose from an old picture book she had. 'Lovely weather we're having, aren't we?' she crooned.

Rani looked up at the feeble grey sky. 'It isn't raining. I suppose it *is* lovely.'

'My son Alan says it's going to rain tomorrow.'

'Oh.' Mrs Woodward worked her son Alan into every single conversation.

'His work takes him all over, you know.' Rani did know – it was mentioned all the time. 'He's in Bristol today, but tomorrow he's going to Edinburgh. Edinburgh! Can you imagine?'

'Wow. That sounds very exciting.'

'I don't know how he does it,' Mrs Woodward sighed, with a mixture of sorrow and pride. 'He's London born and bred. I don't understand how he can stand to be so far away from home, for even a moment.'

Rani didn't say anything. Her picture book had promised

her lovely, welcoming neighbours with interesting stories and delicious cakes on offer. But Mrs Woodward was just another version of Mrs Shukla: nosy, self-important, harping on about her children's dubious achievements. Rani couldn't help but feel that there was no need to get a plane all the way to England just to wind up with the same neighbour she'd had her whole life.

Mrs Woodward tutted, as she often did to punctuate conversation. 'Well, at least he'll be home for Christmas in a couple of months. Are you looking forward to Christmas, Rani?'

The Kapadia family didn't celebrate Christmas. It was Diwali in a few weeks, and they'd be celebrating that, although Rani wouldn't be allowed time off school for it. She looked forward to dressing up nicely, lighting candles and eating lots of food with her parents. She supposed that was what Christmas felt like, for everyone else here.

'Yes, I am,' she said.

'Good girl.' Mrs Woodward nodded, as though Rani had passed some kind of test. 'Well, you really must come and have a cup of tea with me sometime soon, Rani. Your mother too.'

Last time they'd gone for tea at Mrs Woodward's, Rani's mother had spent the entire afternoon afterwards complaining that the woman didn't have a clue how to make a decent pot of tea.

'We definitely will,' said Rani through a rictus grin. She waved as Mrs Woodward strode past her.

Rani arrived home, through the entrance on the side of the house, and latched the kitchen door behind her. The kitchen was a moderate size – most of the downstairs was taken up by the living room instead – but it was well-stocked. As well as the cupboards built into the walls, there were additional wooden shelves which her father had erected. On these stood jars and jars of chilli, cumin, pepper, turmeric, fenugreek, cardamom, cloves, nutmeg, mustard seeds, and many more. In a big bowl at the bottom lived a seemingly never-ending supply of potatoes.

Rani was surprised to find the room empty. Her mother was always here after school, making preparations for dinner. 'Ma?' she called out in Gujarati – her family still spoke Gujarati at home – as she kicked her shoes off by the door and slung her backpack onto the kitchen table.

There was a responding sound from the living room, but it wasn't in any identifiable language Rani knew.

Rani walked in to see her mother sitting on the wide tan leather settee. The room was so vast that the small television, all the way at the other end next to the bay window, was quite difficult to see properly from the settee, especially as the antenna always quivered and made the picture fuzzy. Nevertheless, her mother's gaze was fixed on the screen. Her entire face was wet and shiny with tears, though she'd obviously just tried to rub them off with her sleeve. 'Oh, my daughter. I'm sorry, I didn't realise it was so late already. There's been some very upsetting news today.'

'What happened?' Rani came and sat down, her feet sinking into the plush red-and-gold paisley rug as she did so. But her mother rose to her feet.

'It's nothing. Oh, your father will be home soon and I haven't even started making dinner. I'll do that now. You can go upstairs and do your homework.' Her mother bustled into the kitchen, wiping her face hard with her sleeves.

Normally, Rani obeyed her mother immediately. This time, she resisted. She had to know what had upset her mother so dreadfully. With a sense of apprehension bubbling inside her, she sat and watched the television.

The newsreader was recounting the events of the day. He spoke quite quickly, and Rani didn't catch every word of it, but she gathered that there'd been some kind of horrible accident in a Welsh mining village, called Aberfan. Rani didn't know what a 'slurry' was, but she soon understood that it had been huge and deadly. When it came cascading down from the mountains, it had engulfed a school. A school, just like hers. With children there waiting to learn, just like her. More than a hundred children had been killed, as well as many adults.

No wonder her mother was crying; Rani couldn't stop the tears rolling down her own cheeks. What a frightening thing to happen. These children had arrived at school in the morning, expecting a day full of fractions and spellings and hopscotch, only to never take another breath again. Rani couldn't quite absorb the enormity of the tragedy, but she found herself shaken nonetheless.

'Rani,' her mother said suddenly from the doorway, interrupting the news report. She took the remote from Rani's hand and turned the television off. 'Go upstairs and do your homework. Please.'

Reluctantly, Rani obeyed this time.

The rest of the day passed by uneventfully. Aberfan was not discussed at the dinner table, where instead her father suggested going to see a Bollywood film at the weekend. And that's precisely what they did. The following afternoon, Rani sat quietly as she watched women clad in beautiful flowing saris sing and weep and dance on the big screen. Days continued to trickle by, their routine unaltered, as though nothing had happened.

Some days later, when she reached home after school, she saw another news report. In this one, they were talking about the aftermath of the tragedy. The newsreader pointed out that the Queen had not been to visit Aberfan. At first, Rani wasn't sure she'd heard the man correctly, but he repeated it again soon after – that it had been several days, and Queen Elizabeth II had not yet visited Aberfan.

Rani didn't understand how this could be possible. Here was a woman with all the power in the world, faced with an unspeakable tragedy, and she chose to do nothing? How could this be? Whenever Rani struggled or faltered, full of self-doubt in a new land, she thought about what the Queen would do in her place. Never once did she consider the idea that the Queen would do nothing in the face of such devastation.

She meandered into the kitchen to help her mother with dinner. 'Ma,' she asked as she began to peel potatoes, still feeling a bit stunned, 'why hasn't the Queen gone to Aberfan?'

'I don't know,' said her mother.

'I think she should go.'

'I agree.'

For a few moments, the kitchen contained only the sounds of peeling and chopping. But Rani couldn't contain herself for long:

'I can't believe she hasn't gone. Doesn't she care?'

Her picture book had promised an engaged Queen, waving out at the reader with genuine regard, truly seeing them. The Queen Rani knew was caring and kind. Perhaps that had been a lie, too.

In the flash of a mere moment, so quickly she couldn't control it, all the frustration and pain and confusion Rani had endured since leaving her home half a world away threatened to engulf her. She burst into tears right there in the middle of the kitchen.

Her mother put down her chopping knife, rinsed her hands, and came to place one on her daughter's shoulder.

'My darling daughter, we can never really know what someone else is thinking. I'm sure the Queen cares very much about what happened.'

'Then she should go and see them. So many people died. *Children* died. She should be there for them.'

'I agree,' she said again. 'I think she should be there, and I think it's a huge mistake that she hasn't gone yet.'

'Yet?'

'Well, I don't know. But I think she will go; at least I hope so.'

Rani hated that her eyes were stinging, that she was weeping. After all, the Queen had nothing to do with her. The Queen could spend her life as she liked, and it had no impact on Rani. Anyway, crying never solved anything. She sniffed hard, willing the stream of tears to cease.

'People make mistakes,' said her mother in her soft, lilting Gujarati. 'Sometimes people are so shocked, so panicked, that they wind up paralysed. Sometimes, you spend so long trying to decide what the right thing is to do, that you end up doing nothing at all. It's the worst mistake anyone can make, and yet it happens all the time. We're human. We make mistakes. What matters is how you deal with your mistakes.'

Rani kept her head down, remained silent, and carried on peeling potatoes as she held back her tears.

The very next day, the news reported that Queen Elizabeth II had gone to Aberfan to visit the families who had lost loved ones. The news broadcast images of her sombre, steadfast face, devastated but unwavering. Despite her obvious sorrow, she continued to walk on and meet with everyone – mothers and fathers who had lost their children in a truly terrible way. Rani felt a deep well of sympathy for them, but also a rising sense of warmth at the thought of Her Majesty being there with them; listening, bearing witness in her quiet, stoic way.

That afternoon, Rani was coming home from picking up some milk at the corner shop, when she saw the same menacing boys lurking outside the newsagent's. She didn't even pause; she simply walked past. They made the same awful taunts they always did, but Rani barely listened. She did not look down or quicken her pace; she stared straight ahead and continued her journey entirely unaffected.

In her time in England Rani had learned, acutely, that life isn't a picture book. But that didn't mean she was going to give up. She would keep on turning the pages.

Hour 5: The Shard

'Oh, it's been hours,' moans the older woman in front of us, bending her knees a few times to limber them up. 'If it were anyone else, I wouldn't bother waiting this long. But for dear old Lizzie, I'll persevere. She always persevered, didn't she?'

The woman's name is Agatha, and we've been chatting for a while. She's a combination of my height, my mother's skinny body type, and Harold's age. Her white hair is done up in a frankly unflattering perm, which she unconsciously pats every so often as though trying to ensure it's kept its shape.

'It really is lovely to meet all of you,' she's saying now, patting her head again. 'I'm making so many new friends today. Why, I met the most fascinating man where I was earlier. He was very funny and charming. And so full of interesting stories. He was a veteran, you know.'

'He was?' Harold says. 'So am I!'

They begin to discuss regiments and brigades and battalions, and while I gather that Harold never met Agatha's mysterious new friend, he's chockful of similar stories about the Falklands. Agatha is punctuating his anecdotes with cries of, 'Oh, that's just what the man in the queue earlier said,' and 'That reminds me, the man in the queue earlier said the funniest thing…' Whenever she mentions this man, a sweet little grin adorns her face, making her look twenty years younger, and her eyes cloud over ever so slightly. Then she rapidly pats her perm again.

'Did you get his number?' I ask.

Agatha's face falls, and she's momentarily speechless. 'I didn't think to,' she says eventually, clearly crestfallen. 'I don't have a mobile phone. I carry my notepad and pen with me, of course, but I thought I'd rejoin the queue right where he was. Then I couldn't find him again.'

'Well, maybe he'll come and find you,' I tell Agatha. 'Until then, we'll be your new friends.'

Agatha seems somewhat comforted by this. But she still brings up the anonymous man in the queue. Just here and there. In small ways. Including when Colin mentions that his neck hurts a little, so Agatha says, 'That's such a coincidence – the man in the queue earlier's *back* hurt a little.'

Who says a meet-cute is only for the young? I hope she reunites with him soon, because so far I've learned the man's hometown (Bath), favourite holiday destination (Corfu) and sense of style (he's wearing a suit in the queue today). Before long, I'll be able to write a thesis on him. Perhaps it's not Romeo and Juliet, but I've become quite invested in this budding romance. *Oh, the man in the queue earlier, the man in the queue earlier, wherefore art thou the man in the queue earlier?*

'How did you meet your wife?' Denzel asks Harold, thoughts of romance and flying sparks clearly occupying all our minds. 'You said you moved to London because of her, right?'

'That's right,' says Harold beaming. 'I met Jane at a friend's wedding. She insisted that she could never leave this city. London born and bred. I fell in love with her, and that meant I fell in love with this place too.'

'Did Jane not join you today?' Colin asks.

Harold simply shakes his head and gives a rueful smile, pretending not to notice while Denzel nudges Colin in the ribs. '*What?*' snaps Colin. 'I just want to know where his wife is.'

'Oh, look over there,' Denzel says theatrically, pointing up the queue towards London Bridge. 'Doesn't that woman look fabulous?'

This quick-thinking diversion has the desired effect of distracting Colin, as he seems to possess the glitter-driven attention span of a magpie. There is an Indian woman with ink-black hair, wearing a vivid teal-and-gold sari, ambling down the queue and handing out a flyer to whoever will take one.

'I love that outfit,' Colin says as she comes nearer.

'Thank you very much,' she says, her English sounding melodious in her heavy Indian accent. She hands Colin a flyer.

'Diwali and Nav-uh-rah-tree celebrations,' he reads, squinting.

'Navaratri,' Mum corrects him. 'It's a Hindu festival. *Kya yahaan bahut se tyohaar manae ja rahe hain?*' she says, the language flowing and lyrical. The woman speaks back animatedly. For a few moments, we watch as the two converse, both gesticulating intently and intermittently laughing.

'What are they saying?' Colin asks me.

'They're talking about the celebrations,' I say carelessly.

'Yes, I assumed that much. But what are they actually *saying*?'

At this point in the queue, we are quite close to the Shard. Despite the sun still gleaming brightly in the sky, we are in the tower's chilly shadow. I didn't realise how cold it was, until this moment, and I shrug my coat on.

'I don't know,' I mutter eventually, looking towards my shoes so they can't see my embarrassment.

Agatha blinks. 'Don't you speak Indian?'

'Agatha,' Denzel says, rolling his eyes, '"Indian" is not a language.'

'Oh, I'm sorry,' Agatha says, and to her credit she looks instantly sheepish. 'I'm very sorry.'

'What language are they speaking, then?' presses Colin.

My mother knows fluent Gujarati, but she knows Hindi too. I don't have a clue how to speak, or recognise, either of them.

Mum and the other woman finally finish their conversation, and the woman continues her journey down the queue. 'She was telling me about all the celebrations happening in London,' Mum informs us. 'They start from next week.'

'I've never heard of Navaratri,' Harold says apologetically. 'I do know about Diwali, though. That's the story about good conquering evil, isn't it?'

'Literally every single religious story is about good conquering evil,' mutters Colin.

'What's the Diwali story about, again?' asks Agatha.

'Rama and Sita,' I say. 'Rama is a brave prince, who has to fight a demon king called Ravana to save his wife Sita.'

'The prince has to go and save the helpless princess,'

ponders Harold. 'Doesn't sound very feminist to me,' he adds with a wink in my direction.

'It depends how you look at it.' I explain a particular part of the story: in the middle of a dense green forest, Rama's brother Lakshman is charged with protecting Sita for a time, as Rama has been lured away by the beguiling demon's trickery. The same trickery is employed to mimic Rama's voice crying for help, which in turn distracts Lakshman and calls him away.

'But before Lakshman went,' I say, 'he drew a sacred circle on the ground around Sita, and told her not to leave it.'

'Presumably she did leave it?' Denzel says. 'Or this would be quite a boring story.'

'Exactly,' I say. 'Of course she left the circle. The demon disguised himself as a poor beggar, so she stepped out of the circle to help him. That was when she got captured.'

'As I said,' Harold says with an arched eyebrow. 'Not very feminist.'

'But it *is*,' I insist. 'Sita could have just sat in that circle without moving. She could have just obeyed everyone around her and let fate happen to her, without ever making any decisions for herself. But instead, she made her own choice. She took action. Obviously it didn't work out perfectly, but at least she decided her own fate.'

Mum is shaking her head with pursed lips. 'That seems a bit silly to me. She would've stayed safe in the circle. Isn't it better to stay safe?'

'What's the point in living if you just play it safe all the time?' I ask.

'That's foolish,' Mum reiterates. 'If you *don't* stay safe, then you risk no longer living at all.'

'But if Sita just stood in a circle for the rest of her life, would she really have been living?'

'She'd have been rescued eventually. She just had to have faith and patience.' Mum looks at me pointedly. 'Those are good qualities to have.'

'If Sita had had faith and patience,' I say, my mouth suddenly dry, 'we'd have no *Ramayana* story. We'd have no Diwali.'

Mum's biting her lip and has a pained half-frown on her brow. She looks as though she wants to say something. Instead, she scratches her nose, hiding her face behind her palm as she does so.

Conversation falls silent momentarily. The queue is shuffling forward a fraction more, and now the enormousness of the Shard is all we can really pay attention to.

'It really is an eyesore, isn't it?' muses Agatha with distaste, gazing up at the colossal glass-panelled tower at our side. We're so close to it that its height is both simultaneously exaggerated and diminished: straining my neck upwards I still can't quite see its peak, but its impact is much reduced when not set against the landscape of the rest of the city. 'I much preferred London's skyline before this glass monstrosity came along to ruin it.'

'Are you from London?'

'No, I'm from the Midlands. But I used to look forward to visiting the capital. It was our favourite thing to do, me and my ex-husband. Then they started building all these hideous modern things. So soulless. No character in any of them.'

'Sorry, Agatha,' I say cheerily, 'but I have to disagree with you there. I love the Shard.'

I like seeing it from a distance, because it's so instantly recognisable, it feels like home. And I like being right next to it, walking out of London Bridge station and immediately finding myself in its mighty presence, because of how it so effortlessly dwarfs me, everyone else, everything else. It's existed for less than half of my life, but as soon as it was up there, shaking hands with the distant sky, it felt right to me. Why should New York and Dubai and all those other places hog the limelight for tall buildings? I like the grandeur and the power of a building which says, 'I'm better than all the rest, and I know it.'

'Of course you like it,' sniffs Agatha, not without kindness but not without contempt either. 'You're young. What are you, twenty-one? Twenty-two?'

'I'm thirty.'

'Exactly. Too young to know any better. What about you, Rani?' Agatha jostles Mum a bit. 'I bet you agree with me, don't you?'

I bet she does, too. Mum's always been a staunch supporter of traditional values. She never wants to step outside of the circle.

When I was sixteen, getting ready for my very first ever proper date with a boy – as in, not just clutching each other's clammy hands for thirty seconds at a chaperoned school disco – I wore a brand new skirt I'd bought. It was, as my friend described it, 'Pikachu-yellow', with frills and flares. I paired it with a grey tank top, and fastened a chunky teal belt around my waist. Finally, I affixed my daisy chain necklace and matching bracelets. I scrutinised myself in my bedroom mirror, and I was satisfied: I looked amazing.

The mid-2000s were a strange time for fashion, OK?

I was excited for this date. My parents were trepidatious, and my mother was especially obsessed with asking about the boy's name, address, family, career aspirations, medical history and possibly blood type. But they'd consented. Yes, I could go for pizza and a movie with this boy, and yes, I didn't have to text them every fifteen minutes to confirm I was safe. As long as I was back home by nine o'clock.

I came sauntering down the stairs in my lovely outfit and called a goodbye to my parents on my way to the front door. That was when my mother stepped in front of me.

'You are not,' she said, no hint of a question or a suggestion in her tone, just cold hard fact, 'going out in that thing.'

The skirt was too short, she said. It looked cheap. How could I possibly want to go flaunting myself around in such a manner? Just because everyone else was doing it, did that mean I had to do it too? Didn't I have more dignity?

The skirt, by the way, came to just above my knee. *Just* above.

We argued for so long that I was half an hour late for my date. I only eventually relented and threw on some jeans because I didn't want to stand him up. I couldn't believe it: my perfect, glamorous, ever-so-slightly-sexy look, ruined because my mother was scandalised by knees. Marred by my miserable mood from the start, the date was terrible and I never saw him again.

Mum used to rail against many other 'modern' customs, too. Like when I wanted to wear shocking pink eyeshadow. Or when she started seeing people rapping in Bollywood movies. Or when my dad bought me a flip-phone to replace my old battered Nokia brick. 'But what is the *point* of this?'

she said, glaring at the flip-phone in consternation. 'Why must it *flip*?'

So yes, Agatha's correct. Obviously such a symbol of progress, technology and modernity as the Shard will be downright detested by my mother.

'I'm sorry, Agatha,' Mum says, 'but I must agree with my daughter.' She turns and gazes up at London's contemporary obelisk, a mischievous glimmer in her eyes. 'I like the Shard very much.'

Well, I certainly wasn't expecting that. My mother, embracing modernity? Next she'll be donning sky-high stilettos and asking me to subscribe to her TikTok.

The queue is still shuffling forward, with some unprecedented pace. Within a few more minutes, we are no longer in the Shard's cold shadow. We have stepped back into the sunlight, and behind us, the tower looks as mighty as ever.

Hour 6: London Bridge

Jonny:

Hey, check out the gazpacho
I just made

[SENDS A PHOTO]

Tania:

Don't!!!

That looks amazing

You'll make me hungry

Sorry but I had to send it.
I just had to.

This may be the best
gazpacho I've ever made

I'll gazpacho you in a
minute

Go on then

Gazpacho me, baby

Lol

[SENDS A PHOTO]

LOL, you and your crazy selfies

Will you EVER stop making that face!

Harold just asked me what I'm laughing at

Who's Harold

Is he trying to steal you away???

He's an old man in the queue we've made friends with

And yes, of course he's trying to steal me away

And succeeding

Sorry love, I'm leaving you for Harold

I couldn't resist his twinkly grandpa vibes

His WHAT?

You heard me. His wrinkly gullet is just too irresistible.

Lol

So how are things with your mum

Have you talked about what happened?

Nope

What did she say when you brought it up?

I haven't brought it up yet

I know I should

I will soon

It's okay, I get it

You can't rush it

It's silly though isn't it

What am I doing here

We're both pretending like everything's okay even though we know it's not

Hang in there love

It'll come in time

You're amazing and I love you

I can't wait to get married and officially start the rest of our lives together

It's you and me baby

Gonfka33/

?

Sorry

Dropped my phone

Oh okay

It looked like some kind of secret code

Oh yeah, it is

Gonfka33/ is code for 'I'm leaving you to marry Harold, wedding is in the Maldives next summer, please send expensive gifts'

Ah of course

It's obvious now you say it

I have to go love

I'll text you later

Make sure you eat properly!!!

Love you

I love you

Hour 7: Borough Market

Who doesn't love Borough Market?

Me. That's who. I don't love Borough Market.

Don't get me wrong – I *used to* love Borough Market. I used to insist on going there whenever possible. I once had an office job nearby, and I spent a substantial portion of my pay getting lunch at one of the stalls every single day.

How could I not? The choices, the colours, the intoxicating aromas as you wander around and take it all in. Anything you want, you can find it at Borough Market – it's a culinary bonanza! If you want a falafel wrap with the most delicate yet fragrant spices imaginable, you can find it at Borough Market. If you want crispy deep-fried fish on a skewer, you can find it at Borough Market. If you want a sophisticated but affordable bottle of wine, then go no further. Australian, Spanish, Chilean, Grenadian, Cypriot, Haitian, Malaysian, Russian – it's a veritable smorgasbord of the best food and drink in the world, all served from festive-looking stalls which remind me of Christmas all year round, only without the horrible, gloopy bread sauce. Why get on a plane when you can just go to Borough Market?

I went with Mum and Dad once, years ago, when we were killing time before a show at Shakespeare's Globe. Mum is an incredible cook, and she's always extremely suspicious of any Indian restaurants or catering because she thinks so much of it is low-quality. So when I insisted she try the Gujarati kitchen at Borough Market, she was reluctant, to say the least.

Then she got chatting to the vendor, a nice middle-aged Gujarati man with a beard. Well, I think he was nice – I don't know much Gujarati and I couldn't understand most of what they were saying. But I do know that he started offering Mum free samples. And I do know that Mum kept eating the samples, and requesting more and more, and oohing and aahing in surprise every time she took a bite. Eventually she bought one of nearly everything off the menu. Dad and I felt quite conspicuous later on, with our bursting plastic bags of takeaway food hidden awkwardly beneath our coats while we were watching *Twelfth Night*, but it was worth it. We had foil cartons with cardboard lids, brimming with delicious Gujarati food, stored in our fridge for days.

Ever since, if Borough Market ever came up in conversation, my mother would ask me, 'Is that Gujarati kitchen place still there?'

Here we go. Right on cue. Though the queue doesn't take us directly into Borough Market, we're skimming its perimeter as we continue our riverside path. Clearly, I'm not the only one thinking about what's inside.

'Sure,' I say.

'I liked that place.'

'Do you want to go and get something? You haven't been there in a long time. Maybe you can get some free samples again.'

But she shakes her head and raises her hand to say no, which has by far become her favourite gesture.

'Remember that potato and fenugreek curry? You raved about that for days.'

'It was very good. It could've used a bit more cumin, but it was very good.'

'If you want to stay here, I can go and buy something for you. What do you think?'

Sure enough, the 'no' gesture is repeated yet again. But I can see a flash of longing in her eyes.

Yes, there's a lot to love about Borough Market. Even my mother found something to approve of.

And then, along came Jonny. Four years ago, along came bloody, ridiculous, incredible Jonny.

We didn't have a meet-cute. Our fingers didn't accidentally caress each other over the organic lettuces at the local store. Our eyes didn't find each other across a crowded restaurant or gallery or outdoor fire-eating show. We certainly didn't fall in love at first sight.

Instead, we matched on an app. Oh, yes. What used to be a novelty, a harbinger of our doomed future when robots will enslave us all, is now perfectly ordinary. That is, if you count filtering out the weirdos, perverts, and potential serial killers with shoe fetishes as ordinary. Everyone meets on apps these days, don't they? And like them, we saw some photos of each other, simultaneously thought, 'That person doesn't seem entirely objectionable,' and swiped to have a chat.

Our match wasn't like any other conversation I'd had on the app. Most men I'd matched with started the conversation with a riveting, spellbinding:

> Hey lol

Or:

> U look cool and tanned

No thanks, I don't fancy being some white man's 'exotic' trophy girlfriend. Of course, there was also:

> My house now? I can go all nite

Good for them. Though I was always tempted to respond and ask why autocorrect didn't fix those pesky misspellings for them. But that wasn't what I, personally, was looking for.

Quite removed from all these responses, which truly were a dime a dozen, Jonny went for a different opener instead:

> I see from your profile you like Italian food. It may thrill and delight you to know that I just spilled passata down my favourite shirt and now I'm sad. How's that for an appealing romantic prospect?

It was unprecedented. A personalised, honest, down-to-earth message – and it made me laugh. I remember reading it several times, a little thrown.

I told him I appreciated his honesty, and asked him just how ruined his shirt was. He said it was beyond saving – that tiny violins should be playing for him across the nation.

I suggested he send me a picture, so I could get a sense of just how ruined it was. His response, instead of a passata-splattered shirt, was a selfie that I've still retained as my phone background – Jonny's pulling an exaggerated sad face, with wide shiny eyes and a pouty bottom lip accompanying his knitted brow.

He still pulls that face when he sends me selfies now. And it still makes me laugh.

I'd worried it might be difficult to transition our easy online rapport into a real-life connection, but my eagerness to meet him easily dwarfed my nervousness. He suggested going for lunch somewhere, and I piped up with the idea of Borough Market. This was when I was still going there every day for lunch anyway.

And so I took Jonny, professional chef and food nit-picker extraordinaire, to one of the most bustling food markets in London.

Of course, I didn't know at the time how fastidious he is about food. But I found out very, very quickly.

We met at an entrance to the market and hugged, before going to look for something to eat. 'The great thing about Borough Market,' I said, 'is we don't have to eat from the same place. We can each pick what we want, then go and sit together somewhere else. So pick whatever you fancy, and I'll do the same.'

'Yes, I get it,' he said mildly. 'I may be new to London but I have been to food markets before, you know.'

'Well, I'm sorry, I thought that perhaps you hadn't,' I chuckled. 'Didn't your profile say you're from Essex? I thought you're all basically clueless country bumpkins out there.'

'Er, sure we are. But if that were true, then we'd have a lot of food markets, wouldn't we? How else do you think farmers shift their produce?'

I narrowed my eyes. 'OK, Jonny. You win this round…'

We parted ways briefly to scour food options. I had a burrito craving that day, and grabbed myself a spicy chicken one in about five minutes. Then I wandered to find Jonny, who was squinting at the menu for a salad bar.

'This all looks wonderful, but you've missed a bit of a trick here,' he was saying to the vendor. 'Pomegranates would really have lifted this feta salad. And this parsley's an unusual choice. Don't you think it would be nice to keep the parsley separate, but then also offer people coriander as an alternative?'

Before that moment, I'd never known quite what people meant when they said someone's face looked 'like thunder'. I understood the sentiment of rage being conveyed, but I didn't really grasp how people thought thunder's prophetic booming and rumbling could be written on a human face. That all changed when I saw the salad vendor looking at Jonny that day.

'I'm sorry, I'm sorry,' Jonny said as I dragged him away, mortified. 'I shouldn't have told him what to do. But really, it's mad he doesn't have pomegranates in there.'

'Please, don't tell any more sellers how to fix their food?' I pleaded. 'I'd like to show my face here again.'

'OK, I'm sorry. I don't want to scare you off so soon. I promise I won't tell any more people how to fix their food.'

And he didn't. He just told me instead.

He peered at the mac and cheese at the raclette stand, and whispered to me that it had too much brie, not enough onions. At the Thai place, he inhaled the air deeply and sadly told me the pad thai could use a touch more tamarind. He simply shook his head at the pasta place – he seemed unable to express his grievances through mere words – and hurried me along to the next stall. Stall after stall after stall, he found some concern about what was on offer.

I have to say, Jonny didn't come across as superior or condescending when he critiqued all the vendors. If he had, I think I'd have walked away with my burrito right then and there. Instead he seemed almost excited, as though every meal he saw on offer was a potential project that he wanted to ruminate on and improve, until it was perfect.

'There's so much they could do,' he kept saying. 'I just want to give them a bit of a steer, that's all.'

It was kind of endearing. Yes, OK, it was annoying too. But it was endearing.

'So, are you a perfectionist?' I asked. 'Because that could take some getting used to.'

'I'm not sure.' He shrugged. 'I know I try hard to get as close to perfection as I can. I think that's why I wanted to go on a date with you.' Immediately he turned red and looked away, clearly sheepish that he'd just managed to say something even cheesier than the raclette stand. But, honestly, I didn't find it cheesy at all.

Eventually I complained that my burrito was getting cold, and told him to pick something. Anything. He took one more brisk walk around the market, and then settled on a potato and fenugreek curry from the Gujarati kitchen.

'This could use a touch more cumin,' he said thoughtfully, but he ate it contentedly.

Life is funny, isn't it?

Spoiler alert: Jonny and I became very close after that first date. We texted almost constantly, and I looked forward to each and every date even more than the one before. But he ruined my Borough Market lunchtime routine. Because the next time I went, I thought that, actually, he had a point. The mac and cheese really *would* be better with more onions. And the day after that, I found my pasta salad totally flavourless. By the end of the week I was silently judging everything.

It's absolutely ludicrous, because I know for a fact that Borough Market boasts some of the best food in the country, and arguably the world. Those chefs have all had as much training and experience as Jonny, probably more. Their food is, objectively, incredible. But the truth is, whenever I go to Borough Market now – whenever I go to pretty much any restaurant now – I find myself wondering what little touches Jonny would add to make the food even better.

So, yeah. I mostly eat Jonny's food these days. And I love it. It's as though my love for Borough Market morphed into love for him instead.

I will always, always look back on our first date fondly, of course. It was one of the most important times in my life, the start of something so wonderful and real. I found out exactly who Jonny was on that date, and he's never wavered since that day, not once. Borough Market was the start of the rest of my life.

So deep down, when push comes to shove, I lied: I do love Borough Market really. I may even suggest we hire a Gujarati food truck to cater our wedding. I can't imagine a better nod to our first date.

'Mum,' I say, as the queue slowly creeps past the place I met the perfectionist, perfect love of my life. 'Where did you go on your first date with Dad?'

And here comes the 'no' gesture. Shaking her head, hand raised as though she's holding up a barrier against the very force of my words.

What did I expect? That she was going to start gabbing about what shoes she wore, the butterflies in her stomach? Yeah, sure, and she was going to plait my hair and ask if I want to watch *Beaches* later too.

I don't understand Mum. She and Dad were married for a long time, so they must have had some kind of foundation. But, even when I was a kid, it did seem as though all the expressions of affection and sentiment came from his end, not hers. She was more reserved. She said 'I love you' to me and to Dad, but she never opened up much about her desires, her secrets, her fears. Honestly, I'm not convinced she even has any.

Lately, I sometimes wonder whether Mum's love is just a completely different feeling to most people's love. After all, Dad's not been around for a while now, and she seems almost entirely unchanged. The recent distance between her and me doesn't seem to have affected her much, either.

I know my mother feels love. She's not a robot or a psychopath. She was always there for me, throughout my childhood. She made my packed lunch every day, bought my clothes and supported me with my education and career choices. That's, undeniably, love.

But what is love, without passion? Where are the sparks, the surges of fearlessness, the tears, the rages? I've never seen any of it from Mum. I've seen her stubborn and coolly angry, yes, like when she wouldn't let me wear my yellow skirt. But she's always so controlled, so composed. Where I work in waves, flying up and plummeting down, and experiencing everything life has to offer, Mum always stays on a steady, even, unerring keel.

I'm sorry, but I'll take my tempests any day. I just wish Mum knew what it's like when you feel something with all your heart and soul.

Forty-five years ago

R ani Kapadia had never felt this way before.

She stood there, between the platforms at Tottenham Court Road station, breathing hard.

Things were not supposed to go this way. This was not the plan.

At twenty years old, she lived a good and fruitful life. After leaving school, she had secured an administrative role at a local civil service office, filing papers and arranging meetings. Her office, a short bus ride away, was all cracked bottle-green leather chairs and dusty flickering lightbulbs. There were windows, but they were little more than slits up by the ceiling, so barely any natural light came in at all. Colleagues often complained that it was depressing, but Rani loved it. She enjoyed being part of something wider than her own little world, being useful. She did well, always diligently recording and filing and requesting everything she needed to. All her colleagues liked her, even if she didn't entirely like all of them. She was earning her very own money for the first time, and while she voluntarily spent some of it on her parents and the household, as well as the odd meal out here and there, she was managing to save a bit, too.

One day, she dreamed of living in a home by herself. Not too far away from her family, of course, but still: a kitchen, a bathroom, a living room all of her own. They wouldn't have to be big or grand. Rani would accept the smallest, most impoverished home if she could call it her own. So she saved and saved, and edged further towards her goal with every payday.

She knew she didn't have forever. One day, not too far in the future, she would be married. Her parents had already driven her up to Bradford twice, Leicester once and Birmingham once, to meet potential suitors.

It always went the same way: Rani's mother would help Rani dress up in some overbearingly ornate, itchy sari, and clip giant golden earrings to her lobes. She'd wear more make-up than normal, her lips lined in deep red, her eyelashes dark and endless. Then she'd clamber into the back of her father's car, trying not to drag her sari on the wet pavement. Along they'd go, for many hours along the motorway, Rani sitting stiffly and silently because her clothes didn't allow her to do much else.

Then they'd arrive. They'd ring the doorbell in front of a house which looked not unlike their own, and a jovial Indian man her father's age, usually wearing a hideous brown or green suit, would answer the door. Everyone would embrace as if they were old friends, even though Rani had never seen any of these people before, then they'd be seated in the living room, on sofas sporting garish floral or paisley patterning. Amid the chatter – which Rani never contributed to, nor was she ever asked to – the matriarch of the family would enter, bearing a tray of tea and biscuits.

And then, in would enter Rani's potential suitor, her hopeful future husband.

Each boy was more coarse, more dull than the last. If they said anything at all, it was usually utterly insipid. One of them managed to stutter that he liked Rani's hair, then chewed on his fingernail for the remaining two hours. After the second Bradford visit, even Rani's father commented that the entire family seemed to have two brain cells between them.

Still, the meetings weren't going to stop. Back in India, Geeta, Aniya and Neha were all already married. Rani knew this because her parents kept in touch with their parents, all of whom gloated about their perfect daughters and their perfect lives. Aniya had a one-year-old daughter, and Neha was eight months pregnant. She probably wasn't winning races to the bazaar any more.

Of course, Rani's parents delighted in doing things a bit differently. They were intrepid inhabitants of England, pioneers of the modern way. So, their daughter being unmarried was fine while she was still twenty.

But as she started approaching twenty-five, things would have to change.

The plan was to work, move out by herself in a couple of years, then marry a couple of years after that. She and her husband would live in a big enough house for the children they'd have. She'd like to keep her job, but maybe she'd have to become part-time to juggle parenting duties. She'd see.

That was the plan, and Rani enjoyed plans.

That's why she liked her family's way of doing things. Rani didn't have to run around like her white friends, dressing up to go on torturous, interminable dates with dreary men with whom they had nothing in common. OK, so she had to sit through the odd awkward set-up, but at least she went into an environment where her family, background and traditions were effortlessly understood. Yes, she'd have the right man found for her, from her culture, sharing her values and beliefs.

So what had just happened in Tottenham Court Road station shook her to her core.

Today was her work Christmas party, and to make it an extra special occasion this year, her office had decided to collaborate with some other local services to make it one giant 'extravaganza', as the poster photocopied all over the break room called it. Around two hundred people were expected in the downstairs hall of a big pub near Tottenham Court Road.

Rani knew she wanted to go, but she also knew she wouldn't stay for very long. She didn't enjoy massive crowds. She'd come, say hi to a few of the girls in the office, maybe eat some cocktail sausages, then head back home early before everyone became utterly incoherent.

Rani didn't drink. Her mother didn't drink. Her father very occasionally sipped on a bourbon, but for the most part he didn't drink either. Rani figured that, if it ever appealed, she'd try it. But after the Christmas party last year, where she watched Sherry from the office try to stick her tongue down the boss's throat before throwing herself on the hors d'oeuvres plate and crying for a solid hour, Rani didn't feel any particular compulsion to sample a white wine spritzer just yet.

She didn't put much effort into her appearance – she

wore a simple black shift dress and stockings, plain brown-gold flats, and some subtle gold studs in her ears. When she entered, a pub employee greeting people at the door encouraged her to take her fill from the tables full of wine, beers, spirits, all sorts of things. When she said she didn't drink, he rather apologetically pointed to the one tiny foldaway table in the corner, which bore a few jugs of juices and water.

Rani poured herself an orange juice in a paper cup, found a cluster of her office friends, and chatted a bit. Sherry, sporting a glittery purple number which left little to the imagination, was already looking a bit the worse for wear; her shrill honks of laughter were coming with increasing frequency.

'Jacob is looking delicious, isn't he?' she squawked, before doubling over in stitches. Rani exchanged a glance with another colleague, who raised her eyebrows in bemusement. There was no one called Jacob in their office, and no one had any idea who or what Sherry was talking about.

'Do you mean James?' someone asked tentatively; James was a new accountant who'd joined recently.

'No – James isn't delicious at all!' Sherry roared, gesticulating so wildly that she splashed half of her cup of white wine over the woman next to her. 'Oh, look what you've done,' she whined. 'Now I've lost half of my drink. Get me another one, chop chop.'

At this, Rani decided she'd pour herself one more juice, then head home. She extricated herself with a smile, and went back to the sad little table in the corner. As she lifted the jug, she felt someone approach behind her.

'You're on the juices too, huh?'

She turned to see a man smiling at her. He had light brown hair, with touches of burnt orange when the light hit it just right, and was quite tall and gangly. He was over a foot taller than her, Rani herself only being about five feet tall. His youthful, clean-shaven face bore a wide smile as he looked down at her. Suddenly, bizarrely, Rani felt a jab of self-reproach that she hadn't bothered to wear high heels tonight.

'I think you and I are the only ones,' he said, as he poured himself a lemonade.

'I suppose so,' Rani said. 'Do you never drink, or are you just going sober for this occasion?'

'I *almost* never drink. I like to have a glass of red wine after the turkey on Christmas Day, during the Queen's speech. And I always have a glass of Champagne on my birthday. Beyond that,' he took a deep glug of his lemonade, 'you should've seen how my father drank. Enough to put any boy off booze for the rest of his life.'

'Is your father still with us?' Rani asked, feeling she knew the answer.

'Nope. Died at forty-one.'

Saying 'I'm sorry' would've been so trite, so inadequate, somehow. Instead, Rani lifted the lemonade jug and refilled the man's cup.

'Thanks,' he said. 'What's your name?'

She told him. He said he thought it was a beautiful name. She took a big sip of orange juice and turned to refill her drink, to hide her blush.

'My name's Jim. A pretty boring name, really.'

'Oh yes, very boring,' Rani chuckled. 'I think there's at least three other people here called Jim.'

'Well, none of them are quite as effortlessly charming as me.' He took an exaggerated glug of lemonade, as though he was sinking a glass of whisky, and slammed the paper cup into the table, flattening it.

Rani raised an eyebrow. 'Very smooth, Jim.'

'That's what they tell me, Rani,' he deadpanned.

'Now that you've ruined yours, would you like another cup?'

'Er – yes, thanks.'

As Rani poured Jim another drink, a group of men in suits, over by what appeared to be a half-empty punch bowl, burst into raucous laughter. One of them dropped to the floor and started prancing around on all fours making bizarre warbling noises; the laughter grew.

Jim shook his head with a wry grin. 'Those are my esteemed colleagues. I knew they'd get sloshed tonight, but it's only seven thirty, for Christ's sake.'

'What a shame you're sticking to lemonade,' Rani said, 'or that could be you hopping around on the floor.'

'You see, that's the kind of behaviour I save for a wedding. Or a christening. An occasion of real importance.'

'That's good to know. Shall I hire you to perform at my twenty-first birthday next month?'

Rani's words kept spilling out of her mouth without a second thought. From somewhere in the back of her mind, she admonished herself. How could she be so friendly and familiar with a total stranger? But those stern little chastisements were too easily drowned out by all the noise around them.

Jim seemed appreciative though, as he gestured his approval. 'I'll be there. The big two-one next month, then? Mine was a couple of years ago.'

'Did you have a glass of Champagne?'

'Because it was my twenty-first,' he chuckled, 'I let myself have two.'

'Oh, how very indulgent.'

'That's me. Jim "Indulgent" Nichols.'

'You have to stand out somehow among all the other Jims, don't you?'

His gaze lingered on her. 'I get the feeling you stand out without even trying.'

Rani raised an eyebrow cheekily. 'Well, yes, Jim. Well observed. I *am* usually the only Indian person in the room.'

'Oh.' Jim blushed rapidly. 'I'm sorry, that's not what I meant. I just meant you seem more interesting than most other people here. Like you have more to say. And I don't just mean because you're the only other one here who can currently speak without slurring.'

They watched a while longer as their colleagues cavorted around in glee. Somebody started to bellow 'Auld Lang Syne' at the top of their lungs, and got even louder when they realised no one was going to join in. Meanwhile, Sherry was now trying, and failing, to mount the man who was still galloping around on all fours.

'Well,' Rani said. 'I think I'd best be getting home.'

'Oh, really?' It must have been her imagination, but she could have sworn Jim looked a little disappointed.

'Well, there's not much in the way of food here. I'm quite hungry. It's best if—'

'Please, you're the only person here I can have a conversation with. I'm hungry too. Why don't we both leave, and get some dinner? Then you can head on home.'

She thought of her mother and father at home. She

thought of the stable, solid plans she had for her life, and she knew what her answer had to be.

'Yes.'

That was not what her answer had to be.

It was as though her mouth had taken on a life of its own. She said 'Yes' automatically, as though her mind was momentarily powerless. Now Jim was eagerly saying he'd fetch their coats. She gave him her cloakroom ticket and then stood, immobilised, by the lonely non-alcoholic table. When he returned, it was all she could do to dazedly spin around while he drew her coat over her shoulders.

Throughout the rest of the evening, Rani had a recurring chant in her head. *Stop this now. Stop this now. Stop this now.*

But there was something else going on inside her, too.

She noticed the little crease in the bridge of Jim's nose that appeared whenever he laughed, which was often. Even walking along the street on this freezing, dark winter night, Jim's hair was the colour of crisp autumn leaves, dappled and shining as though the sun shone eternally upon his head.

They settled in a local restaurant which did simple food, burgers and chips and milkshakes. They slid into a shabby booth, the seat padding torn and worn, yellow sponge bursting out in odd places. The table had an old splash of ketchup on it, which no one came to wipe up.

Stop this now. Stop this now. Stop this now. Every time Rani opened her mouth, she heard the voice in her skull imploring her.

But she didn't stop. As they chatted, she found out that Jim had lived in south London for his whole life, and had recently moved into a flat-share with his elder brother. He worked in accounting and finance.

'I like it fine,' he said, through mouthfuls of his burger. 'But I don't believe existence is all about grinding and sweating. Work's not the most important thing.'

'What *is* the most important thing?'

Jim waved his cheeseburger in the air. 'Food. Obviously.'

'If you can call this slop food,' Rani mused, eyeing her own plate.

'Oh, I'm ever so sorry, Your Majesty – we'll go to the Ritz next time,' he said, grinning.

Rani wanted to joke that she probably wouldn't think much of the Ritz's food either – that she generally found English food so bland that she sought it only for fuel, rather than to savour. But she couldn't quite form the words. Her train of thought had been derailed, hopelessly, by the last two words Jim had just uttered: *next time*.

She cleared her throat. 'Seriously,' she said eventually, when she had full control over herself again, 'what is the most important thing in life, to you?'

Jim chewed his next bite slowly, his gaze affixed to nothing in particular in the middle distance, contemplating his answer. 'Having somewhere to call home.'

'I couldn't agree more.' Rani took a mechanical sip of her milkshake, but she didn't taste it at all. She barely noticed what she was eating, she was so swept up by the man before her. The conversation was so much easier than any she'd ever had before, like a river ceaselessly flowing, without effort or toil.

'I miss my home,' Rani said. 'In India. Oh, that's silly – India hasn't been my home for a very long time.'

Jim dabbed his lips with a napkin. 'I don't think home is defined by where you are. I think it's defined by how you feel.'

Stop this now. Stop this now. Stop this now.

Once they'd had their fill, Jim insisted on paying the bill, and they stepped back out into the December frost. 'You're going to the station, too, I suppose?' Jim said, as they headed towards it. 'I'm going south, where you're going north.'

Where the paths to the platforms diverged, they stood and faced each other.

'It was lovely to meet you, Rani. I hope we can spend some more time together.'

'I'd like that.'

She was wary of exaggeration, but in that moment, Rani could only have said that the very foundations of the Earth tilted. That space contorted and rippled, that the laws of physics and gravity broke irrevocably, so that she fell upwards, could not help but fall upwards, to bring her lips to meet Jim's.

It lasted a second. Only a second. And in that second, she travelled through the entire universe. She flew among galaxies, she touched the sun, she discovered what it was to be in the very heart of time itself.

It was only after she and Jim parted ways, office phone numbers exchanged, that she came plummeting back down to the ground. It felt hard, unyielding, beneath her feet.

Things were not supposed to go this way. This was not the plan.

There were two options before Rani, now. Two platforms. Left or right, north or south. Though she boarded the correct train to take herself back home to her parents' house, just as the plan decreed, the forking paths in her life only continued to grow.

She had to make a choice. She knew she did. But neither path seemed easier than the other. Both seemed long, yawning, unending.

Hour 8: Southwark Bridge

On my phone, I'm currently browsing through some news articles published a couple of days ago. They all feature interviews from people who queued for six or eight hours to see the Queen. The comments sections are pretty much what you'd expect:

> *That is WAY TOO LONG!*

> *I'd literally never queue for anything for that long*

> *it should never take EIGHT HOURS to get from southwark park to westminster hall*

> *Why would you queue when you can just get the river boat*

> *Sexy girl want private man fun tonite ?*

I don't think that second-to-last commenter quite understood what the queue is actually for. And that last one was probably a spam bot. Probably.

'Whoa,' Denzel says. I look up from the phone screen

and realise he's clutching my mother's arm; she seems to have tripped over her own feet slightly and he's grabbed her to stop her falling.

'I'm so sorry,' she's mumbling now with a blush, refusing to look anyone in the eye as she steadies herself.

I can feel heat seeping into my cheeks. Eight hours of queuing hasn't had much of an impact on me. My legs ache a bit, but my feet are comfortable in my new trainers. I'm young, and hardy. But my mother isn't. My mum's old. And not exactly athletic, even in her youth. She's not the sort to don some joggers for a quick run around the block – although, to be fair, neither am I.

Harold is old, too. So is Agatha. Not every queue-dweller coming here has the same physical health as I do. Of course eight hours is an incredibly long time to be outside, mostly standing, waiting.

'Mum,' I say, deciding now is the time to put my comfortably trainer-clad foot down. 'We're going to sit down for a bit.'

'No, I'm fine,' she says. Here comes her 'no' gesture. But I gently grab her wrist and lower it to her side, before she can raise it in polite rejection.

'We've been here more than seven hours. You haven't been to use the bathroom once. I haven't seen you eat a single crumb. You need to take a break. You're not a robot.'

'Beep boop,' says my mother.

She doesn't really say that. But she might as well do, the way she sets her jaw in a rigid line and refuses to acknowledge me.

'You should listen to your daughter, Rani.'

Mum doesn't look at Harold, but I can see the rapid flicker of contrition as it flashes across her face.

'Go on, Rani,' Colin chips in. He's currently huddled up to Denzel, arms wrapped tightly around his broad chest, while Denzel strokes his hair. 'You've powered through for so long, you deserve a break.'

'Honestly, Rani,' Agatha tuts, not unkindly. 'Take it from an old lady like me – you need a break every now and then.'

The people behind us are nodding and murmuring and sharing encouragements, too.

Mum doesn't know where to look. Her eyes sweep across the ground as though she's looking for a coin she's dropped.

'Please, Mum.'

She looks at me now.

'All right, my daughter,' she says with a heavy sigh, the fight all sapped from her. 'Let's go. But let's do this quickly. I don't want to dawdle for too long.'

Choosing to bite my tongue rather than make fun of my mother for using the word 'dawdle' – I have incredible self-restraint – I more firmly take her arm and steer her away. Over my shoulder, I call to Denzel that I'll phone him soon so we can find them and rejoin. Everyone waves and Colin blows a kiss.

'We could go back to Borough Market and grab something from the Gujarati kitchen, if you want?'

'No, there's no need to go that far back. Let's just get a sandwich nearby, and sit on a bench.'

First of all, we find the nearest toilets. When Mum enters a cubicle, I silently bet myself that she'll be in there for a reasonably long time, considering she hasn't emptied her bladder for at least eight hours. Almost ten minutes later, after I've peed, washed my hands, and put on some hand cream, I win the bet when she finally joins me again outside. We don't say a word.

Our next goal is food. We source a little newsagent's, tucked away on the South Bank. Mum selects an egg and cress sandwich while I pick up a chicken Caesar wrap and a bag of Maltesers. Neither of us emits so much as a squeak the entire time.

This is absurd. There is so much Mum and I haven't said to each other. I need to take this chance. I need to seize this moment. I need to open my mouth and finally say, in my brashest and most assertive voice:

'Egg and cress is a good sandwich.'

Mum nods at me slowly, her bewilderment apparent.

I froze, OK? I froze.

We are silent again as we wander across the South Bank, looking for a bench or wall to perch on. I keep drawing breath to say something, but then the words catch in my throat. I don't even know exactly what it is that I'm going to say. I have a churning in my stomach, which keeps getting faster and more turbulent, prompting me to say something, anything.

But when I open my mouth, I see my silent, tiny mum, tottering by my side, so reluctant to allow herself this brief, small comfort of a sandwich and a sit-down. I feel as though I'm cradling a fragile, pathetic baby bird in my hands. One sudden movement and it could all go disastrously wrong.

As we sit ourselves down on a low wall and unwrap our food, I hope that eating something will restore a little energy in my mother. Perhaps then, when she's more herself, we can finally have the conversation we need to.

This will be our turning point. Because if a meal and a sit-down can't wake her up a bit, then what possibly can? What force could reignite some life in my mother?

'Did you know, Mum, that the Queen was Britain's longest reigning monarch?'

The squeaky voice carries over the winds and the crowds effortlessly. It's just a snatch, but we both hear it, and we both know what it means.

'Owen,' I say, at the same time Mum says, 'That little Welsh boy who loves the Queen.'

I stand up and whirl around, trying to see over all the people. There are so many wandering back and forth, they all seem to blend into the queue.

'I don't think you'll find them, my daughter,' Mum says evenly. 'There are too many people. They're probably already gone. I'm sorry, but—'

'ELSIEEE!!!' I roar. It feels as though the entire South Bank falls silent and turns towards me. Even the man covered in silver paint and pretending to be a statue breaks character and looks at me. 'OWEEEN!!!'

I'm taking a deep breath to repeat my summoning, choosing to ignore that Mum's teeth are clamped in a kind of frozen cringe, when there they are. From a throng of people in front of us emerge Elsie and Owen, Elsie grinning in genuine pleasure, Owen's cereal box crown tattered but still clinging determinedly to his head.

'Hi, guys. It's great to see you again,' Elsie says, her voice glowing with warmth.

'Hello, Miss Kapadia-Nichols,' says Owen politely. 'Hello, Mrs Kapadia-Nichols.' He gives us a bow, but stoops so low that he nearly loses his footing; Elsie has to haul him back upright by his elbow. Miraculously, his crown does not fall off his head. It must be Sellotaped on tight. He blushes and bites his lip as he finds his footing again.

'How are you guys doing?' I ask.

'OK,' Elsie says. 'I feel a bit like I've fallen into Wonderland.'

She, Mum and I look out across the South Bank. Much of it is the same as ever: street performers blowing giant bubbles, artistic types in vintage clothing headed towards the Tate Modern, families pushing prams and gabbing away in languages from all around the world.

Blessed with the eyes of an uninitiated visitor, Elsie is right. It may be the same as ever, but it *is* a kind of Wonderland here.

Across the river we can see St Paul's Cathedral, its great and stately dome flanked by smaller church spires around it. In the distance behind it, we glimpse the unique silhouette of the BT Tower, its jagged cylindrical shape rising to the clouds. Once again the ancient and modern starkly coincide; in London it seems the most natural thing in the world.

Pedestrians are hurriedly marching to and fro along the footbridge connecting the City to the South Bank. Most are alone, looking at their phones, wireless earphones jammed in tight.

There's a stark contrast, though, right alongside the river, where a determined file of people, sporting wristbands, is slowly making its way towards Westminster. Unlike many of the rushing pedestrians, the queue is more animated, more social. Very few of its inhabitants aren't embroiled in some conversation or another.

The part of the queue currently nearest to us consists of a

group of about ten women in their forties and fifties, some black and some brown and some white. Each one is holding a copy of a paperback; from this distance, the pink glittery cover indicates a romance.

'Are they...' Elsie says disbelievingly. 'Are they doing a book club in the queue?'

Indeed, one person is talking spiritedly, while the others nod or consult their own copies. Then someone else chips in with her view, her strident voice just about audible over the crowds: 'I'm sorry, I just don't think Lucy should have gone back to Hunter after he lied about being an international spy for so long.'

'You would say that,' another woman scornfully retorts. 'You always complain when the man turns out to be a spy.'

'Only because he *always* turns out to be a spy...'

'I suppose it's a way to pass the time.' I shrug with a laugh.

Unlike the rest of us, Owen is not observing the queue. Instead, he's gazing thoughtfully at Mum's almost-empty sandwich carton.

Clearly Mum notices too. 'I've been wondering something,' she says suddenly. 'Do you know what the Queen's favourite sandwich was?'

Owen's contemplative expression doesn't change, suggesting this is the exact question he's been pondering himself. For a few seconds we all regard him, and lean towards him with bated breath. We can practically see the cogs slowly turning in his little head. Eventually, he speaks.

'The Queen ate marmalade sandwiches with Paddington, though Paddington wasn't actually there.'

A beat passes. One glimpse of Mum tells me she doesn't understand a word of this answer. 'I see.'

'I'm sorry,' Owen says, ashen-faced. 'I don't think I know what her favourite sandwich was.'

'That's all right,' Mum says. 'You can't know everything.'

'That's what my teacher said,' Owen responds thoughtfully. 'I said I wanted to learn the entire history of the monarchy, but she said that if I did, I'd lose all the space I need in my head for maths and English and geography and stuff.'

'What's your favourite subject at school?' Mum asks.

'History,' Owen says, as though it's the most obvious thing in the world.

'History is very good,' Mum nods, 'but there's a lot of it. Your teacher's right, you can't learn all of it.'

'I wish I could,' Owen says with a sigh. 'I don't care about fractions or grammar. I just want to know everything about this country.' He raises his arms and gestures around at Wonderland.

'What about other countries? Some of them have had very interesting things happen, too.'

Mum and Owen continue to converse. Elsie comes and sits next to me, emitting a long and low sigh as she does so.

'I can't wait to get home,' she mutters, inaudible to the others.

'We'll keep you company until you can,' I tell her.

'Thank you, that's nice to know. Your mum is very patient with Owen. And that old man, earlier. Howard.'

'Harold.'

'Oh, yeah. They can all humour Owen far longer than

I can.' She tucks a lock of her straight auburn hair behind her ear. 'Sometimes, I think I must be the worst mother in the world.'

'How can you say that? You brought your son all the way down here. You've been queuing for hours. It's obviously all for him. I get the impression you, personally, don't care all that much about the monarchy.'

Elsie looks extremely guilty at this, but I quickly assure her that I'm no raging monarchist myself.

'It's sad the Queen died,' Elsie says swiftly, and I gesture my agreement, 'but in Wales, most of us look at the monarchy quite differently to English people. There's a very complicated history there.'

Mum is saying something to Owen. I don't hear every word, but I hear snatches of 'India' and 'queen' and 'Padmavati'. Owen looks utterly riveted, his eyes shining as he nods rapidly.

'Can I ask you something?' I say to Elsie, maintaining our subdued volume.

'Sure.'

'How come Owen loves the monarchy so much?'

Elsie wrings her hands together, before letting them fall by her sides. Then she wrings them together once more. I sense I've touched some kind of nerve.

'I'm sorry,' I say hastily. 'It's none of my business.'

'It's OK,' Elsie says, looking towards her feet, which are looking pretty snug in stylish faux-leather ankle boots. 'It's not a big deal.'

I've learned a thing or two from my fiancé – and not just how to antagonise the vendors at Borough Market. Rather than asking Elsie again or prompting her in any way, I wait. I wait for quite a while, as Owen comments that my mother seems to share a name with the great Indian queen Rani Padmavati.

As I knew they would, Elsie's words eventually come.

'Owen's dad was English. *Is* English, I suppose,' she corrects herself. 'He's still alive and kicking. He just has no interest in Owen at all. He doesn't want to be in his life.' She raises her head, and as she watches her son the love brimming in her eyes is impossible to deny. 'Owen knows his dad is English. He thinks he's not around because he's busy. Busy in England, doing English things, like eating scones' – she rhymes it with 'gone', the same way I do – 'and drinking tea and hanging out in Buckingham Palace. That's what Owen thinks.'

The little boy is doing some extravagant gesticulating now. I think he may be re-enacting a battle scene which Mum is describing to him. But he's still, somehow, doing it with an air of grace and sophistication, keeping up the same respectful poise he's had all day. He's like a young prince.

'I think he latched onto the Queen as a symbol of Englishness and Britishness. I think learning all these facts, following every royal development with an eagle eye, is his own strange way of connecting with his dad.'

Mum asks Owen something. I don't hear what it is, but the boy looks ever more enthused as he launches into an emphatic speech about Queen Elizabeth II riding an elephant in India.

'One day soon, I'll have to sit Owen down and explain that, no matter how much he learns, no matter how much he tries, his dad is never going to come and be with him. But until that day, I figure, what's the harm in letting him wear a cardboard crown and read royal biographies? If it makes him feel better and more grounded, for now, what's the harm?'

I can't think of any reason to disagree. 'How is he coping with the Queen's death? Has he dealt with grief before?'

'No, he hasn't really. Everyone in my family is alive and healthy, thank God. This is the first time he's…' She trails off, but her hand makes a circular motion, her fingers following a perpetual wheel.

'The first time he's what?' I probe gently.

'Well, I was going to say it's the first time he's lost someone close. But that makes no sense, does it? He never even met the Queen.'

Owen's now listing a bunch of countries the Queen visited. Though he's hesitant, and isn't sure on all the pronunciations, I'm pretty sure he'd get through the entire world map if we gave him enough time. Mum is nodding and smiling along with him.

'Owen's…' Elsie hesitates, searching for the right words. 'Owen's a bit *different* to other kids. When he found out about the Queen's death, he was sad, but he didn't cry. He didn't ask any questions – he seemed to immediately understand that she was gone forever. After a few days, he asked me to bring him here, to see her. Owen almost never asks for anything. So I wrote a sick note,' she says with a sardonic raise of the eyebrow, 'emptied my savings, and here we are.'

I watch the young boy, and I wonder what it must be like to grapple with the enormity of death at such a tender age. Perhaps it's not even possible. Perhaps you have to have lived longer, seen more of the world and its triumphs and beauties and injustices and woes, before you can understand what the departing of a soul from this place really means. And even then, perhaps we can't truly know.

Owen never got to meet the Queen, but he's going to see her, in a way, now.

It'll always be her birthday. Even though she's gone, the day she was born won't ever change.

Whether a young child or an old and wizened crone, don't we all try to defy death? Don't we hang on to memories, dream of our cherished lost one's laughter, relive the days they were here? In a small way, don't we each conquer the finality of death, just a little bit, every single day? Don't we show our strength in the face of its merciless grip, simply by continuing to live and remember? Isn't this very queue proof that life really can triumph over death?

'Mum,' Owen says now, 'Miss Kapadia-Nichols and Mrs Kapadia-Nichols have finished their sandwiches. Can we all go and join the queue together now?'

'Don't rush them,' Elsie tells her son. 'They may still want to rest some more.' She does a bad job of concealing her glance towards Mum.

But Mum, a little slowly, gets to her feet. 'I think you're right, Owen. We've had a good rest, but I would like to rejoin the queue. I've got my energy back now.' She cuts me off with a wave of her hand before I can finish asking her if she's sure.

I retrieve my phone from my pocket and call Denzel to determine their location, as the four of us – two mothers and their children – start making our way back towards Southwark Bridge.

Hour 9: Tate Modern

It's coming up to eight o'clock in the evening, and the daytime is well and truly over. The sun has slowly receded, over to the west, over towards our destination. The sky is a yawning deep navy-blue. All of the South Bank's street performers are packing up now. I hope the book club brought mini torches with them.

Across the river, the crisp silhouette of London – towers and spires and domes and the Gherkin and all – has begun to blur in the oncoming darkness. In its stead, millions of lights are flickering on in each building. The Thames is reflecting those lights, so the mass of distinct beams, like electric stars in a compact constellation, become ripples and contort into a hazy mass.

Denzel and Colin kindly went on a coffee run for us earlier, so most of us are now sipping at cappuccinos or teas. Even Mum accepted their offer – it seems as though that egg sandwich reminded her that consumption of food and drink isn't a sin after all. Despite his plaintive protesting, Owen was forbidden to partake, his reasoning that the Queen used to enjoy a nice pot of tea and therefore he should too falling on deaf ears. Elsie murmured to me that even a hot chocolate would give him more of a sugar rush than she could deal with at the moment. Right now he's eyeing Agatha's polystyrene cup of Earl Grey with undisguised longing.

'I'm sorry, but I don't think it's time to introduce caffeine into your system just yet,' deadpans Elsie. 'On your eighteenth birthday, I'll let you try a nice hot cup of tea.'

'The man in the queue earlier said he always likes a nice hot cup of tea,' sighs Agatha wistfully, and takes a deep sip.

'It's a shame we haven't found him yet,' Denzel remarks. 'It sounds like you had some chemistry.'

'Oh, no, of course not, oh, don't be silly, oh my, no, no,' gushes Agatha, and she spends the next few moments generally making the same incoherent sounds as a flustered chicken.

Harold takes a big gulp of his coffee. 'Don't deny what your heart's telling you, Agatha. That's the biggest mistake anyone can make.'

'What's your heart telling you, Harold?' I ask.

'My heart's telling me…' He looks around at all our expectant faces. 'My heart's telling me to listen to my bladder, and my bladder's telling me I've drunk too much coffee. Back in a mo.'

'I'll come with you,' I say. 'I could use a chance to stretch my legs. And I don't want you getting lost, now it's darker.'

'That's very kind of you, Tania.' He's still pronouncing it perfectly. Better than I pronounce it myself, if I'm brutally honest. 'All right, off we go.'

As well as the portable loos dotted alongside the queue, lots of nearby public venues have made their facilities available to queuers. We're right by the Tate Modern, so we head towards it.

I went to the Tate Modern on a date with Jonny once. It was quite early on in our relationship, and when he suggested it, I didn't want to admit that I don't particularly care for art galleries; I worried he'd think I was a massive philistine. I *am* a massive philistine, but I didn't want him to find that out just yet.

So along we went. For almost ninety minutes, we wandered around the exhibitions, and I'd never felt more uncultured in my life. One of the pieces, given a prime spot in the centre of the floor, was simply somebody's receipt from their grocery shopping: milk, bread, cheddar cheese and organic pasta. Another piece, which I observed fellow visitors ooh and aah at, was a semi-deflated basketball hanging from a door frame on a piece of string. It was called *Slam Dunk*.

Once we'd finished and were leaving the gallery, Jonny breathed a massive sigh. 'Wow,' he whispered. I braced myself: he was going to tell me all about how powerful and subtle and brilliant the art was. I had to seem as though I understood and agreed. In my head I rapidly ran through all the phrases I could use to sound convincing: *So powerful. Utterly insightful. Incredibly moving.*

'That was absolutely dreadful,' Jonny concluded.

I let out a shout of laughter, which must have echoed all the way across the river to St Paul's. 'It was *terrible*!' I crowed with relief, and I linked arms with him as we walked. We cleansed ourselves of the experience by sitting in a nice pub along the river, and we never spoke of it again.

'I hope my fiancé doesn't find out about this,' I giggle to Harold now. 'Me and you going off to the Tate together. He's afraid you're trying to steal me away, you know.'

Harold laughs too. 'Well, perhaps I am. It's his fault really – he should be here to protect you. Instead he's like Rama and Lakshman in the story, leaving you alone to do God knows what.'

Clearly, he sees my face fall. I'm no good at hiding my emotions.

'Oh, I'm so sorry. That was a rude thing to say. I didn't mean it at all.'

'Don't worry, I know you were joking,' I say. 'It's just a bit difficult. Jonny did offer to come today. He's offered over and over again. If I called him right now, he'd leave work and come in a flash. It's just not a good idea.'

'Why not?'

'It's hard to explain. I'm here for Mum, and Jonny would be here for me… but I don't think that chain would stay strong for long.'

'Don't your mum and Jonny get on?'

I don't know how to answer this honestly. I've seen Mum and Jonny getting on like a house on fire before. They have a few silly little things in common, here and there, mostly with respect to food. It's not that they don't get on. After all, with his goofy, performative sense of humour and his heart of gold, Jonny is a lot like Dad. Mum surely must like him – or, at least, must have liked him once.

'Well,' Harold continues, seeing that I've stalled. 'You've got your wedding to look forward to next year, anyway. I've always found that weddings have a way of bringing people together.'

Yes. That is supposed to be what weddings do, isn't it? They bring people together. They bring families together. This is why marriage always solved political conflicts, in history and in *Game of Thrones* and stuff. A violent, centuries-long war could be ended by a nuptial contract, because marriage means two separate clans are melding into one seamless unit.

Except it can't be that way for us. Jonny has a tribe, but I don't. I only have half a tribe.

My grandfather on Dad's side died before I was born, and Grandma died a few years ago. But, through Dad's older brother and cousins, I still have a sprawling family on that side. I don't remember every single random second cousin and relation that I've met, but I know most of them will be coming to the wedding. When I'm up there exchanging vows with Jonny, there's going to be a sea of faces in the crowd, all of whom look just a teeny little bit like Dad, just a teeny little bit like me, who can proudly shed a tear from their eyes and say it's one of their own getting married today.

Then there's the other, polar opposite, end of the spectrum. Mum is no longer in touch with anyone in her family at all. It sounds as though, even when she was younger, they were never particularly close or affectionate with each other. They drifted apart, and no one was particularly hurt in the aftermath.

I'm not stupid. Growing up, I overheard and understood enough to realise that my maternal grandparents most likely didn't approve of my mother marrying a white man. She came from a pretty traditional culture, which expected her to marry a man within the same Indian class and caste as she is. My parents have never addressed it directly, but I can tell their marriage caused a rift.

When I was younger, about thirteen or fourteen maybe,

I asked Mum why she didn't reach out to her parents, to try and resolve the argument.

'There's no point,' she said. 'We're better off this way.'

And that was it. End of discussion. So I never met anyone on her side of the family, or any of her old community from India. I don't know any of the Indian half of my family at all. I've not even seen photographs – Mum says she doesn't have any. It's as though they never existed at all.

I found some of Mum's old, tattered books, piled up in cardboard boxes in the loft. There was Enid Blyton and C.S. Lewis, lots of British stories that were familiar to me. There was a very sweet picture book of London, too, with colourful drawings of red buses and palaces and smiling faces.

There were also books I'd never seen anywhere before, books of curling and mesmerising, beautiful scripts. I understood from Mum that some were Gujarati and some were Hindi. I couldn't read any of them.

Why can I only speak English, and not my mother's mother tongue? Why will almost my entire wedding be white British guests, with next-to-no indication that the bride is half-Indian? Why did we always celebrate Christmas with aplomb – presents and mistletoe and a tree – yet barely acknowledge Diwali? I learned more about Diwali at school than I did at home. Why did Mum have to take that side of my personality, that half of myself, away from me?

Supposedly Mum has her reasons for saying we're better off without them. But I never got to hear those reasons. It makes me wonder whether those reasons exist, or whether it's just Mum's pride keeping her away. Whenever I asked Dad about it, he refused to say a word – except to state that it was Mum's business and I should leave it alone. Leave it alone, leave it alone, leave it alone. Stay quiet and act as though nothing's wrong. Ignore the fact that an entire branch of my family tree was sawn off. Ignore the part of my identity that I never got to nourish.

I wish Harold was right, and that my wedding could be a celebration of everyone coming together. If my Mum could reach out for once in her life – to her family, to Jonny, to me – then maybe that's exactly what could happen. Maybe I could at last know what it truly means to be entirely whole, entirely myself, entirely—

'Tania?'

I snap out of the thoughts rolling through my head. Harold's eyeing me warily. 'Oh… Yes?'

'I understand you're having a moment,' he says gently, 'but you've been staring off into space for ages now. I'm afraid I really do need to visit the old latrine.'

I hastily apologise to Harold, and we resume our walk to the Tate Modern.

Forty years ago

It was the best, and the worst, time of Rani Kapadia's life so far.

From the moment that she and Jim met, laughed, kissed, she was no longer the person she used to be. She fell for him hopelessly, and treasured the hours that they were together. They would eat meals at diners and cafés, and wander the local food market. Jim would often make fun of Rani for being overly picky about the food, but he always did it good-naturedly – and he acknowledged that, thanks to Rani, he was eating much better than he ever did before.

When night dawned and their breath misted in the cold air, they'd pop into a cinema together and watch the latest spy film or romance, clutching each other's hands.

One of the cinemas sometimes showed Bollywood movies, too. Jim would always insist they went to see the latest one, even though he didn't understand a word and there were never any subtitles. He'd make up his own silly little plots, and whisper them to Rani in the dark of the cinema, making her fight to stifle her laughter.

'This man is angry, because thieves stole his wife,' Jim would murmur under his breath as Amitabh Bachchan made some grand, forceful speech on-screen. 'And so he's going to take vengeance, and – oh, now he's singing a song. Hey, where did all these dancers come from?'

They caught a movie once where Dilip Kumar played the lead role of a conflicted father. 'I used to dream that my husband would look like this man,' giggled Rani.

'This old man?' Jim whispered back, his contempt apparent.

'Imagine what he looked like twenty years ago.'

'Hmm, I can see what you mean.'

When the film finished, Rani had to hurry back home in time for dinner. Jim grabbed her arm right after they'd said goodbye and she'd turned to leave.

'Rani, look at me,' he said. 'I know things are complicated. And I know I don't look like that man in the movie. But the truth is, I would dearly love to become your husband.'

It wasn't the first time Jim had said something along those lines. He'd been saying it, here and there, for the past five years. Every single time, Rani hadn't known what to say back. Deep down, she cursed her paralysis. For she believed that surely Jim would one day become sick of her inertia and move on.

But Jim didn't move on. With every passing year, he remained by Rani's side. He didn't mind that she never stayed the night, that she could only see him in snatches at odd times. He didn't mind that he'd never met her family, even while she'd met his mother and brother countless times. He didn't mind that her parents believed she was spending her time with an Indian friend named Prerna, a good Indian girl with good Indian values, who was entirely a work of fiction.

Standing outside the cinema, she looked at this man

who'd come to reside permanently in her heart. As ever, his brown-gold hair twinkled with an ethereal light all its own. To Rani, he looked much more handsome than Dilip Kumar ever had.

'Come home with me,' she said.

'What?' Rani couldn't blame Jim for looking utterly aghast. A statement like this, from her, was utterly unprecedented.

'Come home with me,' she repeated. 'Now. I want you to meet my parents. We'll tell them we're going to get married.'

His jaw almost on the floor, Jim asked her whether she was sure, whether she was *really* sure; whether she didn't want to sleep on it and prepare and plan ahead a bit more. But Rani was adamant. A fire had been lit inside her, and she knew she needed to stoke the flames. It was now or never. Five years had passed, during which Jim had shown her a world of unabashed joy and laughter. He deserved to have what he wanted – what she, too, wanted.

They rode the Tube back to her house in north-west London, Rani's heart beating so fast it threatened to drill its way out of her chest. She gripped Jim's hand tightly, feeling strength flowing from his soul into hers. She refused to let go, even as it meant a thoroughly awkward scene trying to get through the ticket barriers.

Soon, they were approaching the house. Rani didn't allow any time for hesitation – she unlocked the front door and marched straight in, her fingers still intertwined with Jim's.

'My daughter,' her mother called in Gujarati from the living room, when she heard the sound of Jim shutting the door behind them. 'Where have you been? Your father's arranged a meeting with a potential husband. He only lives a mile away, but his family are going to visit India tomorrow so we must meet them now. Come, let me see, do you look decent? Your father's in the bathroom, when he comes back we'll set off.'

Rani was intensely grateful that Jim didn't understand a word.

She walked into the living room, Jim's hand in hers, to find her mother on the settee doing some sewing. Upon seeing this tall white stranger in her home clasping hands with her one and only daughter, Rani's mother looked swiftly alarmed, then utterly dismayed, then a whole new kind of terrified.

'Oh, my daughter,' she said in strangled Gujarati. 'Please don't do this. *Please* don't do this.'

'This is Jim,' Rani said, deliberately speaking in English. 'He is a good, honest man, and he loves me. I love him too. We wish to marry, Ma.'

Her mother shook her head frantically as she rose to her feet, tossing her sewing aside blindly. 'My daughter,' she said urgently, still in Gujarati, 'please listen to me. He has to leave, now. You,' she said to Jim in her somewhat stilted but perfectly competent English, 'you must leave now. Please leave.'

'No, Ma,' Rani said resolutely, ignoring Jim whispering that perhaps her mother was right and they should do this another time.

Rani's mother was now fervently trying to steer her daughter out of the room, but to no avail. Rani kept her feet planted firmly on the carpet, as she heard the sound of a toilet flushing from upstairs. She felt like a mighty mountain, sturdy and unyielding.

Her mother, her eyes giant round pools of bottomless fright, could not speak as thudding on the stairs signalled her father's arrival. When he walked into the room, he started as he saw the tableau before him.

No one spoke for what seemed an interminably long time. It could only have been a matter of seconds, but it seemed as though the expression on her father's face halted time itself.

'Who,' he eventually said in deep, authoritative Gujarati, 'is this white man?'

He used the word *gora*. As a word it wasn't necessarily derogatory, but the way he spat it out, he might as well have called Jim all the very worst curse words known to humankind.

'Pa,' Rani said, striving to keep a tremor out of her voice as she spoke the words in English. 'This is Jim. He's a very decent man. He has a good job and he treats his family well. He treats me well. We wish to be married.'

She glanced at Jim, who looked a bit like someone who was being forced to play Russian roulette. For the first time, he pulled his hand away from Rani's – but it was only so he could extend it towards her father. 'It's good to meet you, Mr Kapadia. I love your daughter very much, and I would like to spend the rest of my life making her happy.'

Rani's father looked down at Jim's extended hand as though someone was trying to hand him a dead animal carcass. Then he turned to his daughter and, in Gujarati, said coldly: 'You're pregnant.'

'No!' exclaimed Rani in disbelief, forgetting to stick to English for Jim's benefit. 'No, Pa, I'm not pregnant. I promise. We haven't... We haven't done that. Jim is a good man, and he knew I didn't want to, before marriage. We haven't done that.'

Rani's mother seemed too stunned to say a word, and had made her way back to the sofa. She sat there, quivering, never taking her eyes off her child. It was a hideous scene: her father's unbridled rage and her mother's frozen fear.

For the first time, Rani wondered if this had been a huge mistake. Surely anything, anything in the world, even eloping or being Jim's secret mistress or having never met him at all – surely anything was better than this.

'If you are not pregnant,' said her father eventually, still in Gujarati, 'then there is no need for this man to stay in your life.'

'I love him,' said Rani in English. 'Pa, I love him.'

'You are being ridiculous. He is a *gora*.'

'I know. But he's also sweet, and kind. He makes good money. He treats me well. He even takes me to see Bollywood films – he respects our culture.'

'You think life is about films?' barked her father, refusing to switch to English despite his fluency. 'Of course you do. You've always thought life is about stories and fantasies. You've always read books and watched films, instead of living in the real world.'

A lump now in her throat, salt beginning to sting her eyes, Rani once again forgot to speak in the language Jim understood. Her vision narrowed to a tunnel; she could only see her father and mother. 'I do live in the real world, Pa. I know what I'm doing.'

'You have no idea what you're doing.' By now, Rani's mother had cradled her head in her hands and was rocking back and forth. In contrast, her father stood tall, immaculate in his suit and unwavering in his wrath. 'What kind of life do you think you'll have with this *gora*? What kind of life do you think your children will have? They'll be half Indian, half white. They'll have no culture. They'll have no home. You'll condemn them to a life of belonging nowhere.'

At this, Rani had nothing to say. She could not string together any words, in any language.

Her father was shaking her head in solemn disgust. 'I bet,' he said scathingly, 'your friend Prerna would never do anything like this to her family.'

Somehow, this unstopped the blockage in her throat. 'Pa,' she said, though her words emerged as a kind of hiss, 'Prerna isn't real. I made her up. I've actually been spending all that time with Jim. I've been seeing him for five years.'

Rani's father was not a man of wild mood swings. She'd only ever seen him in three modes. She'd seen him content, such as when he was munching on dinner and reading a newspaper. She'd seen him hard at work, immersed in action, on phone calls with his office or working out the household's finances. And of course, she'd seen him angry. She'd seen him angry many times, at many things, at many people. He was angry about politics, angry about an inept colleague, angry her mother had spilled tea on his favourite suit. Rani had never seen him as bad as he was right now, but still, her father's temper was not foreign to her.

There was one thing Rani had never seen before, never even imagined. And that was her father being embarrassed.

It was only for a fraction of a moment – so quick most people would never have noticed it – but when he realised that he'd been duped into believing his daughter was spending weekends and evenings with a fictional construct, he looked humiliated. His eyes widened, his brow contorted, his mouth opened and closed in incomprehension. He looked like a stranger.

It was gone in a flash, replaced with his customary uninhibited fury as though nothing had happened. But Rani knew what she'd seen. With her deceit, with her conviction that her parents would trust her every word, she'd humiliated her father. She'd made a complete fool of him.

And her father would never forgive such a thing.

'Get out,' he said.

'Pa, I'm sorry—'

'Five years. Five years of lies. You have disgraced us. You have half an hour to pack up your things, and then you will leave with him. You will go and live your immoral lives together, and you will never, ever come back here again.'

'Please,' whispered Rani's mother, arising from the sofa on unsteady legs, though she was barely coherent behind her tears and her clasped fingers pressed against her mouth. 'Please, she is my daughter. She belongs here.'

He didn't even look at her. 'Get your things, and get out. Now.'

Rani would never be able to remember most details of the half-hour that ensued. She knew she asked Jim to wait outside, and then she stumbled up to her room and began throwing things into a suitcase – random things, any things, useless things. She collected an armful of her books in a holdall, and chucked in a few other trinkets. All the while, she could hear her parents downstairs – her mother pleading, her father bellowing. She stumbled down the stairs with her worldly belongings, and hovered awkwardly at the front door.

Having heard her descend, her mother came to her. She held her by the shoulders, her grip tight. In their shimmering sorrow, her huge eyes were even more beautiful than ever before. 'My daughter, please, stay here.'

'But Pa won't let me.'

'He'll calm down, I promise. You just need to tell him how sorry you are.'

'Of course I'm sorry. I'll tell him right now.'

'Good, yes. And tell him you'll forget all about this white man, and you'll never see him again. Tell him you'll marry the boy he's found for you, no matter who he is. Then I'm sure you'll be allowed to stay home. We can forget all about this.'

Rani looked into her beloved mother's eyes.

'My darling daughter,' she whispered, 'I love you. That's what matters.'

This woman had taught Rani the exact mix of spices to make an aubergine and peanut curry just perfect. She'd taught her how to mend a hole in almost any fabric so you never knew it was there. She'd taught her so much of her reading and writing and her love for stories.

And, once upon a time, she'd taught her:

Sometimes people are so shocked, so panicked, that they wind up paralysed. Sometimes, you spend so long trying to decide what the right thing is to do, that you end up doing nothing at all. It's the worst mistake anyone can make, and yet it happens all the time. We're human. We make mistakes.

What matters is how you deal with your mistakes.

In the *Ramayana*, Sita made the decision to defy the authoritative forces in her life, and step outside her sacred circle. Queen Elizabeth II had faced her own immobilising grief at the Aberfan tragedy, but ultimately did what was needed. Young Rani had feared the boisterous, racist boys at the newsagent's, but she walked on past them regardless. Strong women don't crouch or cower – they move forwards.

No matter how dangerous the world might be, Rani had to experience it for herself. She had to take this step.

Rani hugged her mother as tightly as she could, and told her through her sobbing how much she loved her. And then she turned and walked out of the door.

Hour 10: Blackfriars

Jonny:

Love

I don't want to alarm you

Tania:

???

Something really huge has just happened

And it's not good

?????

Someone asked for my halloumi salad

WITHOUT THE HALLOUMI

Lol

So they just ordered a bowl of leaves then

Errr no

My salad is more than just leaves

Spiced squash, avocado, plum tomatoes, pine nuts, fennel, lemon AND leaves

It's a taste sensation

Oh wow, that does sound nice

Next time I come in I think I'll order a halloumi salad without the halloumi

YOU'RE SO FUNNY

Yeah I knooow

Still on for lunch tomorrow, right?

Of course

At the rate things are going I might have to meet you right after I'm done with this

That's okay

Just remember not to use your phone too much or your battery will run out

My phone will be fine

It's just such a shame, I wanted to come home and cuddle tonight :(

So have you and your mum talked about your issues yet?

'My issues' he says

Ha ha

YOU'RE SO FUNNY

Yeah I knooow

No, we haven't talked

We've had so many chances to, but I keep chickening out

Because it's like talking to a statue

It's weird, I always remember my mum being so sweet and loving when I was small

And there's a little boy here she's really nice and patient with

So is she only nice with kids? Does she just put it on to keep children happy?

Is she not being nice to people?

She was always very nice to me

Until, well, you know

No, she is being nice to people, she's polite and everything

But she doesn't want to talk about anything real

I've tried mentioning you, and dad, but she just clams up

It's worth it though right?

Even if she doesn't say anything back, at least you'll know you tried everything you could

I have to go love, break's over

Maybe I need to learn to be more like her, just stop feeling anything

Okay love

I love you lots you know

Yeah I knooow

Hour 11: Thames Beach

'You say you've been here almost eleven hours. That's a very long time. What's keeping you going?'

'I want to make it to the end,' says Colin. 'But I need to make sure I get to the Golden Jubilee Bridges. That's where I'm going to unveil my surprise for everyone to see.'

'It's not as dodgy as he just made it sound,' Denzel hastily adds.

'What's the surprise?' the journalist asks Colin. She has straight copper-red hair framing a small, heart-shaped face, and she's wearing a frown of concentration. Her bright red puffer jacket matches her fingerless gloves, and she's constantly typing notes on a tablet device, barely looking at anyone when they speak.

'Well,' he responds, raising an eyebrow in utmost incredulity, 'if I told you, it wouldn't be a surprise any more, would it? I don't want it all over your newspaper before I've had a chance to do it.' He pauses for a moment, contemplating something. 'But I would like it in your newspaper *after* I've done it. So, come to the Golden Jubilee Bridges in a bit. You won't want to miss it.'

'Sure,' the journalist says, though she's clearly already lost interest. 'How about you?' she addresses Denzel. 'What's keeping you here?'

'Him,' he says, putting an arm around his husband.

The journalist glances up at Colin with obvious dislike. 'Really? Is that all?'

'You mean, everlasting dedication to the one and only love of my life?' Denzel asks cheerily. 'Is *that* all? Well, what more could there be?'

The journalist temporarily stops typing, to regard the couple with a cool expression. 'Right. So one of you is here for some kind of creepy surprise—'

'It is *not* creepy!' Colin exclaims, sounding sincerely hurt.

'—and the other one's here to support the first one.' She shakes her head, and begins scrolling through her tablet somewhat aggressively, clicking her tongue at her notes. 'This is all totally useless to me.'

We've had a few journalists pop by in the hours that we've been here, but this is the first one to be so openly rude towards us. It infuriates me, because as far as I'm concerned, she has the greatest job in the world. What could be better than talking to different people, unearthing their stories? Yet every time she asks someone why we're here, it's as though she's disappointed by the answer, as though what we say is too frivolous and lacking in substance.

'And you?' she asks me now. 'Why are you here?'

'I… er, well… um, it's… I mean… you know… er…'

Damn it. She caught me by surprise.

'You're here to support your mum, aren't you?' Harold smoothly chimes in. Earlier, a few people came round handing out fold-up deckchairs to older queuers.

Harold graciously accepted and is now sitting in his yellow and white pinstripe chair on the South Bank under the blanket of night, surrounded by determined but exhausted queuers. Still wrapped in his khaki-green raincoat, he looks as though he's on the oddest holiday ever.

I swallow the lump in my throat. 'Yeah, that's right. I'm here for my mum.'

Mum gives a small, assertive nod in the journalist's direction, but resolutely refuses to look at her. I tried to grab a deckchair for Mum earlier, but she wouldn't take it, instead insisting I give it to Agatha.

'That's very nice of you,' says the journalist without feeling. 'So if it weren't for your mum, you wouldn't be here?'

'Um, maybe not, I suppose. But now I'm here, I'm glad I am.'

'I'm here with my mum, too,' says Owen suddenly. He and Elsie have been sitting cross-legged on the ground under a pool of lamplight for a while, playing with a deck of cards Elsie had the foresight to bring.

The journalist eyes the little boy with barely disguised distaste. 'You're here for your mum, too, are you?' she eventually asks, not bothering to stoop to his level.

Instead, he clambers to his feet to face her directly – at least, as directly as he can from his vantage point of about four feet tall. 'I'm here for Her Majesty, Queen Elizabeth II. She passed away,' Owen tells her carefully, as though she's some kind of idiot. Fair play to him.

'Exactly,' Agatha says. She's perched on her deckchair, hugging herself slightly, a tartan blanket draped over her shoulders. 'The Queen was a magnificent woman. She wouldn't care about the dark or the cold. I remember being a young girl, and watching her coronation.'

Agatha describes Queen Elizabeth II's grace and composure with great respect. She talks about how well-spoken and demure the young monarch was, and how her sense of style, accompanied by good education, rendered her a huge influence to British girls and women.

'She was a paragon,' she finishes simply. 'A paragon.'

The journalist folds her arms – an action made somewhat difficult by the fact she's holding a tablet, but she just about manages to tuck it into her elbow. 'OK. She was a paragon, and you adored her. So what will you do now she's gone?'

I'm fully expecting Agatha to bark that she will stay strong, carry on, be everything the Queen embodied and more. I turn to her expectantly, waiting for her to thoroughly school this arrogant journalist. But instead, there's silence. Then a sharp intake of breath. Agatha's bottom lip is trembling. Suddenly, tears begin to stream down her deeply lined face.

'Oh,' she whispers, bringing her gloved hands to her face. 'I simply don't know what I'll do now.'

Colin and I rush to Agatha and each put a reassuring hand on one of her shoulders. Harold hands her a handkerchief, while Denzel murmurs that things will be OK. I see Mum and Elsie simultaneously shooting daggers at the journalist, who at least has a shred enough of decency to look vaguely ashamed.

'Sorry,' she mutters. 'I'm just trying to get a different angle on this story.'

Owen looks her up and down. 'You're not very nice,' he declares with feeling.

Ashen-faced, the journalist hastily thanks us for our time and moves on to speak to someone else.

'I'm so sorry,' Agatha says, dabbing at her face with Harold's handkerchief.

'There's nothing to be ashamed of,' Denzel says fiercely. 'That woman was horrible.'

'But she has a point,' Agatha says, and lets out another choking sob. 'The Queen is gone forever. For almost my entire life, she was my constant. When war and conflict loomed, the Queen was there. When British politics went off the rails, the Queen was there. When my husband left me, the Queen was there.' She shakes her head in dismay. 'Who will be there for me now?'

We all coo in heartening tones, telling Agatha she's not alone. Right now she has us, and surely there are countless others in her life who care about her. But she keeps obstinately shaking her head.

'You're all very nice, and I hope we'll stay in touch. But I'm back to the Midlands, to an empty house, once this is over. I have no children. My friends have no time for me. My life used to be so full of love and laughter, but that time is gone. I don't know what lies ahead any more.'

Colin, who's been patting Agatha on the back, straightens up and places his hands on his hips. 'Now now, Agatha. This doom and gloom just won't do.'

'Colin,' begins Denzel, but Colin swiftly interrupts him.

'After all,' he says with a grin, 'is that what the man in the queue earlier would want?'

Agatha's breath catches mid-sob. She sniffs hard and blinks a few times. 'Oh. No, I suppose he wouldn't.'

'Exactly,' Colin exclaims. 'Think about the man in the queue earlier. Do him proud.'

A small smile greets Agatha's thin, pale lips. 'Oh, the man in the queue earlier was ever so jolly. I bet he wouldn't be sitting around, moping. Why,' she adds sadly, looking down at her deckchair, 'I suppose he wouldn't be sitting around at all.'

'I'm sure he is,' I say hastily, remembering he's supposed to be about Harold's age. 'And why not? I was thinking you guys look like you're on a lovely holiday. Deckchairs,' and I gesture towards the river, 'by the beach.'

We all look at the Thames Beach now, shrouded in darkness. It's a bit of a misleading name, if you ask me. It's just a narrow strip of gritty sand next to the Thames, and even during the day it looks about as grey and dirty as the water itself. A beach in the centre of the capital, at the country's most famous river. It should be so grand, so inviting, yet it has all the colour and life bleached from it.

Still, a beach is a beach.

'I suppose you're right. This really is like a holiday for me,' Harold laughs to the rest of us. 'I haven't been out like this in God only knows how long. I've got to meet so many lovely people. I'm seeing all of London's magnificent sights. This is the best trip I've had for some years. It's lovely being out and about again, after feeling lonely for so long.'

Because his hands are in his pockets, I can't check if he's still wearing a wedding ring. From memory, I think he is.

'My poor wife, Jane,' he says, reading all our minds. 'She was so loved, by so many people. I know I'm biased, but I promise, there would have been a queue of people just as large as this one, paying their respects to Jane. If it had been allowed.'

His deckchair has its back to the river, but he leans out a bit now to turn and look at the sad, lonely Thames Beach. 'Do you all remember the photo of the Queen, at her husband's funeral? Sitting in the empty pews by herself, completely isolated?'

We all nod.

'That's how it was for us, when Jane died. Barely anyone was allowed to come. My daughter doesn't live in our household, and she had a young child, so I couldn't sit next to her and her family. I couldn't even hug her.

'They told us,' and a snort of disdain enters his voice, 'that they could "live stream" the service, so all her family and friends could watch it on the Internet. I'm sorry, but I could not accept that. Jane was so vibrant. She despised the Internet. She said it stopped people talking properly, face to face. There was no way she would have wanted her funeral reduced to some digital spectacle.'

Harold turns away from the beach and now looks over the heads of a queue of thousands, towards Westminster. 'It's important to say goodbye properly. If you can.'

Owen does not tell us what the Queen was wearing at her husband's funeral. Colin does not make a blunt and inappropriate remark. Agatha doesn't mention anything about the man in the queue earlier. None of us know what to say to ease Harold's evident pain.

Almost none of us.

My mother takes a step forward, so she's by Harold's side. She crouches down, so they're face to face, and places her hand on his shoulder.

'I understand,' she says, looking him straight in the eyes.

'Well,' Denzel says eventually, after trying and failing to hide that he's wiping a tear from his eye, 'we'll all be here until the bitter end, won't we?'

'We certainly will,' agrees Harold, as Mum straightens up again. 'That's what Jane would want.'

Denzel gulps and valiantly fights back a sob.

'I think,' says Agatha thoughtfully, the tears now fully dried from her face, 'that that's what the man in the queue earlier would want, too.'

'Her Majesty started using a walking stick last year,' says Owen suddenly, in his understated, calm tone. 'But she wanted to keep going.'

Elsie gets to her feet and gives her son's shoulders an affectionate squeeze.

Colin's been uncharacteristically quiet for a little while. But now, in the relative hush that's settled among us, he opens his mouth.

And did those feet in ancient time
Walk upon England's mountains green?

Wow. Oh, wow. His voice is stunning. Absolutely stunning. From this slender man emerges a booming, captivating sound. I don't know much about music, so I don't know if he's a tenor or a bass or what. All I know is he sounds like a professional opera singer. His voice vibrates and flows with the melody. It's beautiful and haunting, all at once. Its sheer power seems to soar across the Thames. It's bloody incredible.

We are all gaping at him in awe. People several places along in the queue have hushed to listen, too.

And was the holy lamb of God
On England's pleasant pastures seen?

Denzel is the only one whose jaw isn't slack in amazement. 'Oh, did we never mention that Colin sings for a living?' he asks in an undertone, with a chuckle.

And did the countenance divine
Shine forth upon our clouded hills?

As Colin begins the next lines, Harold opens his mouth too. His voice isn't as polished as Colin's – not even close – and to my untrained ear it sounds as though he doesn't quite pitch every note correctly, but he sings with the same level of heart and soul.

And was Jerusalem builded here
Among those dark Satanic Mills?

Now Agatha and Denzel join in too. So do a few others standing nearby.

Bring me my bow of burning gold!
Bring me my arrows of desire!

There's now a huge number of us singing along, myself included. I've never been fanatical about this song, but with all of us here, Colin's powerful voice leading us, it's as though I can't help but sing. I didn't realise I knew the words, but they're bursting forth from me without even trying.

Bring me my spear, o clouds unfold!
Bring me my chariots of fire!

Owen and Elsie aren't singing. I don't think this is a popular song in Wales, and I can respect that. But they look delighted by our impromptu performance, the grins on their faces completely unfaked. Owen reaches for his mother's hand, and she holds it tightly. It's obvious they're singing in their hearts, even if their own chosen lyrics are different. The sentiment of strength, of togetherness, is the same.

I will not cease from mental fight
Nor shall my sword sleep in my hand

There's only one person who isn't swept up. Who isn't smiling. And that's Mum.

Her eyes are perfectly round circles of embarrassment. She's trying to keep her head down, to shrink away into the night itself, but she can't leave.

For a moment, I think she's mortified to be seen with us, and I feel a dart of reproach mingled with anger. But then I notice her mouth moves a little every so often. She's trying to follow along with what everyone's singing. But, like Elsie and Owen, she doesn't know the words. And I realise, unlike Elsie and Owen, she's ashamed.

I've been holding my phone, without even thinking about it, but now I pocket it. Instead, I reach out and take my mother's hand. She looks utterly taken aback for a moment, before quiet but obvious gratitude sets in. The tension dissipates from her face; now, as most of us in the queue around her serenade the Thames Beach, she's smiling. For the first time in a long time, part of something bigger and more profound than herself, I see my mother is glowing with happiness.

Till we have built Jerusalem
In England's green and pleasant land...

Thirty years ago

Rani Kapadia-Nichols was glowing with happiness.

She was wary of exaggeration. But standing here, her perfect little baby so warm and sweet in her arms, she felt more at home than she ever had before.

It hadn't always been easy. Far from it.

Back when she first left her parents' house, ten years prior, she had packed haphazardly. She did not bring any photos of them, or most of the clothes she owned. She took what she happened to lay her eyes on, and only as much as she could carry with ease. Because, at that moment, she had not really, truly believed that she was saying goodbye to her parents forever. She knew she had much to atone for, and she knew it would take them some time to even consider accepting Jim as a son-in-law. But she also knew that, eventually, they would relent.

These were the people who'd made sure to get her a good education, who let her decline mediocre groom after mediocre groom. They'd never before insisted she had to tread the beaten path, a mere clone of everyone else. They'd loved her enough to give her the best of everything. In time, they would see that Jim was simply the perfect man for her. She just knew it.

Rani couldn't bear the thought of getting married without her parents in attendance, and so she begged Jim to delay their nuptials until the rift had been mended. He understood, and agreed. After all, it would likely only be a month or two.

She would wait for her father to reach out. He did not like being pushed; he acted in his own time. If she called too soon, it could make things worse. He had her office number, and Rani knew that one day, he would call.

A month passed, with no word. Rani wasn't fazed, not yet. She hadn't been so stupid as to believe her father would heal quite so quickly.

Now living in a flat with Jim and his brother in south London, she continued her life largely as before: she went to work, she visited the cinema, she cooked and cleaned at home – and was amazed as Jim and his brother insisted that they, too, would cook and clean just as much as her, even if nowhere near as well.

It was wonderful to see so much of Jim. Even though they now slept in the same bed, he still restrained from any sexual advances beyond their kissing and cuddling. Rani could tell it was a struggle for him sometimes, but he never complained. Not out loud, at least.

She herself was scared. In her mid-twenties, she felt woefully inexperienced and useless when it came to the bedroom. She believed marriage would help her relax, but she couldn't marry until her family were there to bless the union. So sex, and all the other tenets of marriage, would have to wait. Not for long. Just until her father reached out.

Then another month passed.

By the end of that second month, Rani felt a desperation

rapidly burgeon within her. She knew that rushing her father was unwise, but she'd never gone so long in her life without hearing his voice, without seeing her mother's smile.

'I was in the wrong,' she reasoned to Jim. 'I should reach out and apologise for the way I handled things.'

While Jim didn't agree she'd done anything much wrong, he didn't veto her decision to call her parents. She waited for the next Sunday night, just after dinner. She knew they'd be home, awake, and not especially busy.

Her finger trembled as she dialled the number, but her entire body seemed to freeze when she heard her father's voice on the end of the receiver, speaking in English: 'Kapadia household.'

'Pa,' Rani managed in Gujarati, through her jaw clamped with nervousness. 'It's me. I—'

Bang. The receiver on the other end was slammed down with such force that she thrust the phone away from her in alarm. She didn't need to tell Jim what had happened; he could tell by looking at her.

The very next morning, Rani spontaneously took the day off work. She had never done such a thing before, and was especially unwilling to now she'd been promoted to office manager, but she was suddenly completely consumed by the need to speak with her parents.

Her father would be at work. But her mother would be home, and she'd listen to reason. Maybe she could get her father to see straight.

From the flat in Bromley, she traversed what felt like the entire city, making her way up to her parents' house in Barnet. When Rani finally arrived at the familiar house, sure enough, her father's car was absent from the driveway.

It felt strange to press the doorbell instead of inserting her own key. She'd never before had to wait outside the door like this, helpless until someone else admitted her. But she stood and waited. And waited. And waited. She prodded the bell again, and waited some more. No one came.

It was coming to ten o'clock in the morning. It would be highly unusual for her mother to be out at the shops right now, but perhaps circumstances had changed. So Rani resolved to stay, until her mother came home.

It was maybe twenty minutes on that she felt a prickling at the back of her neck, as though she had eyes on her, as though she was being secretly observed. Instinctively, she looked up at the bedroom window. The curtains fell shut just as she looked, and she knew her mother had been there, watching her. And she knew, with a certainty that felt like a lead weight dragging her down to the depths of a bottomless ocean, her mother was not going to come to the door.

Rani hovered there, unsure what to do. She was so close; she couldn't give up now.

'Oh, hello, Rani,' she suddenly heard in a saccharine, elderly woman's voice. She started and wheeled around to see old Mrs Woodward tottering along the street. She was in her early seventies or so now, but still wore the same self-satisfied smirk Rani had always known her to.

'Hello, Mrs Woodward,' Rani said, on autopilot.

'I haven't seen you for a while,' Mrs Woodward said, her beady eyes glimmering with intrigue. 'I was worried something's wrong.'

'Nothing's wrong,' Rani said, and gulped. 'I've just moved out to live somewhere else now.'

'But you didn't keep your old house key?' her nosy neighbour said, staring pointedly at her.

Rani could only muster a fake half-smile, which more resembled a grimace, in response.

'Well, good for you,' crooned Mrs Woodward. 'My son Alan moved out when he was around your age. But he always comes back to visit me. He knows family is the most important thing.'

Rani nodded mutely, blinking hard.

'His wedding was the most wonderful night of my life,' Mrs Woodward continued inexplicably, maddeningly. 'And now I'm blessed with three perfect grandchildren. Yes, Alan really has brought me so much joy. I'm so lucky I—'

'Shut up, Mrs Woodward!' Rani blurted out suddenly.

The silence that followed was as palpable and heavy as a tank. Mrs Woodward gaped at her, obviously appalled. Then she shook her head, muttering darkly under her breath, and shuffled away.

Rani looked up at the bedroom window again. There was no sign of life. It was another half-hour before she finally departed the place she'd once called home.

That night, in Bromley, was the first time Rani curled up on her living room floor and cried. The carpet, a stiff and wiry murky green, wasn't particularly comfortable, but she didn't have the strength to get up. Jim's reassuring hand on her back did little to abate her misery.

Over the next few months, she tried many, many times to phone her parents' house, but it was always the same result. During work hours, no one answered. And when her father was home, he simply hung up whenever she uttered a syllable. A few times she tried reaching out to his office and leaving messages, but she never got a call back.

Rani chastised herself daily. If she hadn't so spontaneously brought Jim to meet them, this might not have happened. If she hadn't broken her resolve and phoned her father before giving him time to calm down, this might not have happened. If she hadn't gone all the way over to their house before they were truly ready to see her, this might not have happened. If she hadn't, if she hadn't, if she hadn't...

And then, one day, over a year after she'd first left her parents' house, the pattern broke.

Rani dialled the familiar number late one weekend afternoon. It had become something she did instinctively, spontaneously, an erratic habit. Every time, she'd wonder if this would finally be the breakthrough she was searching for.

For once, the phone was answered without immediately being hung up again.

'Cooper residence, how may I help you?'

Rani blinked and swallowed. 'I'm sorry,' she said, awkwardly, because it felt as though her tongue had swollen to twice its size. 'I must have dialled the wrong number.' When she tried it again, she made sure to be very slow and careful, confirming that every single digit was correct. Then:

'Cooper residence, how may I help you?'

Rani couldn't muster the wherewithal to say anything.

'Ah,' said the friendly-sounding man on the phone in an American twang. 'We only just moved in. Are you looking for the folks who used to live here?'

'Yes!' she said, immediately, urgently. 'Yes,' she repeated, trying to sound more calm and balanced. 'The Kapadias. They've... They've moved house?'

'They sure have,' he said cheerily. 'Unless they're hiding in the walls somewhere.'

Rani couldn't laugh along with him. She felt as though she might violently throw up any second.

'Do you have their new details?' she managed to say in a choked whisper, but somehow, she knew the answer already.

'I'm afraid not, miss,' he said apologetically. 'They mentioned they're moving to India. Otherwise I'd tell you to check the phone book. But I suppose that won't work, will it?'

As he laughed again, Rani felt that this man made too many silly jokes for his own good – or anyone's own good, for that matter. In a daze, she simply put the phone down. It was a little while before she felt bad about how rudely she'd abandoned the conversation, without even thanking the laughing man for his help. But she had too much else on her mind to contemplate it for very long.

She didn't remember her old home address in India – she was so young when they left. She knew the name of the town, but what was the likelihood that her parents had returned to the same home? Her father had made much more money in London, and it was more likely than not that they'd upgraded to a bigger home in a better place.

They had made their choice. They had not wanted their daughter to know where they were. Her flesh and blood were determinedly far away, where she could not follow.

Not for the first time and not for the last, Rani's tears that night almost threatened to flood her flat, Jim cradling her as she wailed.

Jim tried to help, and together they'd occasionally head to the local library to pore over international maps and directories. But it was to no avail. Any time they stumbled on a potential lead, their excitement was swiftly destroyed when a confused Indian stranger picked up the phone at the other end. Their hopes always rose just to be dashed again; their phone bill, stacking up more and more fruitless calls to India, only rose. She wanted to catch a plane and search the country for them, but she knew it would be hopeless – not to mention an expense she couldn't afford.

Rani couldn't pinpoint the exact time she finally gave up. There was no particular moment, no particular trigger. But eventually, as weeks and months and years went by, she stopped trying to chase her parents down. Though she thought of them every single day, and always said a silent prayer in the mornings wishing for their health and happiness, she came to accept that she would not be in their lives, and they would not be in hers.

Though the pain was acute and enduring, Jim made things easier. The two of them moved into their own tiny flat in Lewisham, but still Jim never tried to coax her into doing anything she wasn't ready for. Meanwhile, his mother and brother were very sweet people who always tried extra hard to include Rani in conversations and activities, so dismayed were they that Rani had lost her own family.

Time, as it stubbornly does, marched on by. Though the hurt never left Rani, the joys in her life had the power to distract her enough to make the pain manageable.

Almost five years after she left her parents' house, Rani and Jim decided to get married.

'I want to be Rani Kapadia-Nichols,' she said, when she and Jim discussed finally tying the knot. 'My name is all I have left of my family.'

He understood, and he agreed.

The ceremony was a small, cheap affair. They did the reception in a local pub, so Jim's family, their friends and their colleagues could all attend without significant expense. Rani didn't want to wear white, as it would signal a tradition she wasn't born of – and she didn't want to wear a sari, as it would signal a tradition she'd lost. In the end she bought herself a shimmering but simple golden dress. It hung a bit loose on her, but it still dazzled.

The wedding was such a lively affair, with so much dancing and music and food and laughter that for a brief snatch of time Rani almost forgot none of her family were in attendance. But when she went to pick up some more food and saw the slightly sad skewers of bland, pale cheese and pineapple, her heart yearned for a proper paneer kebab with sticky mango chutney instead, just like her mother used to make.

After getting married, she felt ready, more than ready, to start sleeping with Jim. Now almost thirty, she was quite terrified on her wedding night. However, Jim was careful and considerate – and, as he'd pointed out wryly but good-naturedly before, it wasn't as though he'd had any experience himself the previous ten years anyway. There was pain, blood, and awkwardness on Rani's first night as a wife, but there was also tremendous love and care and connection.

Rani visited her doctor to acquire long-term birth control, and began easing into her new life as a sexually active, married woman. It didn't take as long to adjust as she'd feared. In fact, sometimes in bed, she felt so euphoric that she believed destiny had ordained that she and Jim were meant to be together forever. Such depths of closeness, such heights of pleasure, surely had to be written in the stars.

Both she and Jim wanted children, but Rani remained on birth control for quite a long time. Though she'd accepted her parents' absence in her own life, the sting of it still persevered. She could barely imagine having a child whom her own parents wouldn't know about, wouldn't meet. Could she really do that to a tiny, innocent little baby? Could she bring them into a world where their own grandparents didn't know, didn't care, that they existed?

It was another few years, when Rani was thirty-four, that her doctor warned her that her time may be running out. 'Your biological clock is ticking,' she told her, gesturing at an imaginary wristwatch.

Rani wasn't sure she was entirely ready for a child, but then again, would she ever truly be ready? Her doctor had been quite unambiguous about the sand racing through the hourglass, and though Rani wasn't convinced things were as dire as was being suggested, she felt she needed to make a decision regardless. She was getting older; she and Jim had been married for years. She owed it to them both to make a decision.

Once again, she heard her mother's voice echoing in her mind from a long forgotten age:

Sometimes, you spend so long trying to decide what the right thing is to do, that you end up doing nothing at all. It's the worst mistake anyone can make, and yet it happens all the time.

Once again, Rani decided to move forward through her fear, rather than being paralysed by it. She and Jim decided to try for a baby.

It didn't take long at all. She fell pregnant within a couple of months. Destiny really did believe in Rani and Jim, or so it seemed.

The next nine months went by in a whirlwind for Rani. Her slim physique began to bloom and alter. Sometimes she felt like a goddess, the spark of life unfolding within her like a flower blossoming. Other times, she felt sick and fed up, and wanted to yell at everyone and everything around her. She had always been short and, over time, the weight of an extra person growing inside her proved strenuous. She was exhausted.

Towards the end of her pregnancy, her doctor told her to stick to bed rest as much as possible. She was confined to her home, no shopping trips or dinners out or cinema allowed. It was torturous.

Jim helped. When he wasn't at work, he held her and cooked for her and doted on her. He brought her parenting books he'd bought, peppered with notes as to the parts he thought were the most useful. 'Baby body clock' said one post-it. 'Nipple confusion???' said another. But when Jim was at work, the lonely hours felt eternal.

She had more time than ever before to grieve the glaring lack of her parents by her side. She especially wanted her mother. She had been her guiding light growing up, and Rani wanted to be the same to her own child.

She took to speaking to her mother, inside her own head. As she sat there, bored with magazines, bored with TV, bored with the parenting books which seemed insistent on pointing out how much she didn't know, physically uncomfortable and shattered, she would ask her mother, resident only in her mind and memory, questions.

Ma, she'd think, always in her mother tongue. *What do I do if my child doesn't latch on for breastfeeding?*

Or, *Ma, what if my child cries and cries and I can't help them?*

Or, *Ma, what if my child is lonely and afraid?*

Most often of all, she asked her mother, so many thousands of miles away and unable to hear the thoughts speeding through her mind, one thing.

Ma, what if I'm a bad mother?

Every time Rani asked her mother a silent question, she would hear her voice respond in Gujarati.

Oh, my poor daughter, don't cry, Rani's mother would tell her daughter. *Love your child and protect them. Give them books and let them eat* fishanchips. *You are my blood, and I am with you.*

Her voice didn't immediately abate Rani's fears that she didn't know how to fasten a nappy, or that her child might swallow an errant pebble and choke to death. But it helped. Remembering her as the wonderful mother she had always been, as the wonderful mother Rani one day hoped to be, helped.

The day came. Labour was difficult. Rani did not have wide-set hips, and her body burned in agony as the child fought its way out. Overwhelmed by the physical strain, Rani's mind seemed to disconnect from her body entirely. Entirely unbidden, she floated to the corner of the hospital room and looked down at herself on the bed. She looked so helpless, so lost.

You are your mother's blood, Rani told the version of herself screaming in anguish. *She is with you.*

And now, here they were, a few days on. It was four

o'clock in the morning and Rani was holding her daughter, her beautiful and healthy and perfect daughter, in her arms.

Jim was enjoying some much-deserved rest after days of looking after both his wife and his daughter, barely sleeping himself. Though the baby's cries had roused Rani, she now seemed to be settling. Her little face was all scrunched up and soft. Her skin was the most wondrous colour Rani had seen in her entire life, a dusky pinkish-brown. Her scent reminded Rani of florals and fig trees and Jim, all the most beautiful things she'd ever known.

Her name was Tania Kapadia-Nichols. In the five days she'd been alive, Tania had proved two things without a doubt: she liked to eat, and she liked to make noise.

In the silent dark, rocking her tiny daughter to sleep, an old ghost emerged from the shadows.

What kind of life do you think your children will have? They'll be half Indian, half white. They'll have no culture. They'll have no home. You'll condemn them to a life of belonging nowhere.

But almost instantly, another, softer, voice replied, echoing from the wells of Rani's memories.

My darling daughter. I love you. That's what matters.

Rani kissed her daughter's forehead. Despite functioning on less sleep than she ever had, despite her bruised and torn and fatigued body, despite knowing this perfect child may never meet her own grandparents, she felt a profound peace wash over her. A peace that she had not experienced for a very, very long time – perhaps never before.

A third voice came to her then, that of a young and wise and boundlessly generous man.

I don't think home is defined by where you are. I think it's defined by how you feel.

Rani was home.

Hour 12: Waterloo Bridge

'WHY ARE WE WAITING?!' comes the shrill little boy's voice again, from somewhere further back in the queue. 'WE ARE SUFFOCATING! WHY ARE WE WAITING?! WE ARE SUFFOCATING...!'

Jonny and I have plans to start a family in a few years. But right now, with this chanting drilling into my ears and setting my brain aflame through sheer friction, I cannot imagine why anyone would ever dream of having a child.

'He's been chanting for hours,' Denzel hisses, balling his fists in frustration as he glares towards the direction of the relentless screech. 'Why aren't his parents putting a stop to it?'

'It hasn't been *hours*,' Colin says. He's leaning against the low railing running along the river, scrolling idly through his phone. 'It's been twenty minutes, max.'

'That's long enough,' Harold says. Still in his deckchair, which he gets up and moves every so often whenever the queue's made sufficient pace, his usually genial expression is wearing a frown. 'Kids need discipline. It's not the boy's fault – he clearly hasn't been taught any better. Elsie wouldn't let Owen behave like this.' Elsie and Owen disappeared a while back to get some food.

Agatha, next to Harold in her own chair, makes sounds of agreement. 'The man in the queue earlier wouldn't tolerate this.'

'WHY ARE WE WAITING?!' the voice bellows again, somehow even louder and more determined than before. From where we are, just about to head under Waterloo Bridge, we can't see the source at all. His voice is so loud it's coming to us all the way from God knows where. Maybe he only just joined at Southwark Park, miles back. Maybe this will be our soundtrack for the entire remaining wait. 'WE ARE SUFFOCATING!'

We've all been here for half a day. My trainers, which started off so padded and comfortable, seem to have constricted. Like Colin, I'm leaning against the railing with my back to the river, but leaning doesn't take the burn out of my soles. It's the only part of me which feels hot, though – my fashionable autumn coat wasn't made for the icy onslaught of night-time. I hug myself and hunch down, willing myself to think of sunshine, bonfires, blankets. Waves of tiredness wash over me, and every so often I lurch my drooping head upwards and realise I haven't heard the last few seconds of conversation.

The last thing I need right now is a squawky boy screaming without pause, and infuriatingly reminding us that we're barely halfway through our waiting.

I'm not the only one. Everyone's become exhausted, and even a little irate. The mere fact that the normally calm and collected Denzel is ranting about this kid's noise is indicative that we've crossed a line.

'It's doing my head in,' he says now. 'I can't take any more. I'm going to go and tell his parents to rein him in.'

Denzel makes to stride down the queue towards the source of the voice, when Colin looks up from his phone, reaches out and grabs his arm.

'Come on, honey,' he croons gently. 'He'll tire himself out soon.'

'I'm tired *now*,' barks Denzel. 'His parents, or whoever's with him, need to have more respect for everyone else here.'

'You don't want to start a fight, honey. You don't know what they may be like.'

'WHY ARE WE WAITING?! WE ARE SUFFOCATING!'

'I need this to stop,' Denzel hisses, his eyes wide and desperate.

'OK,' says Colin soothingly. 'Then we'll stop it.' He bends down and plunges his hand into one of the backpacks at his feet. In a fluid motion he retrieves a pair of big, rose-pink wireless headphones and clamps them over Denzel's ears. Before Denzel can say a word, Colin's typed something on his phone and placed it into Denzel's hand. Next thing we know, little green lights are flashing on the headphones' earpieces, and Denzel's look of irritation has been replaced with one of pure delight. A transcendent grin on his face, he begins bobbing up and down, mouthing along with some apparently beloved song. Colin resumes leaning on the railing, now without a phone to distract himself, but entirely uncomplaining.

It's utterly bizarre to see this role reversal. Since we met them, Colin has been the brash and frustrated one in need of tempering, which Denzel has dutifully and lovingly provided.

Colin must see the look of bafflement on my face, because

he shrugs at me now. 'I deal with loud noises much better than Denzel,' he says breezily.

All day it's seemed as though Colin depends on Denzel; it's heart-warming to know it's the other way around, too. I feel a little less cold, suddenly, and I straighten myself up.

I turn around so I'm facing the Thames. This is our last proper glimpse before we are completely under a short tunnel, above which Waterloo Bridge ferries cars and pedestrians across the river. The river's waters have calmed somewhat, no longer rippling from the journeys of boats along its surface.

I crane my neck to see the tunnel. Behind me to the left sits the entrance to the British Film Institute cinema and bar. I look through to the other side of the tunnel and see, nearby, a large outdoor screen has been erected. BFI branding on it confirms the film institute has set it up for queuers to watch films about the Queen. Right now, though, it's a blank and silent white.

During the day, there's usually people with rickety tables in parallel rows under this tunnel, selling piles and piles of all sorts of old books. More than once I've come here with Mum, and wound up spending half an hour with her browsing all the various titles.

Now, the tunnel contains only people – mostly a dogged gaggle of queuers, on their feet and on chairs, set on their destination to the south-west. But there are also other pedestrians, making their way to or from the bars and restaurants of the South Bank.

I swivel my head back around and look to my right. In the distance, the silent glittering city towers before me, and its reflection seems to reach deep into the depths of the water. Right next to me is my mother, equally silent, equally reflective.

Hand on heart, Mum's not looking too good. She's got her hands shoved in her pockets, a posture she used to tell me off for when I was a teenager because she said it made me look 'like a hooligan'. Her torso leans against the railing, and her head is down, her eyes not leaving the waves of the Thames. She's not said a word for a while. In fact, I don't believe Mum has emitted a single sound for more than an hour.

I never properly noticed the sheer number of lines on her face before. On her forehead, below her eyes and around her mouth there are grooves which I swear weren't quite so pronounced when we started queuing twelve hours ago. Maybe it's partly because it's dark now, but I'm positive my mother looks older than she did this morning.

It's almost eleven o'clock in the evening, which I know for a fact is an hour past her normal bedtime. She's been on her feet for most of the time, always bringing out her polite little 'no' gesture when someone offers her a chair. I've spent half my time sitting cross-legged on the ground or perching on a low wall, but she continues to stand, locking her gaze onto the river. As though it's a matter of principle.

As I'm looking at her now, I notice her head drooping further down for a moment before she jerks it back upright.

'Mum,' I say. 'You're falling asleep.'

'I'm fine.'

'WHY ARE WE WAITING?!' comes the stubborn chant. 'WE ARE SUFFOCATING!'

'Come on,' I say, quietly so the others don't hear. 'It's late, and you're exhausted. It's totally OK if you want to give up and go home. I can take you back there.'

Mum lives alone in Watford. I don't entirely fancy heading all the way up there just to get a taxi all the way back down to my flat in Clapham, but that feels like a better prospect than sending her off in the dark all alone.

Mum looks at me, managing to convey a surprising amount of annoyance with her puffy, tired eyes. 'I said I'm fine.'

'I don't believe you,' I say, trying to keep my voice down. 'You almost fell asleep just now. We've got so many more hours left to go. I don't think this queue is worth sacrificing your health.'

Mum doesn't say anything for a while, and I suddenly wonder whether she's even heard me. Maybe she's starting to go deaf? Perhaps that's part of the whole mysterious process of this queue rapidly ageing her. But right as I prepare to repeat myself more loudly, she very quietly speaks.

'If you want to go home, Tania, then go home.'

'I don't,' I say immediately.

'You do,' says Mum, almost as quickly as I spoke.

'I never said that.'

'You don't have to. I'm content here, but you want me to leave. It's just so you have an excuse to leave as well.'

'That's not true. I'm genuinely worried about you.'

'You'd be happier at home though, wouldn't you?'

Well, who the hell wouldn't be?

At home, I could finally kick off these trainers. At home, there's my favourite velvety, Cadbury-purple blanket, just waiting for me to snuggle underneath it. At home, in a tiny flat in Clapham, Jonny is waiting for me. At home, I can intertwine my arms in his and fall asleep in the little nook on his shoulder, where I make my bed every night.

This is the first night in a long time that I won't be falling asleep with Jonny as a pillow. The thought seems alien to me.

'WHY ARE WE WAITING?! WE ARE SUFFOCATING!'

Yes. I'd certainly be happier at home. And I open my mouth to say as much.

But then, looking at my fatigued and stubborn mother, I realise.

Sure, I've got the thought of bright lights and steaming hot food waiting for me the second I step through the door. But Mum doesn't. Mum has to go back to the family home I spent most of my childhood in, except now there's no one else there. Which is better: going to sleep in a lonely house, or powering through the early hours surrounded by friendly, like-minded people? Even for someone my mother's age, I don't think it's an easy decision to abandon the crowd.

But Mum really, truly doesn't look well. She resembles a flower that's wilted. She wasn't stooping this much before. She wasn't frowning this much before. Her strength has been sapped from her, and it's useless to pretend otherwise.

She needs to rest. But that doesn't mean I need to rest. My home will still be there, waiting for me, tomorrow. I came here for a reason, and I will fulfil it.

I steel myself before I next speak.

'Mum, I really think you need to go home and rest. I'll call you a taxi.'

'Tania, what did I—'

'I'll stay here.' I say it as assertively as I can, interrupting her as I know it's the only way she'll listen. 'I'll stay, and I'll

make it to Westminster Hall for you. Don't they have a…'
I'm already speaking softly, but I ensure to lower my voice
even further so Harold doesn't hear the next two words,
'live stream, of the Queen's lying-in-state? I'll text you when
I'm nearly there, and you can watch it online in the morning.
You can see me go by.' I swallow. 'I know it's not the same
as being here, but it'll give you a chance to rest, and you'll
be here, in a way. I'm your blood, so you'll be with me, in a
way. It's practically the same, right?'

My mother doesn't say anything. Even through her
crinkled, exhausted face, she seems a bit bewildered.

'So,' I say, holding my phone ready to take notes. 'Is there
anything you want me to say to the Queen, when I'm there?
Do you want me to pray, or give a message, or something?'

Mum looks a bit like she did when she was trying to join
in with *Jerusalem* – her mouth is moving but no sound is
coming out.

'Do you want me to sing a song for her?' I say, only
half-joking.

'Thank you, my daughter,' Mum says eventually. 'You are
very kind. But I can't give you the message. I have to give
it myself.'

I'm about to ask why, when Agatha begins to try and
arise from her deckchair. She almost stumbles, though, so
Colin and I each grab an arm to help her up.

'Thank you, dears. I believe I'm going to go into the BFI.'

The British Film Institute is one of the many local venues
keeping its facilities open twenty-four-seven for queuers
going by.

Agatha totters off, past a still merrily bopping Denzel,

while we all wave goodbye. Colin murmurs, 'I sure hope the man from the queue earlier is in there.'

'Mum,' I say. 'Why don't we do the same?'

Naturally I'm expecting my mother to bring out her classic 'no' gesture. I'm expecting her to tell me she's fine, she's fine, she's fine. No need to sit down, or rest, or be human in any way at all.

She draws breath to speak. Then:

'Oh my God! Oh my God! Oh my *God! It's David Beckham!!!*'

Again, we hear the screech from somewhere behind us. Again, with intrigued murmurs, we all instinctively hurry aside to reveal the source of the noise. We all see the same blonde woman as before is now pointing further down the queue, hopping from foot to foot with glee.

I crane my neck to follow her finger, as everyone else does the same. And, yes, oh my God, there he is. There he is: tall, dark hair, mighty build. As he turns to face us I take in his leather biker jacket, sunglasses, big bushy beard like a bird's nest, eyepatch—

'Bloody hell,' someone mutters, as the rest of us return to position with a disgruntled murmur.

On the plus side, a phantom sighting of the football legend seems to have finally shut up the little chanting boy. He's probably too deflated to keep it up.

My mum, seemingly, has missed the whole thing. Instead, she's regarding me, with a soft expression I've never seen before.

'I think you're right, my daughter,' she says at last. 'Let's rest for a while.'

Hour 13: The BFI

The bar we're in is quite cosy, with most of the seats done up in a plush deep red. It's situated right next to the bigger restaurant, along which there are views of the South Bank and the river. London never sleeps, and all the twinkling lights adorning the city across the Thames show we're far from the only ones awake at midnight on a Friday night.

After waiting a little while for a table – a small queue in the middle of our big queue, a trippy meta concept which I'm sure could be the basis for some kind of long and incredibly dull sci-fi film – we were seated. Mum doesn't drink except for a glass of red wine during the Queen's Christmas speech and a glass of Champagne on birthdays, and I'm not exactly feeling like going on a binge myself. So she requested an orange juice and I got a lemonade, which we're sipping on now.

And we ordered snacks. Lots and lots of snacks. There's some lovely roasted nuts, almonds and peanuts and cashews. We've got a bit of bread and hummus on the go, too. Then I decided to get a bowl of olives, as well as some lentil chips. And there's a little plate of long-stem broccoli, which has been cooked to perfection in sesame and spices. Although, it *could* use a bit more chilli.

Oh, God. I well and truly have turned into Jonny.

'This broccoli should have just a touch more chilli in it,' says Mum.

It's really strange how alike Mum and Jonny are, sometimes. That's why I can't understand how things went so wrong.

We've so far not been chatting too much, but when we have, it's been about trivial matters. Like the fact our favourite baking competition show returned to TV a few days ago. I spent some time dissecting which contenders are my favourite and which ones irritate me. Mum eventually offered her own, provocative opinion: 'They are all very good.'

But we have to stop procrastinating. Because here we are, sitting together in private. A prime setting for a serious discussion. The problem with Mum and Jonny – the problem with Mum and me – has to be addressed.

I can't waste any more time. I take a deep breath.

'Mum. We should talk about what happened after my engagement party.'

'Oh, look,' she says, blithely ignoring me as though I'm the annoying chanting boy screeching for attention. 'There's a film on.'

She's looking towards Waterloo Bridge, at the big film screen erected nearby, which has sprung into life. We can only see half of it from where we are, and that's if we lean at an awkward angle around our table. From the half a title card I'm contorting myself to catch a glimpse of, it seems this is another documentary about the royals.

'Mum,' I try again. 'About what happened.'

Mum continues straining to look at the screen outside

the window. It genuinely seems as though she hasn't heard me. Perhaps I should try again later, when there are fewer distractions. 'Do you want to go out and watch the film?' I ask.

She sits back and surveys the food in front of her. 'No. I'm sure we'll catch it later. Let's finish eating and sit here for a little while longer.'

Wow. For once, Mum's saying 'no' for a good reason.

'I'm glad you said that,' I admit, after I've eaten an olive so greedily that I accidentally swallow the pit. Mum pretends not to notice.

'Yes, it's nice to sit for a bit. Thank you for convincing me, my daughter. You've been kind today.' She inhales slowly, as though bracing herself. 'Perhaps we should talk about what happened between us, all those months ago. After so long, it must have been very hard for you to come here.'

'Yeah, well,' I say, in between awkward coughs. I'm trying to dislodge the olive pit and only half-listening to what Mum's saying. 'I think standing around watching a documentary about the royals would make it harder.'

Mum dabs a napkin at her lip, wiping up some stray hummus. 'Oh?'

'It's sad she died, and I know it's the end of an era. But I don't like when people worship the royals. They're not gods, they're people.'

Mum looks a little stunned, as though she's surprised the conversation has taken this turn. 'Oh.'

'Think about it,' I press. 'The coverage always fawns all over the royals, except for the royals who dare to do something different.' I scoff, thinking about the way the tabloids treat the different duchesses, ostensibly depending on nothing but the colour of their skin.

'Like Diana.'

I blink in surprise at Mum's interjection. 'Yeah, I suppose so. She did try to be a bit different, didn't she? And they ruined her for it.'

That's what really irks me when I think about the monarchy for too long. The history of prejudice and insularity. I know it doesn't come down to one individual ruler, but I'm uncomfortable with the way the institution characterises some of those things. I tell Mum as much.

'That's one thing I struggle with, now that the Queen has died. The world she was crowned in was so, so different to the one we're in now. Elizabeth brought us through to a much more modern and diverse Britain. Would it be such a bad thing if she was our last ever ruler? Maybe the work of the monarchy is done. Nowadays, it's so much more important to concentrate on respecting people's differences, and other cultures.'

Mum regards me with open, honest curiosity.

'What?'

'Well, my daughter,' she says, 'I'm just wondering. If respecting other cultures is important to you, why don't you mind when people pronounce your name "Tanya"?'

I can't think of anything to say. But I think my face turns as red as the décor around us.

'Tania is such a lovely name,' she continues casually. 'It's much better when people say it correctly.'

I lick my lips, which have suddenly become extremely dry. 'The thing is, Mum, I can barely pronounce it properly myself. I never learned how to speak any Indian languages, did I? You always spoke English at home.'

'Yes, so your father could understand everything.'

'And I didn't exactly have any Indian cousins I could practise with.' I'm now breathing hard, my voice rising both in terms of pitch and volume.

'Harold learned to say it correctly in a couple of minutes.'

'Well, good for Harold. Maybe he's a better Indian than me, OK?'

Mum looks completely uncomprehending. 'What? What does that mean?'

Her tone is so much quieter, more level, than mine. It was always like this, growing up. I'd be furious, or devastated, and it would show in my voice and my actions. Right now I can feel the beginnings of tears.

I hate it. I want to be as cool and unruffled as she is. But then again, her stubborn stoicism is the exact reason I don't know half my own family.

'I wish I knew more about Indian culture, but I don't,' I say, my voice now breaking. 'And whose fault is that?'

'Mine,' says my mother simply.

There's no food left, so I can't hide my face while taking a bite. There's only a bit of orange juice left, but it'd feel rude to reach out and drink it seeing as it's Mum's. So I can't look anywhere except directly at my mother, my disbelief written all over me.

I thought she'd protest. I thought she'd blame me. Instead, she's gone and admitted that this void, this cultural disconnect I've felt for basically my entire life, is her fault.

'It's mine,' she repeats. 'I should've made a bigger effort when you were younger.'

I can't believe this. It's what I've been waiting for my whole life. I've been wondering about Mum's problem with Jonny for a few months, but here in the BFI bar, we're finally addressing the questions I've had since I was a small child.

'OK,' I say, with tremendous effort. 'But *why* didn't you make that effort when I was younger?'

And now she falls silent.

Of course she does. As we're on the cusp of a breakthrough, she decides to clam up.

'Why?' I say again. 'Why, Mum? Please tell me, why did you never reach out to your family?'

Mum's looking out of the window now, as though she's watching the film being screened out there. I know she's not, because she's not leaning around the table. She's just staring at nothing.

And that's when my phone buzzes. I retrieve it, fully expecting it to be Jonny, hoping he can give me some advice on how to get Mum to say something further. Then I see Denzel's name flashing on the screen.

'We're almost at the Golden Jubilee Bridges,' he says in a rush of excitement. 'Colin's surprise is coming any minute. Get back here now. It's like nothing you ever dreamed of, and it's going to change your life.'

Twenty-five years ago

R ani Kapadia-Nichols had not expected this completely
life-changing event.

Normally, Sunday mornings were a jovial time in the
Kapadia-Nichols household. For them, unlike some people
they knew, there were no religious obligations. Jim had
stopped attending church when he was a teenager and
became an atheist. Similarly, Rani had stopped going to
mandir when she moved to England. Her mother had set
up a worship room in the house, where Rani used to pray
to the little idols and paintings diligently, but these days
she preferred to pray to her god silently when she woke up
in the mornings.

Thanks to Jim's hard work and several promotions,
to the point he was now a partner in an accounting firm,
the Kapadia-Nicholses enjoyed a comfortable domestic
life. They'd moved to a two-up, two-down in Watford, so
there'd be more space for Tania who was growing rapidly,
and discovered a community of fellow couples with toddlers
in tow. Most Sundays were spent with these local friends, so
both the adults and the children could have company.

On some Sundays, there'd be a visit from Jim's brother
or mother. Tania's uncle and grandmother absolutely doted

on her, and while many of Grandma's choices for gifts were unusual – the dungarees that were somehow a mix of polka dot, stripes and swirls all at once actively offended Rani's senses – it was unquestionable that Tania did not want for love.

It was an unspoken rule for the family: Sundays were for enjoyment, and enjoyment alone.

This Sunday was to be an especially fun occasion, what with it being the last one before little Tania had to return to school. The plan was to eat a big breakfast, visit the local park and play, and go for a swim at the local baths in the afternoon. There'd be a trip to Pizza Hut for dinner, and if Tania was very very good indeed, she'd get some bonus chocolate ice cream for dessert.

Upon clambering out of bed, Jim headed straight for the kitchen to prepare breakfast. Rani and Tania perched in the living room and switched on the TV. Tania was wearing her favourite cotton pyjamas: bright pink and purple, decorated in hearts all over.

Seeing the news that morning was, at first, like peering through a thick fog, failing to make head or tail of what's there. It all seemed so twisted, so unreal. It had to be a cruel prank. It had to be some kind of collective hallucination.

But it did not relent. The newsreader kept solemnly announcing the details.

'If you're just joining us this morning,' he said, 'we bring you the tragic news that Diana, Princess of Wales, has been killed in a car crash in Paris aged thirty-six.'

Rani couldn't take it in. She was well aware of the trials and tribulations of Diana's time in the royal family – everyone in Britain was, the tabloids made sure of that. Yet she'd seemed so vibrant and strong-willed. In her pursuits, in her fashions, the Princess was a force of nature. Rani had been quite sad when it turned out that, in the end, Diana wouldn't be the Queen's daughter-in-law any more. After all, they seemed so alike in so many ways. It was hard to imagine that such an incredible woman was no longer among the living.

'The Princess is gone,' announced young Tania, in a kind of sad awe.

Rani remembered when she was a child and had seen news of a catastrophe unfold on TV. Staring at the constant coverage had made the tragedy worm its way right into her brain, right into her consciousness. Even now, she often wondered what the Queen might do in any given situation. But she couldn't fathom what the Queen might be feeling today.

She nodded gravely, acknowledging her daughter's statement, before turning the TV off.

'Mummy, what are you doing? We have to watch the news,' her little girl insisted, trying to reach for the remote. 'The Princess is gone!'

She wanted Tania to be strong, and to understand the world around her, with all its complications and messes. But Rani had been older when the Aberfan disaster had happened. Her little one, her precious baby, was still too young to see it all unfold in such a gruelling, stark way.

'The Princess is gone,' Tania repeated.

Rani thought about calling Jim through from the kitchen, but then she reminisced on all the times she'd been upset and her mother, only her mother, was the one who knew just what to say. If she wanted her daughter to be strong, she had to be a good role model.

'Yes, my daughter,' Rani said gently. 'The Princess is gone. She died. That means she won't ever come back.'

Tania looked as though she didn't know quite how to feel. A series of emotions flashed across her face in quick succession; intrigue, sorrow, confusion. She looked all over the room, fidgeting, unsure how to behave, how to be.

'So no one will see her ever again, will they?' she said, after some time.

'That's correct.'

'That's so sad, Mummy.' Tania looked down into her lap for a moment, then looked up again, straight into Rani's eyes. 'If I never got to see you again, I'd cry all the time.'

Rani valiantly tried to conceal that her daughter's simple statement had shattered her heart into a million pieces.

Tania nodded firmly, though a medley of emotions still played on her face. 'Poor Princess,' she said. She slowly reached for the remote and switched on the TV; Rani didn't try to stop her. The screen was broadcasting a series of different images of Diana. 'Oh, Mummy, look at her dress there. The Princess is so pretty.'

'That's true. She was very pretty.'

'She *was* very pretty,' Tania says carefully, concentrating on her switch to past tense.

Her poor sweet daughter. Slowly understanding, for the first time, how someone could go from 'is' to 'was'. It was unbearable.

'Please don't be upset, my daughter,' she said, trying to mend the fracture inside herself, trying to restore joy and stability again for them both.

Tania bit her lip. 'But it's so sad, Mummy.' She gestured

at the TV, which was now depicting a crowd of mourners in Paris. 'Look, everyone is crying.'

'I know. But, please… try not to be sad. It's not good to be sad.'

'Does that mean… I'm not good, because I feel sad?' Tania asked, her face now unambiguously devastated.

'You're very good,' Rani clarified at once.

Silently, Rani rebuked herself. Why was she so verbally clumsy, tripping over her own tongue when her child needed her the most? Her mother was always so good at saying the right thing.

Perhaps it was because her mother's tongue was Gujarati. Perhaps that was a tongue which lent itself to articulation, a tongue you could not trip over. Rani certainly never struggled to find the words in her own head; her thoughts came flowing in her native language like a perpetual stream, and always encompassed exactly what she needed, all nuance and colour intact. It was when she came to voice them, translated, that she sometimes stumbled. Her English was perfectly fluent, yet the meaning wasn't quite her own.

But it was her husband's language and, therefore, her daughter's. She did not want Tania straddled, adrift, between two different worlds, with no home to call her own. So Rani had to make English her own language, too. She had to dampen her Indian traditions, drag them into the peripherals, so that her daughter may thrive unconflicted.

'You're very good,' she repeated. 'You're the best little girl in the world.'

'But I'm sad,' Tania said with a sniffle. 'I miss the Princess. But you said that being sad is bad.'

'I know it must happen sometimes, my daughter. I've

been sad before, too. But what's important is trying to get past the sadness. After all, crying never solved anything, now did it? So don't let sadness win. OK?'

Tania bit her lip, then nodded.

'Will you be my brave girl?'

Tania nodded again.

'Breakfast is ready, my darling girls!' called Jim from the kitchen.

Rani, her heart now scarred but on the mend, took her daughter's tiny hand. Together they headed to the kitchen for their special, last-one-before-term-starts Sunday breakfast. They remained side by side, inseparable, for the rest of the day.

Hour 14: Golden Jubilee Bridges

Mum and I came back from the BFI together, to find Denzel. We are still standing side by side now, nearly an hour later, next to Denzel and Harold. Owen, Elsie and Agatha have not returned, although, as ever, a whole host of new people have greeted us.

We're clustered near the Golden Jubilee Bridges. They're two pedestrian bridges, flanking either side of a railway bridge. They're lit up with spikes of electric-blue light, fanning downwards like fountains from evenly spaced poles across the bridges' span. There haven't been any trains on the railway; I guess the timetable stops well before one o'clock in the morning.

Embankment and Charing Cross are twinkling on the other side of the river. On this side, most of the numerous bars and restaurants are now closed and dim, and there are fewer pedestrians wandering about. The Thames and the sky are the same murky blue-black shade, though the sky is dotted with a chaotic mosaic of wispy grey clouds. I can't see the moon anywhere.

I can't see Colin anywhere, either.

'Denzel,' I say, as sweetly as I can muster, 'I thought you said Colin's surprise would be coming "any minute"?'

'He's getting ready,' Denzel assures us, a tremble of exhilaration in his voice.

'Ready for what?' someone asks.

'*The surprise,*' comes the giddy answer.

Mum has perked up a bit since the BFI and, like the rest of us, she's looking around occasionally to see whether some kind of surprise is making its way towards us, though none of us has a clue what form it's going to take.

A short man, roughly Harold's age or maybe a bit older, has joined us. He's zipped up a shabby raincoat over what looks to be quite a nice, expensive suit. He has a deckchair folded up behind him; currently he's hopping from foot to foot, partly to stay warm and partly in impatience. 'We've been waiting for ages,' he grumbles in a West Country burr. 'Honestly, the woman in the queue before would never have waited this long.'

Harold and I catch each other's eye. 'Oh, really?' I prompt the man.

'Absolutely not. The woman in the queue before, she'd have had no patience for these antics. Why, I bet the woman in the queue before would have given them a piece of her mind by now.'

'I see,' Harold muses. 'Gerry, what was the woman in the queue before's name?'

'I don't know,' Gerry sighs. 'I didn't take note of her name or phone number before we were separated. Silly of me, really. She was such a fiery, fascinating woman.'

'It sounds like you two had a real spark,' I chip in.

'Oh, well... that's... how preposterous... simply... that is... absolutely... very silly, no, no,' he splutters, suddenly quite unable to look anyone in the eye.

'Do we know where Agatha's gone?' I ask Harold in an undertone.

'I'm afraid not. So, the Falklands, eh?' Harold says cheerily to Gerry, who looks quite dumbfounded at this apparent non-sequitur. 'Did you get taken over there by the QE2?'

'Er – yes, yes I did in fact.'

'Me too.' Harold claps Gerry on the shoulder. 'Looks like Queen Elizabeth II's brought us together once more.'

The two of them embark on a war-laden chat, while Denzel gets on his tiptoes and scans the horizon – not the river and city to the north-west, but the South Bank instead.

'You don't have to tell me the surprise,' I say, my patience beginning to wear thin, 'but where *is* Colin?'

'We must be patient,' says Mum. 'We're already waiting – what's the problem with waiting some more? Patience is an important quality,' she adds, echoing her takeaway from the Diwali story it feels like we were discussing a million years ago.

A few people nearby chuckle in agreement. I guess Mum's got a point. But even she can't stop herself glancing towards the South Bank, hoping to catch a glimpse of Colin.

'Ah!' barks Denzel suddenly. He presses his vibrating phone to his ear. 'Hello, are you ready?' He addresses me and Mum, nodding towards the backpack at his feet. 'Can you keep an eye on that? I'll be back in…' But he's already sprinting off towards the BFI, before we can hear the rest.

Back in what, Denzel? Back in a minute? Back in an hour? Back in six months?

'He'll be back in a minute,' says Mum, trying to reassure us both.

'The woman in the queue earlier wouldn't have tolerated this uncertainty,' says Gerry gloomily.

People around us are murmuring that it won't be much longer, it can't be much longer.

'Oh,' Mum suddenly says softly, just about audible amid the hubbub. I turn to look where she's facing, down the South Bank.

Denzel is returning, and there's someone else next to him.

The unfamiliar person has exaggerated, expert make-up applied, stark black and glittery gold outlining their eyes and cheekbones. Tumbling waves of golden-blonde hair fall over their shoulders. And they're wearing an incredible dress with a bright golden skirt decorated with darker chevron stripes that fans out around them; their perfectly shaped nails have been painted to match, while their top half is adorned in a sort of diamond patchwork, bright yellow and blue and pink and orange. It's a striking burst of colour, lighting up the dim surroundings like a firework. The person walks with immense grace, each long stride in their golden heels exuding confidence.

Who on earth is this person? And where's—

'Colin?' Mum breathes in wonder.

She's right. It *is* Colin. Except he's transformed into an entirely new person.

'This,' Denzel beams proudly when they've reached us, gesturing to the glamorous figure at his side, 'is my husband's alter-ego, Harlequeen. She's one of the acts he performs as part of his show.'

'Pleased to finally meet you all,' she says, beaming.

Harlequeen is genuinely mesmerising. Her poise, her

beautifully sculpted face, her outfit. Every single atom of her demands attention.

'I like your dress very much, Harlequeen,' says Mum with obvious sincerity. Of course she does – who wouldn't? It's stunning.

'Thank you,' Harlequeen says in delight, doing a little twirl for us. 'I made it myself. It's a replica of the Queen's Harlequin dress, which she wore at the Royal Variety Performance in 1999.' She looks around. 'I'd hoped Owen might tell everyone that, but I guess he's not here.'

'Harlequeen is a tribute to the Queen,' Denzel adds. 'Not an imitation. That's why she never copies the Queen's hair, or the tiara, or anything like that. Harlequeen is a fan – she's not trying to be the real thing.'

Harlequeen nods firmly.

'I can't believe you made that yourself,' says Mum in wonder.

'Can you make me one?' asks someone else. 'I'll pay you, obviously.'

'How do you do that make-up?' inserts someone else. 'Can you teach me?'

'You're magnificent.' Harold smiles up from his deckchair. 'I've never once thought about remarrying, until this very moment.'

Gerry hasn't said anything yet. He doesn't seem entirely sure how he feels about meeting Harlequeen. He's lurking behind the rest of us, looking determinedly at the Thames, as we all continue to lob our enthusiastic questions and comments at her.

Denzel has bent down to the ground, unzipping the backpack he's been lugging around with him all day. From it, he retrieves a fold-up tripod, and a mobile phone, as well as the oversize pink headphones he was donning earlier. 'This is Harlequeen's phone,' he says to me, as he clamps the headphones on. 'For her business calls, social media... and, of course, her very first ever live stream.'

I help him unfold the tripod and affix the phone to it.

'OK, everyone,' Harlequeen announces. 'My public awaits. You'll have to simmer down a bit while I talk to the camera – but make sure to cheer at the good parts!'

We get some early practice in, most of us cheering manically already as Harlequeen adopts her stance, ready to be filmed.

'OK,' says Denzel, positioning himself behind the tripod and prodding at the phone screen. 'We're almost ready, honey.'

'Oh,' Harlequeen squeaks, putting her hands to her face in mock worry. 'Careful what you say in public, or your husband Colin may find out about us.'

'Don't you worry,' Denzel smirks back as the rest of us laugh, 'I can keep you both on the go. OK, honey, we're about to live stream. Ready?'

'Ready.' Harlequeen gives a thumbs up.

'Three, two, one...'

A hush falls upon the rest of us in the queue. I move to stand beside Denzel so I can see the phone screen. Harlequeen looks enchanting – the local lighting and a small torch on the phone are bathing her in a gentle glow. The colours on her outfit are as bright and dazzling as the gleam in her eyes.

'Go!'

Harlequeen opens her mouth to speak. But no sound

comes out. The glint in her eyes has suddenly morphed into sheer terror.

'Oh, no,' murmurs Denzel.

'What's wrong?' I whisper.

She's still quiet, seemingly unable to move a muscle, her gaze towards the camera rigid.

'I was worried this may happen,' Denzel says, unable to keep the hint of panic in his voice. 'She's performed onstage countless times with no problems, but she's never done a live stream. So many thousands of people could be watching a live stream. She's frozen.'

Harlequeen closes her mouth, and gulps hard. Despite the smooth pale make-up masking her face, it's obvious her cheeks are beginning to turn crimson.

'I'll turn it off,' Denzel mutters, reaching to press the phone screen.

'No,' I say, instinctively, grabbing his hand. 'Wait a second.' I clear my throat, then loudly address Harlequeen: 'Harlequeen, your adoring fans are watching. Do you want to say hello to them?'

'H-hello, everyone,' stutters Harlequeen in a strangled whisper, swallowing again.

'Tell us, Harlequeen,' I say. I'm not thinking at all about what I'm saying. It's just happening, without any deliberation. It feels as though some other, bigger force has taken hold of me. 'Why are you here tonight?'

'I'm here,' says Harlequeen, a smidge more confidently than before, 'because I want to pay tribute to Her Majesty, Queen Elizabeth II.'

'What is it about the Queen that means so much to you?' I prompt.

'Oh, how do I even describe it? I have no time for most of the royals, but the Queen was an icon. She was always so sweet and polite to everyone. I believe she really tried to make things better. Most importantly of all,' and she gestures towards her billowing skirts, 'she was an absolute fashion diva. Did you know' – she seems to be forgetting her nervousness more by the minute – 'that for her coronation, she wore shoes made by Roger Vivier?'

'I did not know that,' I lie with a laugh. 'You've been queuing across London for a long time, haven't you?'

'Oh, yes. I've queued through day and night to reach this very place.'

'Why here?' It's a question I've been wondering all along. I thought the answer would become clear when I discovered what the surprise was, but it's a bigger mystery to me than ever. 'Why the Golden Jubilee Bridges? Why not Tower Bridge, or Westminster? Those places are more associated with the Queen.'

'Because,' Harlequeen says, louder still, her fists curling into determined balls – and rapidly uncurling, probably because she realises she might well mess up her immaculate manicure if she clenches too hard, 'I care about the Queen, but I'm not her. I have to stay true to myself. When I lived in this city, many years ago, I was still finding myself.'

She pauses for a moment, staying a quiver in her voice. 'This is where I was. When I decided to stop pretending, and start being who I'm supposed to be, this is where I was. Harlequeen was born here.'

People in the crowd are nodding and murmuring their appreciation. They start looking up and around at this dynamic and incredible place on the south bank of the Thames, brimming with galleries and cinemas and bars and all life, where someone on the sidelines gathered the strength to become really, truly, themselves.

On the phone screen, I see we've got close to two hundred viewers. Many people have sent little heart emojis in response to Harlequeen's revelation. She's touching people across the country, not just in this queue.

'Well,' I continue, 'it sounds like you've got something big in store for us.'

'Harlequeen always goes big,' she says, seriously. 'I've done some research, and it turns out one of my favourite songs was also one of the Queen's favourite songs. So I'm going to perform it for you all, tonight.'

The live stream is now over five hundred people. The number keeps rising while Denzel lifts the phone off the tripod and carefully films Harlequeen as she solemnly ascends the nearby steps, up on top of the westerly Golden Jubilee Bridge. But he doesn't follow her; he remains with the queue.

Part of me is a bit concerned. Harlequeen is now much further away, high above us all on top of the bridge. She doesn't have a mic on her. Will the sound carry all the way over this distance, through the night's cold wind, to this little phone?

Another, bigger, part of me isn't concerned at all. I know Harlequeen's got this.

She surveys us all, her loyal subjects down below, and takes a deep breath. Then she begins her song.

Listening from the ground, we are instantly transported. We are no longer in the city, in the middle of the night, waiting in the cold. The ground beneath us is no longer rigid concrete. We are in Dover, grass between our bare toes, atop the great white cliffs, watching the bluebirds soar towards the sun.

Not only can we hear Harlequeen's incredible, melodious singing from the ground – I think it must be carrying effortlessly across the entire Thames. It's genuinely one of the most gorgeous sounds I've ever heard in my life. Somehow, her voice is solemn and joyful, sweet and forceful, longing and resolute, all at once. Celestial, drawn from the heavens, the music of the gods, yet right in the centre of my own earthly heart, all at once.

Denzel's filming her very well, despite the tiny size of the device at his disposal. He's zooming in and working carefully up and down the queue, capturing Harlequeen at every angle we can from down here. I follow him, taking turns to watch the Harlequeen up there in real life, and the tiny Harlequeen rendered for the live stream, which is now at nine hundred... nine hundred and fifty... a thousand viewers.

This queue spans miles, so many people across such a vast space. Yet I can hear nothing, nothing in the air or inside my own head, but Harlequeen's song. It's as though the entire queue has fallen silent to witness this performance. In fact, it's as though the entire *city* has fallen silent to witness this performance.

She's nearing the end now, her singing just as strong, just as expressive, as captivating as it has been from the very first word. As she lingers, hauntingly, on her final note, I glance at the recording. I'm momentarily stunned to see that nearly ten thousand viewers have tuned in. But then I realise it's no surprise at all.

When she finishes, we all seem to be holding our breath. Then someone in the crowd whoops. More of us join in, applauding fiercely. The whistling and cheering is so loud, I'm a bit afraid the force of it might cause the Golden Jubilee Bridges to collapse.

Harlequeen slowly descends the stairs, waving at everyone in sight, only interrupting her wide smile stretching from ear to ear when she blows a kiss.

Denzel shuts off the recording and, when Harlequeen is approaching us, leaps over to give her a massive hug.

'You were perfect!' he roars in her ear over the cheers still coming from the ground. 'You had ten thousand people watching!'

'I did?' Harlequeen's jaw drops, and she's momentarily distracted from saying hello to all the queue-dwellers who've come to congratulate her.

'You did. I knew it, honey. I knew you'd be incredible.'

'Do you think she would've liked it?' she asks.

'I do,' Denzel says, and no one has to ask who they're talking about.

Denzel and Harlequeen share a deep kiss, which just gets everyone in the crowd cheering louder. Then I see, fighting his way through the crowd, Gerry is stumbling determinedly towards Harlequeen, an arm outstretched.

Oh, God. Most of us knew that this was intended as a tribute, not some kind of imitation or mockery. But at his age, Gerry doesn't seem like the kind of person who watches Ru Paul, or understands drag at all. Why is his hand out like that? Is he going to hit Harlequeen?

I make to stand in front of him, but I'm too slow – he's

already bristled past me and come to a halt in front of Harlequeen, who's surveying him with trepidation.

'Harlequeen. I would like to shake your hand,' states Gerry, with the clipped, formal tones of a soldier. 'That was one of the most beautiful things I've ever heard in my life. Oh, I wish the woman in the queue before were here to hear it too.'

They shake hands firmly. Among the scattering of the clouds up above, I finally catch a glimpse of the moon.

Hour 15: Jubilee Park

'It wouldn't have happened without you, you know.'

After thanking everyone profusely, Harlequeen headed off back towards the Southbank Centre. In her place returned Colin, a few errant streaks of make-up smudged around his eyes, but essentially as pristine as ever. He came to sit next to Denzel, who's cross-legged on the ground, then promptly fell asleep in his lap.

Harold's chatting to Mum about something. They look quite serious, but I think they're just exhausted. Meanwhile Gerry's on Denzel's phone, where he's now fascinatedly watching the recording from earlier and occasionally murmuring that he hopes the woman from the queue before also gets to see it.

At Denzel's words, I squint, then crouch down to talk to him. 'What do you mean?'

'You knew how to get Harlequeen talking,' says Denzel, absent-mindedly playing with Colin's hair. 'When she froze, you got her back on track.'

'Me? I didn't do anything.'

'You did,' says Denzel. 'You saved tonight. Colin has been planning this for a week. He was so unhappy when the Queen died, because he's always based part of his act on her. So he wanted to do something to pay tribute. When he found out about the queue, he insisted we join. But he also wanted to do something else. Something big.' He pauses, searching for the right words. 'Colin owed this to the Queen, and to Harlequeen. Does that make sense?'

'It does,' I assure him.

'It might not have happened, if you hadn't helped him get through his nerves.'

I shrug awkwardly, which I rapidly learn is a stupid thing to do while crouching on the ground as I nearly fall over. Steadying myself, I say, 'I didn't really think about it. I just knew Harlequeen had it in her, and needed some encouragement to get it out.'

Denzel nods contemplatively. 'Did you say you work in marketing?'

'I do, yes.'

'But you said you don't get to talk to many people?'

Denzel's right. The kind of marketing I do is largely endless tedious numbers. It could be worse, I guess. And I tell Denzel as much.

'But to be honest,' I admit, 'my job's not as much fun as talking to Harlequeen was. When I was doing that, it was instinctive. I just knew what I had to do, so I did it. It felt right. My job's never felt like that before.'

He raises an eyebrow at me. 'Time for a career change?'

'What?!' Colin barks suddenly, darting to sit upright and glaring at his husband in fury. 'You think I need to change career?!'

'No, honey,' says Denzel soothingly, biting back his amusement. 'I wasn't talking to you.'

'Hmm.' Colin's eyes narrow in suspicion, but as he

replaces his head on his husband's lap it isn't long before they're fully closed in sleep again.

I straighten my legs. We're at a much more peaceful part of the South Bank now, next to Jubilee Park. In the day there'd be pretty grass, and trees waving in the breeze. But now the park is utterly dark, no lights at all. I can't even see the outline of a single tree. It's a curious void of blackness in the midst of all the buildings and lamplight.

I wander over to Mum and Harold, by the river railing. Mum seems a bit morose, while Harold is up on his feet, with a hand on her shoulder.

'Everything OK?' I ask.

'Yes, fine,' Harold says, dropping his arm and shoving it into his pocket. 'We oldies are just trying to support each other, that's all.'

Mum smiles at me, but it doesn't reach her eyes. She looks completely drained suddenly, after she'd seemed so lively during Harlequeen's visit. Yet again she stares, as though hypnotised, at the Thames.

'What's wrong?' I ask my mother.

Why hello, 'no' gesture, my old friend. Fancy seeing you here. Again.

To my surprise, Harold chips in a little emphatically: 'Your mum is fine. Don't worry.'

'OK,' I say, though something feels decidedly off.

'You did a very nice thing for Harlequeen earlier,' adds Harold. 'You really saved the day. Or, well, perhaps not the *day*...' He looks up at the ink-like blackness above us, closely resembling the abyss of the nearby park.

'Thanks,' I say. 'Denzel said the same thing just now. He even,' and I attempt a nonchalant little giggle, 'suggested I may want to change careers.' I flip my hair and try to look as though this is a silly, frivolous comment that I've tossed out without a care.

Harold smiles and gives a nod, while my mother turns to look at me, her eyes wide.

'To what?' she says.

'What?'

'Change your career to what?'

'Well, I don't know. It wasn't a serious comment. I just had so much fun doing that mini interview with Harlequeen.'

Mum looks incredulous. She's certainly not as tired as she looked a minute ago, that's for sure. 'So you want to quit your job, to go and make online videos?'

'What? I didn't say that.'

'Online videos don't make money, you know.' Her tone remains cool, unflustered, as it always does.

'Well, they do sometimes—'

'So you're going to risk a stable job for something that only makes money *sometimes*?'

'No' – my voice now several decibels higher than most people around us – 'I don't want to make online videos. Look, the entire time we've been here, I've been really jealous of the journalists coming and interviewing us. They get to chat to people and find out what makes them tick. That's what I *really* enjoyed about talking to Harlequeen. It wasn't about the online video. It was about connecting with another human being.'

'So,' says Mum, her voice still ice, 'you want to be a journalist?'

'So what if I did?' Here it comes, that whine that always stubbornly, irritatingly creeps into my voice when I'm trying to be firm. But I feel like I want to cry. How did a casual chat get so intense, so unpleasant, so damn quickly? 'What's wrong with being a journalist?'

'Nothing's wrong with being a journalist,' says Mum. 'But you're not trained to be a journalist.'

'I could get training.' This is ridiculous. I don't even think it's journalism that I'm interested in. I just know I'm not feeling fulfilled in my current job, and I need something with more human connection. Is that such a crime?

Of course it is to Mum, who instantly decides to be negative about everything.

'You have a good job,' she's saying now. 'I don't know why you'd want to throw that away.'

Harold has been doggedly examining his shoes this whole time, but now pulls his head up to face us. He looks a little winded. No wonder – I feel winded when my mother's being this way, too.

'Well, my dear ones,' he says, 'I'm sorry to interrupt, but I need to pop to the bathroom.'

'Oh, sure,' I say, a bit more quietly than I was just speaking. 'Let me go with you again. We can go to the Southbank Centre or the BFI or—'

'No, no.' Harold cuts me off, oddly assertively. 'I'll go by myself, don't you worry. Stay here, with your mum.'

'But you won't find us again. At least take my number, so you can call me and find us?'

Harold observes me for a few moments, as though he's deciding something. 'Yes, OK,' he says eventually. 'Well, here's my silly little phone. If you put your number in there, I'll make sure to call you when I'm on the way back.'

His phone truly is ancient – a classic early 2000s brick.

Fighting the urge to see whether I can play Snake on it, I instead painstakingly tap my details into his address book. I forgot how utterly awful typing letters on a number pad is.

'Denzel,' Harold's saying as I'm doing so, walking over to where he's sitting, 'you're a wonderful man, and so's your husband. You're lucky to have each other, and I've been lucky to meet you both. And Harlequeen too, of course.'

'Are you going home, Harold?' says Denzel in alarm, trying to shift Colin's head off his lap without rousing him.

'No, no,' Harold says with a dismissive wave. 'I'm certainly not going home. I'm just feeling very fond of you all.' He then moves over to shake hands with Gerry.

Finally, after what feels like forever, I finish saving my number. I hand the phone back to Harold, who pockets it without a glance.

'Rani, Tania,' he says to us. 'Meeting you both has been a great privilege. You are both such good, kind people. Try to be kind to each other, too.'

As he prepares to leave the queue, he sees us all, the worry written unambiguously on our faces. 'I'll see you all very soon,' he says firmly, and gives us a wave before turning and departing.

Harold has temporarily departed to use the bathroom many, many times in the hours we've been here. Obviously. We all have.

But now, as we watch him shuffle off towards the London Eye, a foreboding settles in my stomach.

'I'm worried,' I say to Mum. 'Something doesn't feel right.'

She doesn't stop looking at the river. 'There's no point in

worrying, Tania. You shouldn't let yourself be ruled by your feelings all the time.'

I turn my back to her and watch Harold as he gets smaller and smaller. Then he's gone.

Fourteen years ago

Rani Kapadia-Nichols didn't understand why her daughter had to be this way.

She couldn't believe her eyes, but steadied her tone as she said, 'You are not going out in that thing.'

Her daughter stood before her, wearing a frankly ridiculous outfit which included a tight grey vest and an unnecessarily large belt. The fashions of the day were quite absurd.

Rani could live with most of it. But the skirt? The bright yellow skirt that left next to nothing to the imagination? Rani could not, in good conscience, have her daughter running around town in that.

They argued for over twenty minutes. Rani tried her best to explain her stance. Tania was such a beautiful, precious person. She was different from all the other girls at school. She was special. Her value resided on the inside, not in how she flaunted herself on the surface. But this skirt reduced her daughter from a sophisticated young woman to a cheap tart.

Naturally, Tania wouldn't hear a shred of reason. 'There's nothing wrong with this outfit!' she shrieked, for the umpteenth time.

Rani hated it when her daughter yelled. It was excessive, and bordering on obnoxious. 'Keep your voice down,' she said evenly. 'There's no need to scream and shout.'

'There's every need!' Tania had been crying for a while now. It was devastating for Rani every single time her daughter shed tears, but she just couldn't get her head around why someone would be so emotional over a skirt. It was just a skirt, nothing more. Why couldn't Tania be stronger than this? As she'd grown older, she only seemed to get worse and worse at controlling herself.

'Tania, there's absolutely no need to be so upset,' Rani said firmly. She remained robust, without a hint of a quiver in body or sound. She had to be a good role model for her daughter. 'It's just a silly skirt. You're far better than this.'

Rather than even attempting to listen, Tania screamed about Rani being judgemental and old-fashioned.

'If you believe that,' Rani responded quietly, in a mix of annoyance and perplexity, 'then why do you think I've allowed you to go on this date at all?'

That seemed to catch Tania off-guard momentarily.

'You see? Now stop being so silly. Go and get changed, and enjoy your date.'

That should've been the matter closed. But Tania wasn't ready to give in yet. 'All the girls at school wear clothes like this,' she tried, as Rani knew she would.

'If their mothers are happy with them cheapening themselves in public, then that's their decision. But I am your mother, and I know you can conduct yourself more respectfully than this.'

'I wish I didn't have a mother,' Tania blurted out.

Rani waited a beat, expecting remorse to swiftly alter her daughter's furiously contorted, tear-streaked face. But it didn't come. Mother and daughter glared at each other, the ticking of the hallway clock marking the passing seconds.

'You have no idea,' Rani said, in a voice as cold and even as tundra, 'how lucky you are to have a mother.'

It was then that some thumping on the stairs signalled Jim's descent to the ground floor. 'Oh, girls,' he sighed, seeing the two of them at the front door. 'What's happened this time?'

'Mum won't let me wear this outfit,' Tania spluttered through shallow breaths, indicating her inexplicable sartorial ensemble.

Jim regarded her carefully for a few ticks of the clock. 'You look very nice, angel. But I'm not sure it's the most appropriate outfit for a first date.'

'So you're controlling my life, too?' spat their sixteen-year-old daughter.

'We have to, it's the law until you're eighteen,' Jim replied easily.

'It's all just a big joke to you, isn't it?'

'No, angel.' Jim shook his head. 'I know how stressful first dates can be. It's disappointing to be told you can't wear these clothes when you planned them so carefully. Right?'

Tania nodded, sniffing hard.

'It's OK to be upset. I understand. But,' and he made a theatrical motion of checking his wristwatch despite the loudly ticking clock hanging just behind him, 'you're already twenty-five minutes late. For now, why don't you throw on some jeans, and we can talk about this more later?'

After a glance at the clock, their daughter obediently began stomping up the stairs, muttering something incoherent under her breath. Five minutes later, after she'd returned in some perfectly fashionable blue jeans and slammed the front door behind her, Rani and Jim silently headed to the living room. It wasn't until they both sank down into the sofa that Jim spoke.

'You're a bit too hard on her, love.'

'You're too soft on her,' Rani retorted. 'She's so emotional about everything. She gets hysterical over trivial matters. How will she ever cope with the real world if she doesn't become strong?'

'Expressing your emotions can be its own strength,' mused Jim.

'The time I've spent in my life crying and feeling sorry for myself, was time I wasted.'

'I don't think that's true. You needed to get those feelings out.'

'But they didn't get out.' Rani folded her arms and stared straight ahead at the TV screen, which was switched off. A small mirror image of herself and Jim stared back at her, distorted and darkened by the black sheen. 'I still felt bad. I just learned to get on with things anyway.'

Rani wanted nothing more from life than to see her daughter happy and stable. But Tania was the antithesis of stability, always so quick to end up sobbing and wailing. How could she ever have the discipline and patience needed to forge a steady life for herself? Tears, howling, knee-jerk comments when blinded by a fog of emotions – they could never build a sturdy foundation.

Rani knew that the happy home she and Jim had together took copious time to build. It took graft and focus – things she was concerned Tania wouldn't, or couldn't, embrace. So what then for her precious daughter, Rani's very soul and blood? A life of drifting, never finding her place in the great eternal fabric of existence, never finding a true home? The prospect was more than Rani could take.

Jim put an arm around Rani and gave the top of her head a long, languid kiss. 'Tania gets good grades, she has decent friends, she's always home when she says she'll be. I know she's sensitive, and she never sticks to a hobby, but it's not stopped her getting this far. With all this worrying, perhaps you're the hysterical one, hmm?'

'Tania's right. It *is* all a big joke to you,' huffed Rani, but she didn't pull away.

'I take nothing more seriously than you and Tania,' Jim said, still talking into her hair.

'I know,' Rani said, bringing her fingers up to intertwine with her husband's. 'You're serious when it counts. But I worry Tania isn't mature enough to be the same way.'

'She's still young. She'll learn.'

'But she isn't that young – she's almost a woman. If she keeps behaving this way she'll never finish her education, or hang on to a job, or find a good relationship. She could wind up all alone.'

In the hazy dark reflection of the television screen, Jim

shook his head firmly. 'You're wrong. She'll never be alone, Rani – she'll always have us. We'll never leave her.'

'Of course we won't. But one day she might leave us.'

Jim's confusion was apparent by his furrowed brow in the television reflection. He opened his mouth, clearly about to ask his wife a question – but before he could make a sound, Rani got to her feet and left the room.

Hour 16: The Queen's Walk

Tania:

Why does my mum always feel so far away from me ☹

Jonny:

What happened?

You're far away too

Well then, I'll come and find you

Where are you?

No, it's okay

It's 3am, why are you even awake?

I did sleep for a bit but I woke up again

It's weird trying to sleep without you in the bed

Sorry

You seem really off, love. What's wrong?

Nothing

The whole Harlequeen thing before was fun, did you watch the link I sent you?

Yeah it was great. Genuinely one of the best singers I've ever heard

And that dress was amazing

I know, it's beautiful right? Think I could pull it off?

Yeah, and I think I could pull it off you too

Yeah yeah, it's the middle of the night and I've been standing around on a footpath on the Southbank for hours, let's maybe save the dirty talk for another time

Fair point. You did a good job interviewing you know

Everyone keeps saying that

Love I'm wondering if I need to think about a career change

I get it

You should think seriously about it

You're the best

I wish mum supported me

She always shoots me down

She shoots us both down

Seriously love, why am I even here?

I get what you mean

You've been doing so well though, you'd be mad at yourself if you gave up now [MESSAGE UNDELIVERED]

I know things are hard with you and your mum but I really believe that breakthrough's around the corner [MESSAGE UNDELIVERED]

??? [MESSAGE UNDELIVERED]

Love can you read this? [MESSAGE UNDELIVERED]

[MISSED CALL]

Love? [MESSAGE UNDELIVERED]

Hour 17: The London Eye

For over sixteen hours of queuing, my phone battery made it through.

It got me all the way to this westerly section of the Queen's Walk, the sweet little promenade lined with trees – now nearly stripped bare of leaves – along the South Bank which leads to Westminster Bridge. Now, we're right under the London Eye, the colossal optic organ of the city scrutinising us all, judging us all. At night it doesn't revolve, but its entire circumference is lit with a pinkish-red light, like a giant wheel that's aflame.

It looks pretty spectacular. But I can't take a photo, because my phone's dead.

As I look up at the London Eye, its perfect circular shape seems to wobble and distort. I blink hard, but everything is warped. I try to think of people like Agatha who don't use a mobile at all, but I simply can't relate. Because I can no longer browse through social media or read the news or talk to Jonny, or generally remind myself that there's still a living, breathing world beyond the queue. It's not just my phone that's dead – my very lifeline is dead.

'Don't worry,' Mum says from somewhere in my blurry

peripheral vision. 'You'll be fine without your phone for a few hours.'

Yes. I know 'I'll be fine'. As in, I'll survive. But I don't *feel* fine. Not right now.

'What if Harold tries to ring me, though?' The thought's only just occurred to me, but it's true. Harold could be trying to return to the queue, and thanks to my dead phone, he might not be able to find us. He could be wandering up and down the queue, lost and lonely, a disoriented old man in the middle of a vast crowd.

Denzel's shaking his head. 'He had my number, too. I gave it to him ages ago. But he hasn't called me. He left nearly two hours ago, Tania. He was looking pretty tired. I think we have to accept he went home.'

I don't want to accept it. I don't want to accept that Harold is gone, that I can't talk to my fiancé, that I'm stuck in this queue at four in the morning.

'Maybe I should go and look for him.' I don't really plan the words, they just spill from my mouth anyway.

'I don't think you'll find him,' Mum says in her trademark level tone. 'It's best to stay here.'

'I miss him,' I blurt out, my mouth still making decisions entirely uncoupled from my brain. It's like what happened when I interviewed Harlequeen, except way less fun. When I was doing that, I felt a kind of lightness in me. The words came because I was entirely at harmony with the world, as though I actually knew what I was doing for once. Right now, though, the words are coming because I feel I might explode if they don't.

'Yes, he is a very nice man. But he had to go. We can't dwell on that.'

'According to you, we can't dwell on anything!' I fold my arms and plant my feet so I'm squarely facing her. She looks back at me blankly, hands still loosely in her pockets, the fact that she's slightly hunched over lending even more weight to her general indifference. 'According to you, emotions are useless, redundant things to be squashed.'

'That's silly,' she says, not getting remotely louder, faster, or shorter of breath. 'Everyone has emotions.'

'Guys,' Denzel begins reluctantly, but I swiftly cut him off:

'Except you, Mum.'

Mum looks up into the sky, which is still an endless gaping abyss of night, no daylight in sight. She takes a few deep breaths. When she regains eye contact, she still sounds entirely unchanged. 'I just don't believe there's any point in expressing every single little thing that's on your mind. I got where I am by being strong.'

'And where's that?' I snort. 'Living alone and miserable?'

'Tania!' Denzel and Colin chorus in shock.

'What?' I spit. 'It's the truth. She abandoned her family before I was born. Then, last year, she abandoned my dad, too. No rhyme or reason. She just spontaneously decided to end their marriage, after over thirty years. He's still devastated.'

Denzel visibly bites his lip, and then trains his gaze on the London Eye towering over us.

His husband does not demonstrate similar restraint. 'Wait,' he says, looking between me and Mum rapidly, before his eyes settle on me. 'Your dad is alive?'

I'm so surprised that I'm motionless for a moment. 'I'm sorry, what?'

'Your dad is alive?' Colin repeats insistently, ignoring Denzel trying to drag him away. 'I thought he was dead.'

A contorted brow, for just a moment, indicates Mum's disquiet, though when she speaks it's not conveyed in her voice. 'Why would you say such a thing?'

'Well,' Colin shrugs, 'you said things aren't the same without him. You both seem like you went through some big event you're trying to process. And,' he addresses Mum, 'when Harold said he was here for his wife, you said you understood. I assumed that meant—'

'My dad's not dead!' I shout. A fair few people nearby turn, looking a little alarmed. I clear my throat and try to adopt a lower volume. 'I'm getting lunch with him and my fiancé tomorrow. I mean, today.'

'That sounds nice,' Denzel says, a valiant attempt at jollity in his voice ringing false.

'It *is* nice,' I say, wiping a sleeve across my nose which has started running. 'Dad's always been wonderful to Jonny. Whereas Mum hates him.'

There. I've finally said it.

This isn't the way I wanted to do it. I wanted to be articulate and sensitive. I wanted to discuss it in a private place, away from everyone else, so we could be truly honest with each other. I believed this queue was going to be our breakthrough. I really did.

'I don't hate Jonny,' Mum says, and for the first time in a long time, I actually hear a twinge of something, other than disinterest, in her words. It sounds suspiciously like hurt. Genuine hurt.

I'm not a monster. I want to give my mum a chance.

Perhaps we still might have our breakthrough. Perhaps it's going to happen right now.

'OK,' I say, trying to subdue the tremor altering my voice. 'But if you don't hate him, can you please just explain why you said those things you said? Six months ago?'

Evidently, *Jerusalem* is far from the only time Mum struggles to find the words. She opens her mouth and closes it again. Then, like Denzel, and even like Colin who seems to regret the Pandora's box he's unleashed, she also decides to start a taciturn staring contest with the London Eye.

'Please,' I say. 'Just tell me why you did it. Tell me you're sorry.'

No one moves. A veil of silence falls between us yet again. And I'm sick and tired of it. I'm sick of feeling like the only one ever to reach out, to try to bridge the ever-widening gap between us. I'm sick of feeling like half of a lost whole.

'OK!' I yell. 'Fine! You don't have to tell me why you did it. I *know* why you did it. You didn't really love your parents, so you cut them out of your life. You didn't really love Dad, so you cut him out of your life. You don't know what real love is, do you? You never have. So it's no wonder you don't want me to marry Jonny. You don't understand what we have, because you've never experienced it.'

The fight slowly draining from me, my next words are in a fatigued, matter-of-fact near-monotone. 'And when it comes down to it, you don't really love me either. That's why we didn't even speak for six months, not until this stupid queue came along.'

It took an event as historic, as momentous, as the Queen's death to finally bring me and my mother together again. It felt like proof that there are bigger, more important things than our own personal arguments and grievances. In coming here, I was grateful for the renewed perspective I'd earned. A woman of worldwide renown is gone, a woman who was more than a monarch. She was a daughter, a wife, a mother. It made me realise that I have to cherish the time I have with my own mother.

But I'd falsely believed she'd gained perspective, too. I thought my mother was also realising that life is too short, and was preparing finally to open up. But that's not why she's here at all. I have no idea why she's here. I suppose the Queen, and her sophistication and stoicism and strength, always meant more to her than her overly emotional daughter.

Finally, like the others, I gaze up to look at the London Eye. Ferris wheels are a bizarre thing, when you think about them. Ever spinning, ever moving, but getting nowhere. Like trying to have a conversation with someone who's plugged their fingers in their ears.

'Maybe it was better when we weren't speaking,' I say. I turn to look at the people by my side.

They almost look like statues, they're so captivated by the London Eye. I can see Colin blinking away tears, though, and Denzel looks as uneasy as I could ever imagine him to be. Though they stand stock-still, there's so much emotion in their features, so many feelings just beneath the surface.

But my mother's face has not altered. Though the lines in her flesh indicate her age and her fatigue, there is not an iota of expression beyond a hint of cool irritation. Her lips form a stiff straight line. Her jaw is set. Her eyes are dry and cold.

She will not look at me. She will not see me.

I think it's time for me to stop hoping that, one day, she will.

I don't want to yell any more. I don't want to cry. I just want to go home.

'See you, guys,' I say, to no one in particular, to everyone in the vicinity. And before anyone has a chance to respond, I'm rapidly walking away, finally granting Mum the solitude and silence she's always favoured.

Five years ago

Rani Kapadia-Nichols was having a perfectly pleasant Saturday, all by herself.

She was at home, enjoying a cup of tea. She made it the way she always did, carefully boiling the pan of water on the stove.

Jim was out at the pub with some friends, a gathering she wasn't in the mood for. Not because she felt sad or awkward, or anything like that. She was happy. She wanted to sit and bask for a while, by herself, in peace. Jim was the very definition of an extrovert, and always wanted to go out and mingle whenever he was in high spirits. Rani, by contrast, preferred to take some time to herself. Sure, she could've gone and had a laugh with Jim and the rest of them. She would've enjoyed herself, no doubt. But the prospect of relaxing, in blissful solitude and quiet, was far more appealing to her that day.

So often in her past, she'd felt lost. So often she'd wondered where she belonged. But she'd found her answer. She belonged here, in Watford, in this beloved house, with her beloved Jim. Tania had long flown the nest, but was enjoying a successful life in London, and came to visit regularly.

Tania could still be a bit erratic, a bit immature. She often let her imagination run away with her, and would dwell on trivial things. Not surprisingly, she was somewhat ill-equipped to deal with the more serious parts of life. Rani still cringed – partly with pain, partly with embarrassment – when she remembered the scene Tania had made at Jim's mother's funeral a couple of years back. She sobbed so loudly that the priest had to stop his eulogy midway and wait for her to quieten down. Certainly funerals are always a dreadful thing, but it's important to retain some level of poise, isn't it?

Now though, at twenty-five, Tania was starting to settle into herself. In fact, she'd just the previous week been offered a new job at a marketing firm. It had a decent salary, helpful benefits, and a defined career path. After hopping from job to unhappy job in the years following her university graduation with a degree in business, Tania now had a proper foundation, a real focus.

Her daughter was thriving. Her husband was the same calm, kind, jovial soul he'd always been, an unwavering constant. Though Rani had lost a family once, she'd since gained another, and she knew this one would be by her side for all eternity.

Rani Kapadia-Nichols was wary of exaggeration. But sitting here, thinking about how the dramatic, sometimes terrible, twists and turns of her life had led her to this place, where she and her loved ones were content and free, she wondered if she was perhaps the luckiest woman in the world.

An idle gossip show was playing on TV – Rani faintly discerned that some bland-looking celebrity had cheated on some other bland-looking celebrity with yet a third bland-looking celebrity – but she wasn't really listening. She was in her own head, indulging in the singular comforts of home.

It was then that the phone rang. Its harsh trill cut straight through Rani's serene Saturday.

'Hello?'

There was no answer. Rani could just about discern some very, very quiet breathing on the other side.

'Hello?'

She was on the verge of putting the receiver down, when a man spoke Gujarati in a deep, commanding timbre, only mildly affected by the burdens of old age. 'Is it you, Rani?'

She would have dropped the phone, had her fingers not frozen to the extent that she couldn't move them. She couldn't move anything.

'Rani, I'm phoning to tell you some news.'

In the future, she would never, ever be able to articulate what happened in the brief pause before he, this echo emerging from a distant past, spoke next. For there undoubtedly was a pause, if only for a couple of seconds. And in that pause, Rani was an oracle. She assumed powers only the gods and the prophets can boast. She could hear the next sentence before it was spoken. She knew precisely what had happened, even before she truly could know. The relentless, awful knowledge became resident inside her bones, never to leave again.

'Your mother has died.'

Rani blinked, and blinked again.

'It was a peaceful death in her sleep, after a short battle with cancer.'

She blinked hard. But she could no longer see her

surroundings. She could no longer see the photo hanging up in the hallway, of her and her family at the seaside together, laughing in the sea-salt breeze in north Wales.

The voice at the other end cleared its throat. 'That's it. Goodbye.'

'No!' Rani yelped; both the sentiment and the use of her mother tongue were automatic, immediate. She was too trapped in this awful moment to be surprised by the volume of the sound she'd emitted, and instead it reached her ears as a muffled, abstract, wordless noise. 'Please, wait. I want to come to the funeral. When is it? Which city? I'll come to India now. Please.'

'You can't come to the funeral.'

'Please, Pa. I know it's been a long time, but this is more important than everything else. Please, let me come. I have to be there.'

'You can't come to the funeral, because it was last week. We've already scattered her ashes in the sea. I'm phoning to convey the information, nothing more.'

'Pa,' Rani whispered. 'Please, wait.'

'I have to go now. Goodbye.'

She tried returning the call, but he'd dialled from a private, blocked number. She could not connect.

Over the days and weeks and years that followed, Rani would wonder many things. She'd wonder about the big, obvious things, of course. Things which kept her up at night, which rocked the very core of her being.

But she'd also wonder about sillier, smaller, stranger things.

How much effort did her father go to, to find her phone number? The house was listed in directory enquiries, but it still must have been an endeavour from India. Her father must have really tried. He must have poured copious time and toil into finding her at last.

Then again, perhaps he didn't. Rani wasn't entirely sure how much information was held on the Internet, but perhaps all it took was a quick online search. Come to think of it, perhaps a secretary or assistant did the job for him. Perhaps the extent of her father's efforts culminated in the sixty seconds they were on the phone together. Perhaps he forgot all about her as soon as he hung up. She could not know. She could only wonder.

And she often wondered, inexplicably to herself, what her mother had been wearing when she died. It was peacefully in her sleep, her father said. Was she wearing the long, tattered, white nightdress she used to love, which she always said was so cosy and warm?

No. Of course she wasn't. Because thirty-five years had passed, and somebody did not hang on to a nightdress for thirty-five years. Rani didn't know what clothes her mother was wearing, or what food she mostly ate, or how she'd spent her days in the run-up to her passing. She didn't know if the cancer had been painful, if she'd been surrounded by love when she drew her last breath. She could only know that her daughter had not been there.

Because thirty-five years had passed. And there was nothing, nothing, she could do to change that.

Over the days and weeks and years that followed, Rani would get on with her life. She worked part-time in a local government office, and she did her work as diligently and reliably as ever. She spent time with her husband and her daughter. She lived her life. She did everything that she always did.

Over the days and weeks and years that followed, there was one thing, one conspicuous thing, which Rani did not do. Because she knew from bitter experience that crying never solved anything.

Hour 18: Westminster Bridge

I've cried a lot over the last six months. Not speaking to my mother this whole time hasn't been easy. I've wanted to reach out, almost constantly. I've picked up the phone several times, only to abort at the last minute. Because, after the things she said, it isn't fair for me be the one to reach out. She should've been the one calling me, apologising to me.

I waited, every day. I waited and waited.

Yesterday, at seven in the morning, just as I was about to clamber out of bed and get ready for work, my phone vibrated. I blearily wiped the sleep from my eyes and reached for it. When I saw the word 'Mum' flashing on the screen, I wiped my eyes again, because surely I wasn't seeing straight. Then I looked at Jonny, his straw-coloured hair flattened against the pillow next to mine. He smiled at me – not a joyful or relieved smile, simply an encouraging one.

I answered the phone, and my mother asked me to join the queue. Though I wasn't convinced at first, by the end of the conversation I said yes, and I meant it. I made the commitment. Four hours later, there we were, together, in Southwark Park. I thought it was the beginning of the mend of our rift.

Mum and I have clashed many, many times before. We're like ice and fire. But since last year, when she so callously and abruptly left Dad without explanation, it's been harder to maintain a peaceful relationship with her. Her treatment of Jonny should've been the last straw. But I came here anyway, trying to afford her one more chance, trying to find our way back to our once-decent relationship. Because I'm an idiot.

I'm not going to be a fool any more. I'm not going to waste all my time and energy on someone who doesn't support me in my relationship or my career. I'm getting out, and I'm moving on.

I'm walking towards Westminster Bridge, whose white lamp lights glimmer in the dark water of the Thames. But, of course, I'm moving at a pace about a billion times faster than the queue, overtaking it. I really should've done this hours ago, but instead I foolishly hung on, hoping my mother would defy a lifetime of habit and actually open up to me.

I'm at the easterly end of Westminster Bridge now. Across the river the Palace of Westminster shines through the inky black. The vast and infamous building is a majestic castle, all turrets and pillars and grand flourish. Within its halls, as well as the Houses of Parliament, is the ultimate destination, the place where the Queen currently rests. But rather than crossing Westminster Bridge and approaching it now, queuers instead have to progress further on to Lambeth Bridge, then cross the river and backtrack, such is the extraordinary length of the queue.

Big Ben stands solemn and proud, perhaps the only icon of London famous enough to beat Tower Bridge or the Shard. And the only one of those landmarks which has the audacity to remind me that I'm currently hovering on the South Bank at almost five o'clock in the morning.

The queue along this end of the South Bank has mostly been fairly subdued for several hours; after all, it's the early hours of the morning and everyone's been here a long time. But at Westminster Bridge, I see the stirrings of reignited enthusiasm. Though a few people are napping in their deckchairs, there's generally much more chatter, more smiling. By Westminster Bridge, it's obvious that the journey's nearly complete, the end finally in sight.

'Why can't we just cross the bridge now?' I hear a middle-aged man grumble to the woman at his side. 'It's right *there*.'

'Patience is a virtue,' she sings calmly back at him.

There's a little bit of my heart which shines with warmth as I see them all there. So vast an array of people, men and women, of different races and body types and ages. I want to go over and mingle with them, be a part of them, discover their boundless depths. How are they feeling now that, after so long, they're nearly there? I know they must have tremendous stories, each and every one of them uniquely special.

But the truth is, I'm wiped out. My legs and feet are sore enough as it is; I cannot remain by the Thames any longer.

And it's cold. The wind nips at my face and neck, making me wish I had a scarf.

I only have one remaining desire: to go home.

At home, I can cuddle up with Jonny and maybe even get a decent rest in before we head out to meet Dad for lunch in Soho. Dad and Jonny have always got on, from the very first moment they met and joked about, well, me. They laughed about how I compulsively buy shoes which I never wear (not true, I always get to each pair eventually). And how I once saw a spoof trailer for a *Titanic* sequel, which was actually made up of clips from other Leonardo DiCaprio films, and fell for it (that wasn't my fault, it was very convincingly made). They also went on and on about my singing in the shower (which is frankly pretty good, so I don't know what their problem is).

Obviously all their mocking was gentle and affectionate. I think Dad saw, right from the start, that Jonny cares about me just as much as he does. As a rule, Dad is a lot like Jonny: a kind and fun-loving guy, always cracking jokes and believing the best of people. He's the type of man who can provide comfort in almost any situation.

Like at Grandma's funeral many years back, when I couldn't stop crying. Throughout the entire service, I wept unabashedly, often inadvertently drowning out the sermon with my sobs. Afterwards Dad and I walked out of the quaint little stone church together, to hover on the gravelly path with the rest of the congregation. Mum was talking to Dad's brother near the car park, when I saw her glance towards me and bite her lip. She was too far away for me to hear what she was saying, but I could tell she was mortified by my excessive crying.

As a fresh wave of sobs engulfed me, Dad turned to give me a gentle hug.

'I'm embarrassing... myself,' I tiptoed to whisper haltingly in his ear, in between shuddering gasps. 'I'm so sorry... I'm making a scene. She was... your mother. I should be... here for you...'

'Tania, you *are* here for me,' he murmured gently, with a sniff.

'I should… be stronger. I just can't believe… she's gone…'

Dad pulled back from our hug then, so he could look me straight in the face. 'Tania, you're one of the strongest people I've ever known. Showing emotion isn't weakness. It shows how much you care, and that's the greatest strength anyone could ever have.'

Finally, for the first time that day, I didn't want to cry.

Dad is still the same wonderful, insightful man. But ever since he and Mum separated, it's as though a spark has gone from him. He never admits it – he always shrugs off any enquiry as to his well-being, he won't even discuss the specifics of what happened between them – but it's obvious he's not the man he once was. Where he used to crack up in booming shouts of laughter, now the best he can usually manage is a tired smile. He walks with a bowed head, as though a weight is dragging him down. He's got the same heart of gold as ever, but it's been tarnished.

It's my mother who caused this. Dad is so overcome he can't even speak about it, but I know Mum broke his heart somehow. The same way she broke mine.

A while back, I realised my mother will never understand people like me and Dad and Jonny, or the flame of life and love and laughter that burns in us. With every interaction I have with her, a little bit more of my flame goes out, shrinking under her unrelenting cold. I realised I had to break away, once and for all, before I ended up lost and broken, dimmed like my poor father.

For six months, I left the door open for her to come after me. It could have been the start of a healing process that's been a long time coming. With this queue, I thought the day had come. But I was wrong. And now I'm closing that door.

I don't know what to do right now, with no money and no phone. I'm too drained to even feel worried about it. I think I'm going to find a bench and rest for a bit, consider my options.

I head south, past Westminster Bridge. Each aching step makes my feet protest, but I keep going.

As I walk, I tear off the green band which has been wrapped around my wrist for eighteen hours, and I drop it in a nearby public bin.

Hour 19: St Thomas' Hospital

Soon, I've left the immediate noise of the queue behind me. I can see the back of a wooden bench, near a little patch of grass, and I make my way towards it. Sitting for a while will ease my feet and my mind. Perhaps I can use the time to rewatch Harlequeen's stream on my phone…

Oh, right. No, I can't. Well, sitting and staring into space it is.

I approach the bench, staggering slightly as I swear my trainers are spontaneously shrinking with each step. As I round it, making to sit on it, I realise I can't – at least, I can't without being incredibly inappropriate. Someone's already lying there.

'Oh, sorry,' I mumble, even though I'm not sure what I'm apologising for. The person doesn't seem to have noticed me at all. He's facing the back of the bench, so I can only really see his back, which is covered in a khaki-green coat.

Wait a minute. I know this coat. This is a coat which I was looking at for hours and hours and hours, from Southwark Park, to a striped deckchair by the beach, to a sudden and foreboding exit by Jubilee Park.

'Harold!' I cry. My dismay is so loud in the surrounding quiet, it seems to bounce and echo across the river.

To my relief, he stirs. He looks up towards where I'm leaning over him. 'Tania,' he says, feebly.

'Are you OK?'

'Was... tired... just... quick... rest...'

Between every single word he pauses to heavily wheeze. He's speaking so quietly, I have to lean close to him to hear a word.

'You need help.' I stand up straight. To my right stands a large, square, pale grey building adorned with clusters of windows. At the top, in neat black lettering, it proclaims: St Thomas' Hospital.

'Were you trying to get to the hospital, Harold?'

'Yes.'

Poor, poor Harold. He'd seemed so resilient, so unbreakable, the time we'd spent together. The thought of getting to the front of the queue and honouring his wife had lent him almost superhuman strength.

But Harold's an old man, one who's seen grief and conflict and tens of thousands of sunrises over the decades. He must be so, so tired.

When he left the queue, he must have known he couldn't make it. The fatigue and sickness must have been growing for a while. And so he tried to make his way here, to the nearest hospital, no more than half a mile from where he bid us his goodbye.

That was hours ago.

Harold's now attempting to turn around, so sluggishly that I'm worried he's going to slide straight off the bench. I take his arm as he shuffles round and reaches his feet towards the ground. Painstakingly he starts straightening his spine so he's sitting up; I gently prop his shoulders to help him. When he's sitting, it seems as though he might fall off to the side, so I sit beside him and hold up my hands against his arm to bear his weight. He feels frail, fragile, his bones paper-light with age.

'How long have you been here?' I ask, after he's taken a few ragged breaths.

'Don't... know... Long... time... Daylight... now...'

I look up, and see the sky is a strange kind of blue, dark and bright simultaneously. I'm not usually awake in time to see the sun rising, so it's a curious thing to behold. As though somewhere beneath that deep blue blanket, there is light waiting to burst out.

'So when you got here, it was dark? OK. I think you must have been on this bench a long time. You've done an incredible job getting to the hospital all by yourself. You're almost there.'

'My... daughter...'

'Sorry?' If Harold's entered a state of delusion bad enough to think I'm his daughter, I truly don't know what to do.

'I... called... her...'

'Oh. OK, Harold, that's good. She must be on her way. I'm going to reach into your pocket now, and pull out your mobile phone. I'll use that to call some doctors to come and get you. Is that OK?'

'Not... there...'

'Harold?'

'Phone... robbed...'

'*What?*'

'Called... daughter... then... phone... robbed...'

'Harold... are you saying you were here, on the phone to your daughter, when someone mugged you?'

'Yes...'

I can't believe it. Harold, this kind, sweet, unwell old man, managed to make his way right next to a hospital before he ran out of energy. He sat here to call for help, and someone came along and robbed him?

'How could someone do that?' I hiss. 'How could someone be such a coward?'

I'm absolutely enraged. I'm shaking.

'I hope they rot in hell!' Before I know it, I'm on my feet, pacing furiously. 'I can't believe someone could be so cruel and selfish. What kind of world are we living in, for someone to take advantage of a sickly old man like that? You don't deserve for someone to do that to you! You deserve to be cared for!'

A soft *thud* comes from behind me. I turn and see Harold has gradually tilted over, while I wasn't there to hold him up. The sound was his head coming to rest against the bench.

'Oh my God!' I rush over and help him to sit up again. 'I'm so, so sorry.'

I guess now isn't the moment for me to get distracted by rage and sorrow. I'll have time for that later. Right now, I need to take action.

'Listen to me. My phone isn't working, and yours is gone. It's not even six in the morning and I haven't seen anyone coming by, so I think we're on our own for now. I suppose I could run over to the hospital and ask for help, but I don't think it's right to leave you alone again. And the queue is too far away for me to shout for help. So, I need to take you to the hospital. It's really close, so we can make it. OK, Harold?'

He makes a sound that I can't quite interpret.

'We'll go really, really slowly. You can lean on me the whole way, and we can take breaks. But we have to go.'

Harold doesn't say anything, but I think he understands.

Getting him to stand is the most difficult part. I'm not particularly strong, and Harold's not particularly bulky, but it takes every iota of my strength to remain standing as I haul him upwards by his armpits. He totters for a moment but, with a hand on each of my shoulders, he stays on his feet. He keeps one arm draped around my neck, and I wrap one of mine around his waist. Slowly, intertwined, with me in the lead and Harold bent on me heavily, we begin to shuffle towards St Thomas' Hospital.

I feel absolutely horrible making this poor man stand and walk even more than he already has. It can't be doing him any good. But what are our options? There's no one here. I have no idea whether he was able to tell his daughter his location before his phone was robbed, so if and when she'll turn up is a mystery.

She must be worried sick, I know that much. And so am I. I can't let her poorly father sit around on the lonely bench he got mugged on, with no idea when anyone might come by to help.

The hospital isn't far at all. It's right before us – Harold almost completed his journey alone. But with every fraction of an inch we shuffle forward, it feels to me like it's not getting any closer. Still, we keep going. We keep moving forward.

Sometimes – many times – Harold's wheezing turns into erratic spluttering, and immediately I stop and let him rest for a while. At these times he bends over, almost double, and I bend with him, taking his weight on my hands and shoulder.

I wish I could sweep him up in my arms and carry him to St Thomas'. I can only hope he got sufficient rest when he was lying down on the bench – although I admit, I don't think passing out from weakness is the same thing as taking a good long nap.

'Port Talbot...' he rasps suddenly. At least, I think he does. I'm not sure I've heard him correctly.

'It's okay, Harold,' I murmur. 'One step at a time.'

'Yomped... fifty... miles... All... our... gear... This... is... nothing...'

I have no idea what Harold's talking about, and can only hope he hasn't become delirious. But whatever he's saying, it seems to have spurred him on. He's gripping on tighter than ever, but he keeps going. We keep going.

I don't know how long it takes. I don't turn around to look at Big Ben. I focus only on Harold.

After what seems like a very long time, we make it to the automatic glass doors of A&E. We're shuffling through so slowly at first, that the doors start to close on us before rapidly opening up again. It's not long, though, before a nurse with closely cropped black hair comes rushing over with a wheelchair. He and I both help Harold into it, and as Harold's weight is at last taken off me, I realise just how much my limbs and back are aching.

As though it matters. I'm young, and I'm hardy.

Inside, it smells of indistinct chemicals and bleach. The floor and walls are all a dull grey. In a cluster of stiff-looking navy blue seats down the corridor I see various people sitting, waiting to be seen. Most are alone; all are quiet.

Nearby is a reception desk, jutting out from a wall. The nurse steers the wheelchair as we take Harold over to be signed in. As we're approaching the desk, Harold's breath falters and he begins to emit small moans.

'Oh God, is he all right?' I ask in fright.

The nurse crouches down and surveys Harold. 'I think he's trying to say something.'

He's right. Harold's obviously so depleted that focusing on his task is taking everything he has left, but he perseveres. Soon, the words come.

'Thank... you... Tania...'

Even now, after all the weariness and pain, after all the strain both mental and physical, after age and exhaustion have sapped nearly every last ounce of strength from him, even now Harold pronounces my name perfectly.

One year ago

Rani Kapadia-Nichols was drained of the very last vestiges of her energy.

Sitting on the bed that late summer afternoon, her throat dry from shouting, she didn't know how long she'd been there.

On the face of it, since that phone call from her father four years ago, life had carried on just as before. She went to her job, and performed her tasks to a high standard. She saw her work friends for dinner or brunch sometimes. She cooked food and cleaned the house, alternating duties with her husband in the same way they always had done. She and Jim each sipped a glass of Champagne on birthdays, and a red wine during the Queen's Christmas speech.

She saw her daughter on occasional weekends and evenings, when they'd visit Borough Market or browse the books on sale under Waterloo Bridge. She had frequent phone catch-ups with her, too. A few years prior, she met her daughter's boyfriend Jonny for the first time. He was the first man who'd been in a relationship with Tania for longer than about six months.

Rani liked Jonny. He wasn't all that much to look at, in her opinion, but he was sweet and attentive, and had seemingly unlimited reserves of patience for Tania's peculiar impulses. He also knew a thing or two about good food, and Rani enjoyed swapping ideas and tips with him. In fact, as time went on, Rani realised Jonny was quite a handsome man after all; it just took time to see it. She had to admit, she was proud of her daughter for seeing it from the very start.

Yes, on the face of it, life had carried on just as before – perhaps better than before, with her daughter grounded by a good job and a good partner. But beneath the surface, a different story was unfolding.

When Rani Kapadia met Jim Nichols, so many moons ago when they were each so young, so incomplete, the very universe conspired to bring them together. That's what she'd always believed. That's what she'd always known. The forces of physics rippled and ripped; space distorted beyond humankind's earthly understanding; all that had existed and would ever exist honed into a single point, a single moment, a single first kiss in Tottenham Court Road station. She and Jim were not just written in the stars – they were written in time itself. That's what she'd always believed. That's what she'd always known.

But the past few years had taught Rani an important lesson: the things she believed and knew meant nothing. Nothing at all. Not if fate had other plans.

Once, the sound of Jim's voice brought her solace. Once, the sight of his face brought her hope. She had loved this man with every atom of her being. But the constellations had since misaligned. Now, his presence, the mere thought of his presence, brought Rani a very different kind of passion.

They fought constantly. Rani couldn't fathom how she'd never before realised how selfish Jim could be. He constantly forgot to do the things he said he would, whether it was taking out the rubbish or getting the car MOT'd. He was always so relaxed about everything – nothing ever seemed to faze him or throw him off course, even when it should have. Jim had this unique ability to remain balanced, because he always, stubbornly, infuriatingly, insisted everything was going to be OK.

Rani detested it. How dare he? How dare he say such a thing? How could he fail to understand that nothing was ever going to be OK again? That everything stopped being OK when Rani made the decision to turn her back on her own family, on her own mother, and walk away?

Where Rani once closed her eyes and inhaled the sweet, heady comforts of home, she now only saw ugliness and isolation. Drab wet roads, unfriendly faces turning away from her, and a cold which ran through her very blood. That cold stayed with her, even as she opened her eyes again, ruthlessly reminding her: Rani had no home. She'd left her home behind, a long time ago.

She sat there at the foot of the bed, the one she'd shared with her husband until their ceaseless arguing resulted in him moving his things to the spare room. She sat there alone, her fists and jaw clenched tightly, staring at nothing. She did not cry.

They'd fought again earlier. Rani had seen the utensils and plates he'd washed up after lunch were covered in soap suds. Perhaps it seemed a trivial matter to him, but she'd told him myriad times to rinse them properly, and he never did. And that was the real issue. Why didn't he listen? Why didn't he use the tiny amount of energy required to do it properly? Why didn't he care?

She had shouted. He had protested, then also shouted. Back and forth they went, their voices rising to meet one another in defiance. Then Rani simply came up here, to her own room where he knew better than to follow, and sat down.

She wasn't sure how long she'd been sitting there on the bed – a minute? An hour? Half a day? – when, to her surprise, the door slowly opened. For the first time in a long time, Jim entered what was supposed to be their bedroom.

Like Rani, like anyone, he'd aged in the time that had gone by, with his hairline shrinking while his belly grew. Unlike Rani, he still retained a boyish glint in his eyes, however clouded it had become at this particular moment.

He approached her and sat by her side.

It really did seem as though that phone call with her father had given Rani prophetic powers, because she knew what her husband was going to say before he said it.

'This isn't working, my love.'

She felt no need to object. How could she? No whining or pleading could change the truth.

'I love you very much, Rani. But ever since your mother died, you've been so, so angry with me.'

'I know.'

'I can't imagine how it must have felt for you when you found out. I'll never be able to know. But, my love, I don't deserve this. You act as though you hate me. But I haven't done anything wrong.'

Though they were the same words repeated, Rani struggled a lot more to say them the second time. But, after steeling herself, she did:

'I know.'

It was the truth – it wasn't Jim's fault. He didn't drag her out of her parents' house. She made that choice all by herself.

'I think we should try counselling.' It was not the first time Jim had suggested this. Rani, however, could not conceive of anything less helpful, anything more useless, than sitting around in a room ruminating over her every thought and feeling. What good could that possibly do? For the thousandth time, she said as much to Jim.

He sniffed, then, and dabbed at his eyes. 'I love you so much, Rani. But I can't live like this. Every move I make seems to start a fight. We simply can't go on like this.'

The next moments went by in a kind of dreamlike haze. Jim went over how he would look into renting a flat elsewhere. Perhaps in south London, where he grew up, near where his brother still lived. He and Rani started discussing various logistics: finances, routines, legal considerations.

Neither of them wanted any kind of conflict. The thought of an exhaustive, exhausting divorce was anathema to them both. They agreed to keep things largely the same – except for ceasing to see each other any more.

When almost everything had been considered and decided, Jim posed the one question Rani had been pondering the whole time but was reluctant to lend voice to:

'What do we tell Tania?'

They both knew it would be impossible to maintain a

ruse that nothing had changed. Their daughter had to be told they were separating.

'She'll want to know why,' Jim said, eyeing Rani pointedly.

'I don't want her to know about my mother. I don't want her to know anything about my parents at all.'

'I know it's painful. But maybe it'd help us all if Tania knew about it. She doesn't even know your mother died. You've been grieving for four years—'

'I have not been grieving for four years. I hadn't known the woman for most of my life when she died. She was a stranger.'

Jim looked aghast. 'That's not true. Of course you've been grieving, my love.'

'I haven't been grieving. I've been thinking about the decisions I made in my own life. It's nothing to do with grief.'

He shook his head in disbelief. 'Rani, you never got to say goodbye to your mother. You've been taking it out on me, and I understand why. But if you're not willing to admit it, to get counselling to work through it, then you'll be grieving for the rest of your life.'

She felt so tired, suddenly. She wanted to lie back and sleep.

'We don't have to tell Tania every little thing,' she said. 'We'll tell her you've been unhappy for a while and decided to move out. It's the truth.'

'I don't want to tell her that,' Jim said. 'I know it's true, in a way. But I believe we could still be happy together, if we worked on making you happy first.'

'Well, then, tell her *I* was unhappy, and I kicked you out.'

'I don't want to tell her that either.'

'For God's sake!' Rani had had enough of this. If he was going to leave her, couldn't he just do it? Couldn't he take some kind of responsibility for it? 'I'm not telling her about my parents. My mind is made up. Beyond that, tell her whatever you want. She'll blame me anyway.'

Anyone else in the world might have walked away at that moment. Rani wouldn't have blamed them – again she was getting emotional, speaking without thinking, making a fool of herself.

Jim, however, put an arm around his wife and kissed her hair.

'Tania loves you very much. She just gets confused, because there's so much about your life she doesn't know.'

'Telling her would make it worse, not better. How am I supposed to tell her that her own grandparents didn't care what happened to me, didn't care that they might have a grandchild one day? Tania is so sensitive about everything. I don't think she'd cope.'

Jim still held her. 'OK, my love. I understand. It's your business, and I won't tell Tania anything.'

'Thank you.'

'But I think you should consider telling her yourself one day.'

He held her for a long time, then, and Rani didn't pull away. She didn't know how many minutes ticked by, as the room cooled around them. Eventually, Jim gave her a final squeeze, before getting to his feet and heading to the spare bedroom to pack.

Hour 20: Lambeth Palace

I waited with Harold for close to an hour. The reception staff were extremely apologetic, saying there was limited resource available for Harold to be seen any sooner. He dozed off in his chair, which I really hope brought him some deserved respite.

It was then that a woman, around fifty years old with short wavy golden hair, came urgently striding into the hospital. She was in casual clothes, black joggers and a matching big jumper which didn't quite suit her, as though she'd thrown on anything she had to hand in a hurry. She charged up to the reception desk and I couldn't hear much of what she said in her clipped received pronunciation, except snatches of 'father' and 'phone'. Then the receptionist pointed our way. Upon sight of Harold, his daughter came rushing over and fell to her knees in front of him, taking his hand and examining his face. His eyes flickered open briefly, and I think the corners of his mouth turned up in a smile, but it was difficult to tell.

Her name was Marlene, she told me. Her father had phoned her in the early hours saying he was unwell, when the call had been cut off. She'd spent the last few hours in a panic running around the queue route, trying to find him. Her husband had stayed home to look after their son.

'Thank you,' she told me more than once. 'Thank you so much for helping Dad.'

I emphasised that I didn't do much really, that it was all down to Harold's own strength and courage.

'You must be exhausted,' Marlene tells me now. 'Please feel free to go home, I can take it from here.'

I'm supposed to be meeting Jonny and Dad in less than five hours for lunch, and I'm acutely aware that after a day and night almost entirely on my feet, I am sweaty, smelly, and entirely unpresentable. Marlene and I swap numbers so she can update me on Harold's condition, then I bid her goodbye.

'Goodbye to you too, Harold,' I say, squeezing his hand very gently. 'Thank you for being my friend in the queue. I hope we can meet again soon.'

He says something, but despite leaning in and straining my ears, I sadly can't tell what it is.

The sun has come out in full force while I've been at St Thomas', and the sheer brightness of daylight makes me blink. Apart from the queue over by the river, I see many other people milling about; joggers and dog-walkers and even some tourists waving their cameras around – which is positively rude at such an ungodly hour.

I ask someone who looks like a London resident – in other words, he's frowning as though he doesn't want to talk to anyone – how I can best walk to Clapham. The frown doesn't leave his face, but he's nevertheless very helpful, taking out his phone and showing me a map. His phone instructs me to keep following the embankment south, which will take me to Vauxhall, and then take the main road down towards Nine Elms and Wandsworth, before turning towards Clapham. A little over an hour, the map estimated. With my tight stiff trainers, maybe it'll take me closer to two.

I thank the man and set off, still parallel to the semi-distant queue for now, marvelling at how I am heading home by essentially retracing my steps from the day before. Maybe, all this time, I was actually just waiting to go home.

I'm now outside Lambeth Palace, an ornate and regal-looking place with towers and turrets. I slow down, distracted by its splendour, when:

'Tania!'

I swivel around to see Marlene running towards me. Literally, she's running, as fast as her legs will carry her. She's wearing appropriate clothes for running, but she's clearly not equipped beyond that; when she reaches me she hunches over, hands pressed against her knees, huffing and puffing.

'What's happened?' I cry in alarm. 'Is Harold all right?'

'He's... fine...' In gruesome, entirely accidental mimicry of her father earlier, Marlene is currently unable to say more than a single word without pausing for breath. 'He's... with... doctors...'

I wait for a bit, so her lungs can resume normal activity. After a minute she stands up straight, seemingly much less winded.

'Sorry about that,' she says. 'My dad is fine. He's with doctors right now, who are giving him a proper check, but they think he'll be OK. He exerted himself too much, they say.'

'I'm glad he'll be OK. Thank you for telling me.'

'That's not why I'm here,' Marlene says. 'My dad asked me to give you a message, immediately.'

'He did?'

'It was hard to make out, but he got there in the end. He really wanted me to give it to you now, rather than later. I tried phoning you but seems like your phone is switched off.'

'The battery died. What did he want to tell me?'

'Well, that's the thing. He didn't technically want to tell *you* anything – he wanted to tell it to someone named Rani. Do you know someone called Rani?'

'Erm,' I mumble, reluctant to admit that it's highly likely I'll never be speaking to her again. 'Yeah.'

'OK, good, that means I heard him correctly. He wants Rani to know something straight away. That's why,' she added, a slight disgruntled tone entering her voice, 'I had to run all the way here to catch you.'

'What does he want Rani to know?'

She clears her throat, and speaks the next words with a deliberate care. '"You can remember the dead without forgetting how to live."'

'What?'

'That's my dad's message for Rani. "You can remember the dead without forgetting how to live."' Marlene folds her arms. 'Dad would know. When my mum died he was inconsolable for months. We all were, to be honest. It took us ages to get back to anything resembling normality again.'

'That's very sad,' I manage, through the giant, solid lump which has formed in my throat. 'I'm sorry.'

'Thanks. It was especially hard because of all the rules

at the time. We couldn't do a proper funeral.' She takes a sharp inhale of breath. 'Mum and I had drifted apart before she died. It was complicated, but she wasn't always very supportive of mine and my husband's plan to adopt our son. The thing is, looking back, I think she always *did* support us really. She absolutely doted on our son, the little time she got to share with him. She was just worried that we might get hurt. In her own, clumsy way, she was trying to protect us. I wish I'd seen that at the time.'

Quite abruptly, she wheels round and gazes up the river for a moment. Instinctively, I know where she's looking. I passed it earlier, outside the hospital, directly across the river from the Palace of Westminster: the wall adorned with red hearts, upon each one a dedication to a lost loved one. Beautiful and devastating, grief incarnate and a testament to the power of enduring love, all at once. Without needing to ask, I know Marlene's mother's name is on that wall.

When she turns back to me, she seems to inwardly compose herself a bit, and holds her head up straight. 'Anyway, I promised Dad I'd find you and give you his message. Will you pass it on to Rani?'

The lump in my throat has grown so large that I can no longer speak. I nod.

'Thank you,' Marlene says with obvious relief that her task has been successfully completed. 'I'd best get back. I'll call you later.' She turns and heads back towards the hospital.

You can remember the dead without forgetting how to live.

Colin was right. Mum *did* seem to understand what Harold was saying, about how important it is to say goodbye properly if you can. At the time, I simply assumed she was referring to Dad, and how she could've afforded to say goodbye to him more kindly. But now, I don't think that's correct at all.

I remember now, that when I was flying high after Harlequeen's performance and contemplating a career change, Mum and Harold had been having some kind of serious conversation. He'd had a hand on her shoulder, comforting her. Then when I came over, they both insisted everything was all right.

I think Mum shared something with Harold. Something which she hasn't shared with many people, if anyone at all, before. Something which she tries to keep locked inside. Something which Harold understood, but I could not.

You can remember the dead without forgetting how to live.

There's so much I don't understand. But I am certain, now, that the Queen isn't the only person Mum is mourning.

I want to understand. And when I finally do, maybe I can help. Maybe, as my dad keeps telling me, everything really will work out OK.

But there's only one way it can happen.

I have to give Mum Harold's message. I have to make sure she hears it, really and truly hears it. And I have to be there for her, until the very end.

I have to rejoin the queue.

Hour 21: Westminster Bridge (again)

Oh, God. This is really unpleasant. Of all the low points in my life so far, rooting around a public rubbish bin might be down there with the very worst of them.

Right now, I can't even contemplate the herculean task of finding my mother in the queue again, when I can't phone her and I have no idea how far along she is. I can't get to that yet, because it's pointless unless I have a wristband and can join her.

Unfortunately, I tossed my wristband into a public bin. And I can't remember which bin.

I know I was somewhere here, near Westminster Bridge. So I came running up, and started rooting around in the first bin I could spot.

Predictably, it's really, really gross. I can't do it properly, because the bin doesn't have an open lid – there's just a small slit for posting rubbish through. So I've had to squat, stick my hand in and feel around, hoping desperately that my fingers will feel the thin strip that is my wristband. Passers-by are staring at me and, understandably, giving me a wide berth.

My hand has come into contact with wet, sticky, mushy things – I don't even want to know. On occasion I've gripped a thin piece of paper and yanked it out in triumph, but it's just been a receipt or a leaflet.

I don't know how much I want to stick my hand deeper into the mass of filth, and I'm not sure there's really any point in trying.

I retrieve my hand from the bin to see a bit of wet grey chewing gum affixed to my little finger. Great. I try shaking it off, to no avail.

My breath is quickening and my eyes are stinging. Still squatting, I concentrate on the ground, trying to centre myself. But there's not much point.

This is hideous. It's just hideous. I got upset and deserted the queue without thinking, without being patient. Now I'm literally elbow-deep in rubbish, and all I've got to show for it is a revolting, dirty, smelly hand.

As I'm watching the ground, a tear drips off my nose and falls to leave a tiny stain. Then another. And another. Then…

'Miss Kapadia-Nichols!' I hear a call from the vicinity of the queue.

I look up, and to my shock, I see Owen and Elsie have disentangled themselves from the queue to approach me. Owen looks as calm as ever, while Elsie looks alarmed.

'Are you all right?' she asks uncertainly. It's a fair question, seeing as I'm crouching next to a bin with someone else's chewing gum on my hand.

'Oh, er, yeah,' I stammer, hurriedly wiping the gum onto the ground and dragging a sleeve across my wet eyes before I stand up straight.

'Do you need some help, Miss Kapadia-Nichols?' Owen asks in his melodious Welsh accent.

'Oh, no, don't worry,' I say, fumbling in my bag for hand sanitiser.

'Where's your mum?' Elsie asks, ever shrewd.

I squeeze some sanitiser into my palm and begin cleaning my hands, again gazing down as I do so. But I can't conceal my sob.

'What's happened?' Elsie asks urgently.

'I messed up,' I say in a choke. 'I got mad at Mum, and I left. I threw away my wristband and I can't find it again.' I'm trembling now. 'I abandoned her when she needed me. I need to find her, but I can't. I need to join the queue again so I can be with her, at the end. But I can't.'

I gulp hard, trying to stop myself from openly crying. Owen's just a child. He doesn't need to be faced with this intensity.

'I'm so sorry,' Elsie says with obvious feeling. 'I wish we could help, but we took quite a long break to rest. Your mum is probably much further ahead than us.'

'It's OK,' I say, shaking my head. 'It's my fault. I have to deal with it.'

It's the truth. I have to deal with it. I have to live with the fact that I left my mother to grieve all alone. Another sob escapes my lips, before I bite down, clamping them shut.

Owen clears his throat, then takes a step forward. His cereal-box crown looks faded, but it's still determinedly perched on his head.

'Miss Kapadia-Nichols,' he says. 'Please take my wristband.'

Elsie and I both stare down at the little boy. 'What?' we say in unison.

'Please take my wristband.' Before either of us can say

another word, he's carefully torn it off his wrist and is holding it out to me.

'Owen,' Elsie says carefully. 'That's a lovely offer. But are you absolutely sure you want to do this?'

'No,' I say immediately, before Owen can answer. I lightly take his outstretched arm and lower it again, crouching down so we're eye to eye. 'Owen, thank you so much. It's a very kind offer. But I can't accept. You've come all the way down from Wales. You've been queuing for almost a full day. The Queen means the world to you. You'll never get another chance like this again. Please, go back to the queue. If you stick with your mum, no one will question that your wristband's come loose.' I take a deep breath, and I smile at him, this unbelievably sweet and generous young boy. 'But thank you, Owen. I will never forget this.'

'I'm sorry, Miss Kapadia-Nichols,' he says. 'But I also think you'll never forget your mum being all alone.'

My cheeks redden. Elsie grits her teeth, as though making to admonish her son, but she holds off.

'What I mean to say,' he continues, 'is sometimes, duty calls. The Queen tried her best to put everyone else's needs above her own. I'd like to be the same way.' Once more, he holds out his wristband to me. 'I really want you to take my wristband and find your mum. I think that's more important.' With his other hand, he intertwines his fingers with his mother's. 'I already have my mum with me. I'll be OK.'

Elsie breaks into a huge grin, tears shining in her eyes. 'Oh, my sweet boy.'

'Please, Miss Kapadia-Nichols. Go and find Mrs Kapadia-Nichols. She needs you.'

Owen takes another step forward and pushes his wristband into my limp hand. He refuses to pull away, until I've gripped on to it.

'Now, we'll need to fasten it on with something sticky,' he says matter-of-factly. 'Is that why you were getting that chewing gum?'

'Erm…'

'It's a little bit horrible,' he says. 'But I think it will work.'

Numbly, I bend down and retrieve the horrible sticky gum I wiped on to the floor. I wrap Owen's wristband around my wrist, and place the chewing gum where it overlaps. I press down on the paper, and when I draw my finger away, it just about resembles an intact wristband.

'Splendid,' says Owen, beaming.

'Owen,' I say again, barely above a whisper, 'I *can't*—'

'Please, Miss Kapadia-Nichols,' he interrupts. 'I won't change my mind. The Queen once said, "Good memories are our second chance at happiness."' He looks at his mum, and then around at the queue and across the river to the bright, bustling city of London. The city is well and truly awake now; a host of cars and people are zipping back and forth along the roads. Every window of every building, whether ancient and ornate or clean and modern, is twinkling in the morning light. 'I've had a very nice time in the queue, and I'll always remember it. I want you and Mrs Kapadia-Nichols to have a good memory of it, too.'

Elsie is furiously dabbing at her eyes, trying to stem her tears. Her son looks up at her now. 'Shall we go home, Mum?'

She manages a smile and nod. 'Yes, my sweet boy. Let's go home.'

I try to thank Owen again but he keeps shrugging it off. Elsie gives me a hug and we exchange social media details. Then they walk off, in the opposite direction of the queue, towards Waterloo so they can get the Tube up to Euston, and catch a train home.

I watch them as they go, hand in hand. Though he says he wants to be like Her Majesty, it's obvious that the Queen's not the only tenacious, kind woman who inspires Owen. He would not be the strong, big-hearted boy he is, if it weren't for the unshakeable bond between mother and child.

Six months ago

Rani Kapadia-Nichols felt very, very nervous.

She'd spent the afternoon at Tania and Jonny's flat. It was a small place, made even smaller by the forty-odd guests they'd crammed in. White bunting with 'We're engaged!' printed on in cursive black was strewn haphazardly around. Everyone was laughing and joking and clinking each other's glasses.

Besides Rani, Jim was the only other one who wasn't clutching a glass of Champagne. When she caught his eye across the room, he gave her a sad half-smile, which she returned.

She wanted to go over and talk to him. They were on perfectly good terms, and still had a friendly phone conversation here and there. She was grateful for those calls, occasional though they were, because she missed him. She missed his eagerness to help out, his easy way of defusing a situation, his silly little jokes. She even missed the way he said everything was going to be OK. Rani's house was silent now, and no one ever told her that everything was going to be OK.

She couldn't go over there and talk to him, though. Tania would read too much into it. She'd think her parents were reconciling. Rani knew that couldn't happen, and that Jim's return to the house would only result in more misery, both hers and his own. It simply couldn't happen. That time had passed.

So she carefully avoided her husband, stepping in a different direction if it seemed like he was approaching. She mostly clung to the walls for the whole party. She made benign chit-chat with Jonny's parents, who she'd met before and were perfectly nice people, but she excused herself as soon as she had the chance to. She didn't want to talk to them. She didn't want to talk to anyone. But there was one person she had to talk to.

There was a yawning dread opening up inside Rani. It had started when her daughter phoned her a couple of days earlier, excitedly gushing that Jonny had proposed and she'd accepted. The party would be on Sunday, she said. Could her mother make it?

Rani said yes. Of course she said yes. She didn't want to come, but she knew she had to. She had something important to discuss with her daughter, and she needed to seize her chance as quickly as possible.

That chance was not forthcoming during the party itself. Tania was too busy talking to anyone and everyone in sight, shrieking about her beautiful ring (Rani personally found it a little gaudy, with its cluster of diamonds on a gold band) and discussing potential wedding plans. As the party dragged on, Rani busied herself tidying away empty glasses, and reattaching a bit of bunting when the Sellotape had peeled off. She couldn't leave until she'd had the chance to speak with her daughter alone.

The time came eventually, as guests started peeling

away. It was a late Sunday afternoon, and everyone seemed quite drunk. Jim gave everyone a hug and waved a goodbye to Rani before leaving. Before long, Jonny's parents announced that they fancied heading out to the pub for a further drink, and extended an open invitation for everyone else to join, which the happy couple enthusiastically accepted.

'Wait,' Rani said, striding over. It was now or never. 'Tania, could we please have a quick word first?'

'Um, are you sure? Can we do it at the pub?'

'Do it here, while it's quiet,' said Jonny breezily. 'We'll see you both at the pub in a bit.'

Rani didn't love the way Tania and Jonny were always intent to kiss so deeply and passionately in public, but she politely averted her eyes as they said goodbye. When the door shut, Rani was left alone with her daughter.

'I'll help you clean up,' she said automatically, starting to reach for bunting and wrenching it down off the wall.

'We can do that later,' said Tania, sounding obviously puzzled. 'What's going on, Mum? Is it about Dad?'

'No,' said Rani. She was standing behind the sofa, near the kitchen, at the opposite end of the room to where Tania stood, hovering at the front door.

'What is it, then?' Tania asked, with a hint of her trademark impatience.

Rani only hesitated for a second. But she knew she needed to speak now, or everything she had – what precious little there was left – would come crashing down around her.

'My daughter, I know Jonny's a good man. But I don't think you should marry him.'

There. It was said.

There were other daughters in the world who would remain calm, who would listen, who would understand. In a flash, Rani found herself remembering her old friends, Geeta, Aniya and Neha. What were their daughters like? Rani had a feeling they were demure, respectful, and accepted that their elders had accrued wisdom they were yet to learn.

Tania had never been that kind of daughter.

Rani mentally braced herself – and even physically, she adopted a slightly wider stance, firmly planting herself on the ground.

'What?' Tania sounded uncharacteristically quiet.

'I don't think you should marry him.'

'Um…' Tania had been glugging down her glasses of Champagne, so it was no wonder she was now slightly swaying. She placed a hand on the wall to steady herself. 'Why are you saying this? What's wrong with Jonny?'

Rani knew she had to tread very carefully.

'Nothing is wrong with Jonny. He's a nice man, and I'm glad he's treated you well. But it can't last. He's not from your culture.'

Tania looked puzzled. 'What, because he's from Essex? I know they can be a little weird over there, but their culture's not that different from London.'

'I don't mean that. I mean the fact that you're Indian.'

Tania's eyes seemed to open a little wider in recognition. 'Oh. I see. Mum, don't worry. We're not planning to move to Essex. We both love it here in London. We both want to stay in a more diverse community. It's sweet of you to worry, but you don't have to.'

Tania's mind always ran off on tangents. She always

answered questions which hadn't been asked, made assumptions that took her miles away from the focus at hand. Rani wished she'd just listen.

'Please, my daughter. Take it from me. I've made a lot of mistakes in my life, and I don't want you to make the same ones.'

Her daughter's brow was furrowed. 'What mistakes?'

What mistakes? Rani couldn't, wouldn't, put it into words. But she knew all too well the pain and loss of falling in love with the wrong person. It was far better to remain within your own culture, with your own people.

'I'm trying to warn you, Tania. It would be better to marry someone who's more similar to yourself.'

'What?' Tania spat in contempt. 'Half Indian and half white? I have to marry a mixed race man?'

'No, I'm not saying that,' Rani sighed. Why wouldn't her girl hear her? 'I know you're half white, and that's an important part of your culture too. But you can't completely abandon your Indian roots. You should marry someone who understands them, who respects them.'

'Jonny *does* respect my Indian roots, though. He makes a special effort to cook Indian food, and always wants to know more about Gujarati cuisine. He talks to you about that all the time, doesn't he?'

'You think life is about food?' Rani was floored by her poor daughter's naivety. 'I'm talking about much more important things than food.'

Tania shook her head, and took a few, slightly unsteady, paces towards her mother. 'How can you tell me I need to stay in touch with my roots? You never stayed in touch with yours.'

Rani opened her mouth to speak but, as ever, her daughter barrelled on.

'I wish I knew how to speak Gujarati. I wish I knew my Indian relatives. It's because of you that I don't have any connection to my Indian culture at all.'

That's not true, Rani wanted to say. *You have me. Right now, you still have me.*

But she didn't say it. She knew her daughter was right. Rani should have made a bigger effort to speak Gujarati at home, to teach Tania about Indian books and music and films. Rani should have realised how much these things would enrich her daughter, rather than reminding her of a family who chose not to know of her existence.

The British Raj had ended long before Rani was born. Yet, through her fear, through her decision to default entirely to the new culture she'd assimilated into, the same cultural power struggle was now playing out within the very soul of her own daughter. Half Indian, half British, and the Indian half had been losing for decades.

Rani knew all of this. That's why she needed to take action, now.

'You're right, you *should* have more connection to your Indian culture,' Rani said, evenly and steadily, in contrast to her daughter's short and irregular breathing. 'But marrying Jonny will only take you further away from it.'

'So it was OK for you to marry a white man, and not me?' Tania burst out, tears pooling in the corners of her eyes.

How could Rani answer this honestly? How could she say that, actually, no, it was *not* OK that she'd married a white man? How could she say that abandoning her family for him was one of the greatest regrets she'd ever had? How could she say that, when she heard the news about her daughter's engagement, she knew with a blood-deep certainty that Tania was on the verge of repeating a dreadful, heartbreaking, and utterly irrevocable pattern?

How could she say all this, while it was also true that she'd spent many, many happy years with Jim? While the most important thing of all was that her daughter, who only existed through Rani and Jim's physical and metaphysical unity, was the greatest joy in her life?

Rani Kapadia-Nichols regretted nothing, and she regretted everything, all at once. How could she convey all these conflicts, all these frictions, to Tania when she could barely comprehend them herself? How could Tania, who was so much more fragile than her mother, ever cope with them if even Rani barely could?

So Rani did not say these things. All that mattered was rescuing her daughter from a life of solitude and loneliness.

'I don't believe this is about culture at all.' Tania folded her arms. 'I think you've just got something against Jonny personally. Tell me what it is.'

'Please listen to me, my daughter,' said Rani. 'I don't have anything against him. But you mustn't marry Jonny. He might make you happy now, but in the future, he won't.'

'Just because you got sick of Dad for no reason, doesn't mean I'm going to do the same to Jonny,' her daughter replied. 'I'm not like you.'

No, Rani had to admit. She wasn't.

A couple of coat hooks were affixed to the front door, each with a few coats hanging from them. Tania stepped towards it now and reached for her nearest coat, a dusty pink-brown jacket.

Rani remembered her beautiful baby daughter in her arms, her skin a colour unlike any she'd ever seen.

'Tania,' Rani said, fighting to keep her voice calm so she'd be credible. 'I'm warning you. Do not marry this man.'

'I am going to marry Jonny!' shouted Tania. 'He's a good man, even if you don't think he is. I love him, and if you can't accept that, then I don't want you in my life!'

She slammed the door on her way out. Five minutes later, Rani let herself out of the flat, gently shutting the door behind her.

Hour 22: Lambeth Bridge

I want to run along the length of the queue, shouting Mum's name, but my shoes have now reached a level of discomfort so great that I can only really travel in sad little half-skips and jumps. Nevertheless, once I've fully accepted Owen's kind gift, I begin racing as fast as I can along the length of the queue.

From Westminster Bridge, I find myself running along past St Thomas' Hospital again. I hope Harold's OK. Then I'm back at Lambeth Palace, and it's here that I realise the pain in my feet is starting to get matched by the pain in my bladder. I haven't gone to the bathroom in absolutely ages.

There are some toilets set up for queue-dwellers nearby. I'm momentarily torn between going, and making sure I find Mum before it's all over. I can't afford to waste any more time than I already have.

Then again, I don't think it'd be appropriate to witness the Queen's lying-in-state whilst wetting myself. Not to mention that the spectacle would be broadcast online for the world to see. Maybe Harold's late wife Jane was right, and the advent of live streaming really is a menace.

I hop frantically over to the toilets, which fortunately

don't have too much of a queue. When I've relieved myself and washed my hands, I'm ready to resume my search with renewed vigour.

'Oh, Tania, hello!'

As I exit the toilets, I see Colin and Denzel approaching.

'Hey, guys,' I say in surprise and delight. 'I'm so glad to see you.'

Denzel looks a bit pained. 'Is your mum OK?'

'Why?' My heart literally skips a beat, I swear to God.

'She just seemed quite tired when we last saw her. We left the queue a while back, to get some rest. We wanted to find her again, so I asked her to put her number in my phone. When I checked it later she'd put in a landline, not a mobile number.'

Of course she did. For God's sake, Mum.

'Where did you leave her?'

'Not too far from here, but that was a while ago,' says Colin. 'Tania, I'm confused about something. If your dad's not dead, then who is?'

'Where do you think she'd be now?' I say, blithely ignoring Colin while his husband shushes him manically. I faintly think about how strange it is that Harlequeen never seemed to place her foot directly in her mouth as much as Colin does. But I digress.

Colin surveys the queue. Not too far from where we're standing, the queue takes a turn, figuratively and literally. From its southerly trajectory it travels a ninety-degree corner, west across the low, even, unassuming Lambeth Bridge, whose metalwork is painted in a bizarre clashing coral and navy.

'She's probably on the bridge,' says Colin thoughtfully.

'Unless she took a long break. If she did, I suppose she could be somewhere behind us.'

'She won't have taken a long break.' I'm a hundred per cent sure of that. 'She might not have taken another break at all.'

'Well,' Denzel says. 'Considering how slowly the queue's been going, Colin's probably right. I'd guess she's somewhere on the bridge.'

'Thank you, guys,' I say. 'I'll text you sometime, OK?'

They both give me a wave. They're arm in arm, and as I wave back I find my heart swelling with warmth. Colin and Denzel truly are a couple for the ages.

Then I embark on my swift way to find Mum, half-jogging and half-skipping. As I reach the easterly end of Lambeth Bridge, I prepare myself for the set of stone stairs that will take me to the top of the bridge itself. My feet pulsate in pain as they each take my entire weight up the steps in turn, but I keep on going. On every step stands a member of the queue, chatting with a friend or relative.

Once I'm on the bridge, I begin my search. It's a squeeze. Lambeth Bridge has pavements flanking a road, which means there's traffic as well as pedestrians to contend with. I'm barging past a tight concentration of people, searching every figure for the one I'm looking for.

'Hey!' someone yells. 'Don't push in!'

'I'm looking for my mum!' I roar back.

I hold up my wristband, Owen's wristband, like some kind of talisman. Mercifully, I spot a semi-familiar face here and there, and no one else tries to kick me out. I know I left for a while, but in my heart, I'm just as much of a queuer as these guys. I think they understand.

After eventually making it up the entire length of the

bridge and then heading all the way back down, I can't spot Mum anywhere.

I know what she's like. She wouldn't have gone for a big break. She certainly wouldn't have given up and gone home. She's here somewhere. She *has* to be here somewhere.

I take a deep, deep breath. I fill my lungs with as much air as they can possibly take.

'*RAAAANIIIIII!!!*' I bellow, beginning my jog up the bridge once again. '*RAAAANIIIIII!!!*'

Up ahead, I can see some people jostling and murmuring. In their midst, a little Indian woman's head pops up from below. She must have been sitting down.

'Mum!' I cry out, and half-limp over to her as quickly as I can. Again, I wave my wristband around to prove my validity. But it's obvious I'm with Mum, so no one seems overly fussed either way.

She looks completely and utterly dazed by my presence. She also looks drained. I can't imagine how tired she must be, after queuing for almost an entire day, at her age. No wonder she was sitting – from the looks of it she's brought Harold's old yellow-and-white deckchair all this way, and thankfully thought to make good use of it.

She looks so, so small. My mother has always been a short woman, but she seems to have shrunk in the hours since I last saw her.

'My daughter… You came back?'

'I'm sorry I left,' I say. 'I should have stayed with you.'

'I don't blame you for leaving,' she says, while making her old familiar 'no' gesture, raising her hand in a humble rejection of my apology.

'You left your mother all alone?' a tall man standing just in front of us jabs at me. 'How could you do that?'

I open my mouth to acknowledge he's right, and that I'm a scumbag. But Mum gets in first:

'My daughter has done nothing wrong. Mind your own business.' She seems to ponder something for a second, and then adds: 'Please.'

The man snorts, and eyes us both with undisguised dislike, before turning his back to us.

'What have you been doing, all this time?' Mum asks. 'Did you rest? Did you eat?'

I describe, briefly, the whole thing, including taking Harold to hospital, and meeting Harold's daughter.

'I'm sorry I started using Harold's chair,' Mum says, mildly red-faced.

'Why? Chairs are for sitting.'

'It was Harold's chair, not mine. I only brought it along in the hope he might return.'

'He won't be coming back, sadly,' I confirm sombrely. 'To be honest, I almost couldn't come back myself. If it weren't for Owen, I wouldn't be here.'

'That little Welsh boy who loves the Queen?'

I tell her about Owen's incredible sacrifice.

My mother gasps. 'He gave you his wristband? But he *loves* the Queen.'

'I know. But he thought it was more important that I come and be with you.'

We're silent for a while, both of us thinking about how such strength and compassion can come from one so small.

'What about you?' I ask. 'Did you rest or eat?'

Mum's awkward half-smile tells me all I need to know.

'I did break to use the bathroom, at one point,' she adds quickly, before I can begin telling her off.

'That's something,' I say, 'but you must be starving.'

Like a lightbulb going off in my head, I have a memory of being handed a pack of ready-salted crisps, back when I felt as though I was starving.

I reach into my bag and withdraw the extremely battered half-packet. 'Why don't you finish these, Mum?' I shove them in her hand before she can begin her 'no' gesture. She relents, and begins to eat, never once complaining that most of the crisps have been crushed to the size of her little fingernail.

'Thank you,' she says, after a couple of bites.

'Thank *you* – they're your crisps.'

'I had no right to ask you here,' Mum says. 'It was very kind of you to come at all.'

'Of course I came,' I say. 'I'm glad you asked me.' I silently chide myself for the lump forming in my throat. Now is not the time. I cannot cry now. There are more important things at stake.

'Mum,' I say. 'Harold wanted me to give you a message.'

Mum's eyebrows rise. I can't tell if it's in panic, or in intrigue. Probably somewhere in between. Eventually, she swallows. 'What did he say?'

I give her the message. *You can remember the dead without forgetting how to live.*

Upon hearing it, Mum doesn't move for a few seconds. Then she turns around to look down at the waters of the Thames, flowing beneath us. Once again, she seems to be concentrating very hard on the river.

'Mum, what did he mean? I know Colin assumed

Dad was dead, but I don't think Harold believed that. I think you're mourning someone here today, besides the Queen. You told Harold.' I draw myself up, so my spine's straight and my stance is strong, while the waves of the Thames are reflected in my mother's eyes. 'Can you tell me?'

A familiar silence greets me.

'Mum,' I say gently. 'A lot's happened between us. I want us to get past it all. But that can't happen unless you start being more open and honest with me.'

At last, she stops looking at the Thames, and instead looks at me. But the water I saw in her eyes has not wholly disappeared. For the first time in my entire life, I see my mother's eyes are shimmering with tears.

'I failed,' she whispers. 'I failed as a daughter, and I failed as a mother.'

'That's not true,' I say automatically, though I barely understand what she's saying to me. 'That's not true at all.'

She smiles at me, a smile full of sincerity even as it's quivering.

'Mum,' I say, one more time. 'Please will you explain it all to me?'

An age seems to pass within a few seconds.

'Yes, my daughter,' she says at last. 'I will.'

Hour 23: Millbank

It's over an hour later, almost ten in the morning. I insisted Mum sit back down on her chair, and once again I'm standing alongside her. Mum has explained everything to me. Everything.

How she felt so lost and alone as a little girl in England. How she devotedly obeyed her parents, who'd always been so good to her, letting her forge a different path to that which most of the highly domestic young girls she'd known had traversed. So, she did her duty. She played her part. And her parents never pushed her in any way.

But then she got older. She met Dad, and she fell in love. At that age, at that time, her parents could not accept it. They'd always believed she'd eventually find the right, Indian, man for her. They couldn't cope with the alternative before them.

I can't imagine what it must have been like for her, having her family cut contact and disappear. She didn't do anything wrong; all she did was fall in love. All she did was follow her heart, and she was punished for it so severely.

'I should not have lied to my father,' Mum said ruefully as she conveyed this part of the story. 'He was a proud man, and I should never have lied. That was my downfall.'

'But kids lie to their parents all the time! Er, I mean,' I hastily add when she gives me a piercing look, '*most* kids do. Not me, of course. But your lie wasn't so bad. It was only to buy you time, so you could get ready to tell the truth. You told them about Dad in the end.'

'Yes,' she sighed. 'In the end.'

When I was born, she remained quietly afraid of her father's warning that I'd be split apart by two cultures, and wind up homeless. She didn't even realise it, but the fear had wormed its way right inside her. So she made sure England would be my home, and English would be my language, and fish and chips and the pub and tea and biscuits and saying sorry for no reason and queuing, of course queuing, would be my culture.

After all, the Indian half of my family never wanted to know me, never even wanted to know whether I existed. How could I adopt a culture whose adherents had so blithely turned their backs on me?

That's what Mum wondered, anyway. And then, five years ago, she heard that her mother had died.

And she grieved – for everything she'd lost, for everything I never even got to have. Eventually, she left Dad, because he seemed to symbolise everything which had torn her apart from herself.

'I treated your father very badly,' she said, blinking hard. 'He must hate me.'

'He doesn't,' I say, honestly. 'Whenever he mentions you, it's obvious he misses you.'

When Mum learned I was planning to marry Jonny, she went into panic mode. She thought I was doing the same thing: marrying a man who'd take me far away from my own roots, from my own culture. She wanted to salvage what chance I had left of embracing my Indian side, before it really was too late, and my Kapadia name dissolved into oblivion.

'I didn't handle it well,' she says now, which I have to admit is somewhat of an understatement. But at least she's said it. 'I really am very sorry, my daughter.'

'Thank you,' I say.

'I do like Jonny, very much. I believe he'll make you happy. My own fears got in the way.'

We're now edging along the upper side of the Thames, back a little northwards. We can see the Palace of Westminster closer than ever, the colossal grand and iconic building which is synonymous with the city we call home.

Again, I don't know much about architecture. I think I heard someone else saying it's a Gothic building, whatever that's supposed to mean. But I can tell that it's, you know, old.

In its halls, laws are created and broken and passed and rejected. In its halls, our politicians make decisions which make or break our lives. In one of its halls, right now, lies Queen Elizabeth II, a symbol of so much of our country's stoicism in the face of great hardship.

I'm no royalist, but over the time I've been here, I'm starting to understand the appeal of stoicism in the face of great hardship. It's through that stoicism that an entire nation can be led from war and terrible loss and fear into the light of modernity and progress. Sometimes, that stoicism is the only way you can survive. It was certainly the only way Mum could survive.

'Mum,' I say, 'did the Queen mean a lot to you?'

'Yes, very much so. She exemplified everything my parents came to this country to find. Sometimes, when I wasn't sure what to do, I'd think of her strength and it would guide me.'

'I get it.' I fold my arms and squint up at the Palace of Westminster again, golden in the morning sunlight. 'I'm glad I'm with you to see her, Mum.'

'I'm grateful, my daughter. I'm glad you're with me too.'

'Of course, I would have preferred not having to queue for an entire day,' I add with a chuckle.

Mum doesn't say anything. She looks down into the Thames again.

'Sorry. I was just joking. I didn't mind queuing really. I had fun, and I met so many great people. But you have to admit, it would've been easier if we'd just walked into the palace.'

'Yes,' Mum says distantly. 'It would have been easier.'

'Mum? What is it?'

She snaps out of her temporary reverie, and looks at me again, catching her breath. For a minute, she seems to struggle with herself. But then she says, 'The queue itself has been very important to me.'

'Really? Why's that?'

Once more, she eyes the Thames, the grey-green water churning away. 'Rivers run to the sea, don't they?'

'Um, yes.' This is the very last situation where I'd have expected an impromptu geography lesson, but I'll go with it.

'And so all the rivers and seas in the world are connected, aren't they? It's the same water.'

'Um, yeah, I think so.'

She nods, not really in agreement or confirmation, but

in a kind of faraway acceptance. 'My father told me they scattered my mother's ashes in the sea. I knew the queue would be alongside the river for most of the duration. That's why I didn't want to take too many breaks. I wanted to…'

She trails off. But I don't need her to finish. I finally understand why she's been so preoccupied with gazing at the river, all this time.

'We're almost there, Mum,' I say. 'Soon, you'll have your chance to say goodbye.'

You can remember the dead without forgetting how to live. I think my mum is finally beginning to learn Harold's lesson.

I've learned a lot too, this fateful day. I've learned to be more thoughtful. From now on, I will stop repeating patterns. I will stop making the same mistakes—

'Oh my God! Oh my God! Oh my *God! It's David Beckham!!!*'

'Ooh, maybe it's *actually* him this time!' I yelp with glee, hopping to my tiptoes despite the pain it causes my feet, swivelling around to find the familiar blonde girl and see where she's pointing. I catch a glimpse of her up ahead, desperately directing everyone's attention to the opposite side of the street.

Oh wow. This is it, at last. This is really and truly it. There she is…

Wait.

'That's a woman,' my mother helpfully confirms.

Yes, that's a woman on the other side of the street. A tall, athletic woman who looks very suave with her buzz cut and smart dark suit. But it's undoubtedly a woman.

'For God's sake!' shouts someone in the queue as we all resume our positions.

'I'm sorry, my daughter,' my mother says. 'Perhaps we'll see him soon.'

'We won't. I'm pretty sure he finished queuing ages ago.' I sigh. 'But I keep wanting to believe her, damn it.'

'That certainly would've made the queue more exciting.'

'It's been exciting enough,' I say, not maliciously. It's the truth: with the journalists coming to and fro, with Harlequeen's appearance, with Harold's health scare, I think I've had enough excitement for a lifetime.

I think again about Harlequeen, and how I helped her calm her nerves for her big performance. I wish I had my phone so I could check if her video is trending.

As though she's read my mind, my mother speaks. 'If you want to change your career, my daughter, then I support it.'

'Oh,' I say weakly. I'm unsure what to say.

'You should find something you love to do,' she persists. 'Don't waste your life only doing what's expected of you. That's the easy route. You're stronger than that.'

'Yeah,' I say, after I've swallowed hard. 'OK.'

We're edging nearer to the Palace of Westminster now. I can see people entering the huge, imposing doors.

I can also see people who've clearly just left, milling around in the garden nearby. It's a large square patch of bright verdant grass. A rare snatch of peace and nature in this, one of the most busy and iconic parts of the capital. A few pebbly paths mark out routes for pedestrians through the garden, lined by low bushes of all kinds of green and purple-ish leaves. Some people walking the paths are in tears, many are solemn.

And then, I see... at least I *think* I see...

'Oh,' says Mum with a chuckle. 'It's the man in the queue earlier, and the woman in the queue before.'

She's right. Agatha and Gerry are shuffling along a path, hand-in-hand. It's a bit difficult to tell from this distance, but I don't think they're talking. I suppose they're lost for words when they're not pining for each other.

'My daughter,' asks Mum suddenly. 'Why did you come here today?'

'To be with you.' Is this some kind of trick question? Maybe I was supposed to say something else. If Owen or Agatha had been asked that question, they may have said 'To honour the glory of the Queen' or something like that.

'I know,' Mum says with a fragile smile. 'And it means very much to me. But I was so awful to you about Jonny. We hadn't spoken in such a long time. When I phoned and asked you to come, why didn't you say no?'

I think back to that call, yesterday morning. I think back to the moment I decided to say yes. The reason I said yes was, ultimately, a very simple one. But I can't say it explicitly, because it would sound so blunt, so coarse.

'Because,' I say eventually, 'on that call, you did something I've never known you to do before. It felt like a turning point.'

Mum doesn't ask me to clarify. I think she knows what I mean.

One day ago

R ani Kapadia-Nichols knew what she had to do.

Since she'd awoken, at four in the morning, she'd known. The knowledge had come to her in her dreams. She'd glimpsed a beautiful, cobalt blue ocean, but it was far in the distance. She had to walk, and wait, following a twisting and turning river for a very long time, before she could reach it.

Now, a few hours later, she sat, dawn fully broken in the sky, her mobile phone in her hand, the display scrolled to Tania's name. She needed to press her thumb down, and make the call.

Rani Kapadia-Nichols was wary of exaggeration. But she was the most terrified she'd ever been.

She hadn't spoken to her daughter in six months, and it was all entirely her own fault. But every time she'd thought about reaching out, she'd decided against it. Because, her entire life, she'd only made things worse for the people she loved. Her parents, Jim, and now her daughter. Tania was living a very good life, with a very good man, and Rani could only ruin that.

If her daughter ever needed her, she'd be there in a heartbeat. Of course she would. But in what twisted, imaginary universe could her daughter, could anyone, really need Rani Kapadia-Nichols?

Jim was gone. Tania was gone. She was due to retire pretty soon. No one needed her. When she was young, she'd craved solitude. Now she had it in abundance and she could hardly bear it.

Then the Queen died.

Rani had been at home, seeing the news as it broke on TV. In the afternoon, it was obvious something serious had occurred: the BBC were doing continued coverage of the situation, while the royals were travelling to Scotland. Rationally, Rani knew what had happened. But she still felt a stunned start when it was confirmed.

By the early evening, they announced it. Queen Elizabeth II had died peacefully at Balmoral, aged ninety-six.

Rani didn't cry. She didn't feel much of anything. It wasn't until another week had passed, after the Queen had been transported to London and the queue to view her coffin had begun, that the realisation began to dawn on her. When she awoke from her dream that Friday morning, with the memory of that distant blue ocean so enticing and peaceful, she knew she had to join the queue.

And she knew she had to ask her daughter to be with her.

She'd probably say no. Rani already knew that. Tania wasn't a fan of the monarchy, and doing something like this was absolutely alien to her character. But Rani knew she had to ask.

Not allowing herself any more time to linger, she jabbed her thumb down onto the screen, and raised her phone to her ear. It rang for a little while before she heard her daughter's sleepy voice on the other end.

'Mum?'

'Tania.' She cleared her throat. 'I know this is unexpected. But I would like to ask you a favour. A big favour.'

'Are you serious?' Of course Tania sounded disbelieving. After everything that had happened between them, how could her mother have the gall to request a favour? Rani understood, she really did. But she also knew she had to queue, and it was now or never. She knew the unique pain of a mother and daughter's bond being broken, and she had to do her very best to mend this before it was too late.

The queue was the only way to do it. Her dream had told her as much, and she believed it. She didn't believe much these days, but she believed that.

Rani ignored her daughter's question, a valid one though it was, and instead asked her own. 'You'll have seen that the Queen died?'

'Well, yes. We're not living in a cave.'

'I would like to join the queue to view her coffin.'

'What?' Tania exclaimed. She didn't sound sleepy any more. 'Since when are you a royalist?'

'I'm not. But I want to do it.'

'OK.' Tania sounded entirely incredulous. 'Fine. What's the favour?'

No need for frills or fuss. No need for silly hyperbole. Just say what you mean.

'I would like you to join the queue with me. Please.'

There was silence at the other end, which was wholly unusual for Tania. 'Excuse me?' she said eventually.

'I said—'

'Oh, I heard you. I just can't believe you asked me that. After everything you said to me, after telling me not to marry Jonny, you go and ask me to stand in a queue with you? For six whole hours?'

Oh, dear. Perhaps her daughter really did live in a cave if she believed the queue was only going to be six hours long.

'Why would you do this, Mum? Tell me, why?'

But Rani, after sixty-five years and a lifetime of uncertainty, was out of words. She could not speak any more. She could not answer her daughter.

Instead, although she really and truly believed that it never solved anything, Rani Kapadia-Nichols couldn't help herself – she began to cry.

She tried to stop herself from making the sounds, but her sobs escaped her lips regardless. She sniffled and gasped and struggled to regain composure, but she was quaking so much she kept bumping the phone against her ear. She cried for all the things she could not say. She cried for the Queen. She cried for her mother. She cried for her daughter. She cried for her husband. After so long refusing herself this release, Rani Kapadia-Nichols cried for herself.

Several minutes later, Rani regained a hold on herself. Her gasping slowed, and she wiped her eyes dry.

The sound of breathing in her ear told her Tania hadn't hung up yet. Then, she heard her daughter's voice, tender and concerned:

'OK, Mum. I'll come and queue with you, no problem. Tell me when and where to meet you.'

Hour 24: The Palace of Westminster

We're here. We're finally here.

We raise our wristbands at the doors. I spin mine around so the crude chewing gum fastening isn't as visible. Fortunately, we're waved through with no problems.

As we enter Westminster Hall, which is cavernous with its high ceilings and echoing stone walls, the queue splits into two sides. Mum and I are funnelled towards two different branches – she takes the right, and I take the left, each of us following a vast grey wall around the main focus of the room. We are opposite each other as the queue moves slowly forward, every mourner pausing to pay their respects before moving on.

The coffin sits atop an elevated crimson platform. It's shrouded in regal purple, with a red royal flag draped over the top. It's flanked by guards, who are all clad in a splendid red and gold.

It's hard to believe that she's resting here. The woman whose face adorns coins and bank notes. Who people would crowd around their TV to watch speaking every Christmas afternoon. Who saw no fewer than fifteen prime ministers come and go. Who had to deal with both the triumphs and the blights of her own family while the entire world watched.

Who ate marmalade sandwiches with Paddington, though Paddington wasn't actually there.

As I move forward to stand before the coffin, first of all I say a little prayer from Owen in my head. On his behalf, I thank the Queen, for reminding us all that "Good memories are our second chance at happiness".

I did manage to learn a thing or two about the Queen myself today, even without Owen's help. I think he'd be proud of me for that. And so, in my head, from the bottom of my heart, I tell Queen Elizabeth II that I really like her Harlequin dress from the Royal Variety Performance in 1999.

Standing here, to my own surprise, I don't want to cry. I feel sad, I feel fatigued, I feel overwhelmed, but I don't want to cry. Sometimes, it really is better to hold back a little bit. I never believed that before, but I've come to realise it now. Sometimes, there is real value in emotional fortitude and calmness.

Opposite, though, I know my mother is crying. I can't currently see her, but I saw her begin to weep on her approach. I have never before, in my entire life, seen my mother cry. Yesterday was the first time I'd ever heard her cry, and today is the first time I've seen it. And, though it breaks my heart to see my mother sad, I'm grateful. I think she's been waiting for this release for an unspeakably long time. I know I have.

I put my hands together in a prayer gesture, by way of saying goodbye, and progress to move on and out of the building. As I walk towards the end of the room, my mother comes into view, still lingering at her side of the coffin. Tears streaming down her face from her tightly shut eyes, she also has her palms pressed together in a prayer gesture. She raises her hands up, and then she drops them. Opening her eyes, she wipes them roughly with her sleeve. Then, still crying while I remain stoic, she comes to meet me.

At last, at long last, we have joined each other.

Outside, the sun is shining brightly. It's a mere twenty-four hours on from Southwark Park, but I feel as though I've lived an entire lifetime in a day.

'Mum,' I say. 'I'm meeting Jonny and Dad for lunch in an hour.'

'Oh, they must be worried that they haven't heard from you. Would you like me to call Dad and explain?'

'Maybe later, but don't worry about that. Jonny predicted I'd probably run out of phone battery, so I don't think he'll be too worried. What I wanted to ask was, would you like to come along?'

Mum raises her hands, and for a frightening moment I think the 'no' gesture has returned. But instead, she's simply wiping some stray tears from her cheeks.

Then she smiles at me. 'Yes, my daughter. I would like that very much. There's a lot I want to say to Jonny. And to your dad.'

'OK, great.' I look around. 'We can catch the Tube towards Soho, if you don't mind lending me a bit of cash?'

'Of course I don't mind.'

'Thank you. Oh, and on the way, can I ask you a few questions? For my wedding planning. I want to make it a bit more Indian-influenced.'

Her eyes widen in surprise, and pleasure. 'Really?'

'Yes. Why not?'

'That sounds wonderful, my daughter. We can talk about

Indian wedding clothes, and food, and music. Although, you might not want it to be *too* Indian-influenced – or your wedding will wind up lasting three full days.'

I laugh. 'Well, Mum, I never thought I'd stand in a queue for one full day. So anything's possible, isn't it?'

Though our feet are aching, though our bodies are tired, we are rejuvenated. The waiting is over.

Mum and I begin to walk, side by side, in the direction of the place that we call home.

Acknowledgements

Ever since the day I learned what an "author" is, I've dreamed of being one. And even though the profession is all about using words, I'm not sure I'll ever be able to find words strong enough to convey the depth of gratitude I feel for every single person who's contributed to making it happen.

Thank you to Rosie De Courcy, my astonishingly smart and insightful editor, for your expertise and belief, as well as your warm humour. Thank you to Bianca Gillam for your unwavering efficiency and enthusiasm. Thank you to every single awesome member of the publishing team at Head of Zeus: Yasminn Brown, Emily Champion, Becky Clark, Karen Dobbs, Victoria Eddison, Rachel Faulkner-Willcocks, Zoe Giles, Daniel Groenewald, Clemence Jacquinet, Jo Liddiard, Ayo Okojie, Jessie Price, Megan Rayner, Meg Shepherd, Nikki Ward, and Amy Watson. You have each helped this book on its journey, and it means everything to me.

Thank you to Max Edwards and Sara O'Keeffe, my infinitely talented and supportive agents. You brought resilience and creativity out of me I never knew I had. Thank you to everyone else at Aevitas Creative Management who helped this book come to life, including Gus Brown, Vanessa Kerr, Tom Lloyd-Williams, and Allison Warren.

Thank you to Sabrina Osborne, my Hindi teacher, for helping me with the Hindi used in this book and for continually providing opportunities for me to get involved and immersed in London's Indian culture.

Thank you to my spectacular friends. All of you who've given me eager words of encouragement during drinks and dinners and parties: you're all my lifeblood. Thank you especially to Laurence Makins, for your genius suggestions I would never have thought of alone; and to Chan Murali, who was with me when the idea for this book began in the middle of an intensely crowded Gatwick Airport, and who is with me at all times (even when you're living on the other side of the world).

Always and forever, thank you to my incredible family: my brilliant and generous uncles Swarup, Yuvraj and Dharmendra; my lovely aunt Nayana; my kind and clever cousins Vishal and Vishakha; my amazing and almost annoyingly intelligent brother Rahul and sister-in-law Hannah; my sweet and teeny-tiny nephew Aditya; and my inspirational, caring, eternally strong mother Prathna. Thank you all for being there no matter what, for infusing me with the pride and passion of India, and for always letting me be unabashedly me.

About the Author

SWÉTA RANA was born into a Gujarati family in Birmingham, and now lives in south London. She studied Philosophy and Theology at Oxford before doing a Master's in Publishing at UCL. After working briefly in editorial at Orion, she moved into designing and managing commercial websites.

Swéta has enjoyed writing ever since she was a child, always taking any opportunity she can to write fiction pieces, film reviews, or articles on Indian culture. *Queuing for the Queen* is her first novel. In her spare time, Swéta takes Hindi language classes, sings soprano in a chamber choir, and volunteers for a mental health charity.